The Side Ways: Awake

ANDY HAVENS

For Dave, Sally, Chris & Dan.

With thanks to Neil, Jon and Doug
for early reading, proofing and inspiration.

CONTENTS

Chapter 1. Illusion

Apple blossoms.

That was the sight, and the smell, that greeted Kendra White when she woke to the ringing of her alarm on a cool morning in June. It was also the scene that Solomon Monday, the Librarian, would associate with Kendra after he entered her mind and scanned her memories of that day.

* * * * *

The white flowers filled Kendra's vision as she tried to smack the alarm clock in just the right way to silence it without knocking it off her bed stand. If she knocked it off, odds were good that it would keep ringing as it rolled under the bed. She managed to make it shut up after hitting it just three times.

Better'n average, she thought, sitting up in bed.

It wasn't really summer, not quite. It was late June, sure, but school had only been out for two weeks and it was still comfortably cool in the city. But the apple tree outside Kendra's window always blossomed late, and so the white petals were the first thing she saw in the morning as she stretched and woke up for real. And because the air was so nice and cool this time of year, her mom let her keep the window open. So she awoke not only to the sight of white blossoms, framed in pale, yellow curtains, but to their sweet, heavy smell as well.

Do other people have that in-between-time? That moment between sleep and wakefulness when light seems solid and heavy, a pressure on your eyes, sure... but on your chest and hands and feet too?

That fuzzy time always seemed to last longer in the summer to her.

Kendra cracked her jaw and rolled her head, trying to loosen up the stiffness from yesterday's work. Anybody who thought gardening wasn't hard work hadn't ever done it for real, she thought. Her calluses were coming along nicely, and her knees had begun to toughen up, but her neck always seemed to get the worst of the deal.

Well, jeez, she thought, shuffling into the bathroom, *if it was easy it wouldn't pay so well, I guess.*

Bathroom prep in the summer took less than half as long as it did during the school-year. Almost no make-up. No real work on the hair, except to shampoo it and towel dry. It wasn't long enough in back for even a little pony tail and the long bangs she liked did hang down annoyingly while she worked, but it was a price she was willing to pay for her personal curtain. Being able to hide behind a thin wall, even one made only of hair, was an advantage she wasn't prepared to give up.

White t-shirt, overalls and thick, white socks. She always remembered what Mr. Vernon had said when he'd offered her the job: "No matter how hot it gets, always wear thick, white socks." She wasn't sure why they had to be white, but she didn't argue with the guy. He'd been a master gardener for more than thirty years. If he said white socks, then white socks it was. Last year's Keds finished the outfit and it was downstairs for breakfast.

The real estate person that had found this place for her mom had called it a "town home." Kendra's friend Shama called it a condo. In Kendra's mind it was an apartment. It shared walls with another family's place and didn't have a yard all to itself. That made it an apartment. A big apartment, sure. One with three floors and a "semi-finished" basement, yes. But not a "house."

"We don't need a house," Kendra's mom had told her when they'd moved to the city five years ago for her work. Kendra hadn't cared much about the house itself. But it had meant leaving friends, teams, a school she knew well, all for a strange and crowded place. A place with fewer trees and more funky, unpleasant smells. A place where you couldn't go for a walk at night just because you felt like it. A place where her keychain had a small can of mace on it, her book bag contained an air-horn alarm and she – and all her friends – carried cell phones as much for security as socialization. One of the girls a year ahead of Kendra wore a bracelet (a nice bracelet) with a tracking chip in it. Her father was some big-deal international banker and connected guy. The rumor was that the daughter of somebody else at his level had been kidnapped. Thus the Tiffany GPS.

Had it been a school day, Kendra would probably have missed her mom on the way out. Kendra was a morning person and usually had a club of some kind or band practice before school and had to be out and on her way by 7:00 am. Her mom wasn't usually up until at least 8:00. They often missed each other on the back end of the day, too. Kendra was usually in bed by 10:00 pm or so, and though her mom worked mostly at home, she was often out on errands and doing research until well after 11:00 pm.

But in the summer, Kendra slept in until 7:00 or 7:30, as Mr. Vernon didn't like her to get to any of his clients' gardens before they were awake or out for the day. So as she jogged downstairs, Kendra heard her mom pulling a chair across the linoleum floor in the breakfast nook to have her morning coffee. Said "nook" being a corner of the kitchen with a card table and two folding chairs.

Kendra waved absentmindedly at her mom as she passed into the kitchen and began poking around the pantry, seeking something that would qualify as "what I want" for breakfast. Unlike her mom, who had the exact same thing every morning, Kendra liked variety. She was about to really consider some yogurt with granola mixed in when her mom spoke up from behind her copy of the Harvard Business Review.

"Don't forget… it's Tuesday."

Tuesday… Tuesday… Tuesday… The day after Monday. The day before Wednesday. Not trash day. Not the day I pick up the dry cleaning on my way home. Not mom's night out with the girls. Not… Oh, crap.

"Dr. Lyonne."

"Right. Tuesday. Moved by your request during the summer from Friday mornings so that you'd be able to do some long-weekend trips with what's-her-name."

"Tania."

"Right. With the cabin upstate. Which is fine. But if you miss your appointment…"

"We still pay. I know, I know."

All this from behind a magazine. About a year ago, Kendra realized she had almost no eye contact with her mother. Every now and then she'd try to catch some, but it was tough. They spent almost no time together. Twice a year they went out together for dinner so that mom could find out "what's going on in your life." Even then, Kendra had realized at the most recent of those outings just a few weeks ago, her mom barely looked right at her.

Kendra glanced at the digital clock built into the microwave. 08:14. Her appointment with Dr. Lyonne was for 9:00. Which gave her a bit less time than she needed unless she took a cab. And mom didn't pay for cabs. Just for the metro pass. A cab would cost Kendra half of her day's pay.

Screw it, she thought, *I can make it on the metro.* She grabbed her backpack from the counter and was about to hit the door when her mom said, again from behind the magazine, "Don't forget your meds."

It wasn't in a calling voice, the same way you'd call to a kid, out the back door, "Don't forget your lunch." It was the way one grown-up would talk to another. "Don't forget your briefcase. Don't forget your car keys." No emotion, not even any chiding. Just straight-up info.

One hand on the door, Kendra paused. She didn't like lying to her mom, but she was about to do it. Again.

"Thanks for reminding me," she said and went back to the sink.

She took the brown pill bottle off the shelf below the window and shook three pills into her palm. She put them in her mouth, turned on the water and ducked her head under the faucet. The water ran into her mouth and she swallowed it. Water off, face wiped on the back of her hand, backpack swung up on the left shoulder, right shoulder through the door. Mom never even looked up.

Kendra was out the door, down the steps, and all the way to the end of the service alley that ran next to their "town home" before she spit the slightly soggy capsules back into her hand. By that point the view to the kitchen was blocked by their bank of mailboxes, a telephone pole and a large utility van.

She kept the pills in her palm, even thought they were a little slimy, until she was four blocks away. Then, as she ducked and wove between the early morning sidewalk traffic, she pretended to trip while walking up over a sewer grating. She went down on one knee just for a second, and as she pushed back up to her feet, she dropped the capsules carefully into the sewer, making sure they fell through the mesh into the darkness below. She fought the urge to wipe her hand on the leg of her overalls until she'd gone another two blocks.

Paranoid? Sure. Crazy? Maybe.

Down the narrow stairs that smelled of urine (even in the middle of winter), down into the subway system that always made Kendra think of Minos' labyrinth or the early Christian catacombs. All the mechanical sounds of the subway were so loud that personal communication was impossible. So while it was loud enough to hurt her ears, there was no talk, just the sounds of wheels and brakes and steam and scrape.

She was able to skip the lines of people waiting for tokens and use her metro pass in the QuicKard lane. She'd put the Kard on a zip-line that attached to one of three carabiners locked on the inside of her backpack. She'd got the carabineers at a six-week backpacking, hiking and rock-climbing camp two summers before. Those things were good for lots of stuff.

She ran down the second set of steps, past the newsstand and the guy selling flowers, and just made her train as the doors were shutting. An old man in a long, black coat stepped nicely out of her way so that she wouldn't get pinched by the closing doors. Usually the sensors gave you a break and let the doors open before you got smooshed. Usually. It was nice of the old guy to help out, anyway. She smiled at him and he smiled back.

And she had her first hallucination of the day.

The train rocked forward and back and then forward again as it jostled into gear. You got used to it. The *hucka-hucka-hooo motion*, Shama called it. As she shifted to get her feet into a good balancing position, Kendra's hand came to rest on the arm of the old man's coat. This was just as he was smiling back at her, and his face seemed to become somewhat… transparent.

No, thought Kendra. *That's not the right word. I can't see through him. I see other things that shouldn't be there, with him in the middle of them.* Like curling ram's horns. His white, collar-length hair seemed to flow from his widow's peak into a pair of beautifully tapering, spiraled horns. They almost looked like nautilus shells, she thought. They had that mother-of-pearl, rainbow quality. And his glasses, which had seemed like normal, round John Lennon specs, were now attached to his face with dozens of tiny tendrils like some cybernetic prosthesis. But he was still smiling that "nice old-guy" smile, so

Kendra kept smiling back. She nodded a quick, "Thanks," for getting out of her way, and turned to get a better grip on the hand-rail.

It wasn't the strangest thing she'd ever hallucinated. Not by a long shot. She was just surprised it had taken it so long to happen this time.

She checked her watch. 8:52. She was going to be a little late. Frankly, as long as she was there in time for at least half the session, mom probably wouldn't complain.

The train leaned hard going around a curve and she used the motion to mask a quick look at the old guy. Same long, black coat. Which was a bit weird, as it wasn't really cold, only cool. Even warm in the subway. Same grey, corduroy pants. Same white, men's dress shirt, unbuttoned at the collar. But... yup. Big ol' goat horns were still there. Still radiating color like neon and rainwater rippling over a pool of gasoline. He was staring out the opposite window, so Kendra got a chance to study the glasses-things a bit more carefully. They were cylinders of metal, not glass, pressed or joined into the flesh of his cheeks. And the wires she'd seen briefly before linked the rims of these cylinders to his cheeks. They were like whiskers, maybe. But growing up into the...

She looked away as he began to turn his head toward her. The train came to a stop with a screaming squeal. Her station. As soon as she felt the doors open, she backed out without looking at the old guy again.

According to Dr. Lyonne, her hallucinations were somewhat unique in their stability. Many schizoids' visions changed from moment to moment or, at least, from episode to episode. Not Kendra's. If the crossing guard at the posh private school across from the art museum had a glowing nimbus and six arms on Monday, he'd be tricked out the same forevermore in Kendra's damaged brain.

At least I'm consistently crazy, she thought as she jogged up the steps and into the light and relative quiet of the street. *I'd hate to be a raving, disorganized loony.*

Two blocks over, one block up. This was a slightly better part of town. Smaller buildings, nicer architecture, more landscaping, more brick, less concrete. There were trees in big pots at regular intervals along Dr. Lyonne's street. Lots of the first floor window boxes and small, front-yard gardens. The black, wrought-iron security fences were even kind of artsy-pretty. In a mildly spiky, threatening way.

By the time she got to the steps in front of Dr. Lyonne's building, Kendra was a little winded. She was in good shape from running track last year, but she didn't usually run with a backpack full of 25+ pounds of crap. The overalls weren't great for running either. They chaffed a bit.

Time? 9:05. Not bad, not bad at all. She decided she could take a minute to catch her breath, so she sat down on the top step, leaned back on her backpack and began to breathe deeply, enjoying the slight breeze that had found its way between the densely packed buildings.

Hallucination #2: Across the street, the plate glass window of a deli split open along a horizontal line like a giant clam. It even made a wet, sucking sort of sound that Kendra could hear from across the street. Huge billows of deep pink and blue steam came rolling out of this giant, glass mouth and into the street. The fog crept down onto the sidewalk. As people walked through it, their passing made whorls and eddies in the colored clouds. The fissure in the window opened wider and even larger puffs poured out.

It looks like the techies got out of control at a junior high production of Midsummer Night's Dream, Kendra thought. Nevertheless, as the fog began to creep across the street, she decided she'd had enough of this particular delusion. She stood, brushed off the seat of her overalls, and turned to ring the buzzer for Dr. Lyonne's apartment. Without anyone asking who was there, she was buzzed in.

Kendra shouldered open the heavy, brass door and walked into the small, cool lobby. The pink and blue fog rolled into the street behind her.

* * * * *

Dr. Lyonne's office was also her apartment. It was a regular apartment building where people lived, not an office complex or medical center or... *whatever.* Kendra had been coming to see Dr. Lyonne for more than three years, always at this address, and so she'd long ago begun to recognize – and be recognized by – some of the neighbors. Not by name, of course. She didn't know if they knew what kind of doctor Dr. Lyonne was. Of course they had to have some idea. She couldn't very well be a brain surgeon or research physician up in her own two-bedroom flat, could she? They probably knew.

There was the old lady on the first floor who was always dressed like she was going to church. Very nice, almost formal. Dark dresses, a shawl, nice shoes, gloves, the whole bit. She was very sweet and always smiled at

Kendra, but didn't say anything. The apartment next to Miss Manners, which was what Kendra called the nice, old lady in her head, had had at least three tenants in the last few years. The latest was a nervous young man who stammered, "G... g... g... g... g... g... good... good... good... good m... m... m... m... morning," to Kendra every time they chanced to meet. No matter how long it took him to get it out, she waited patiently and responded with exactly the same words, albeit without the stammering.

Dr. Lyonne was on the third floor. Kendra always took the stairs, and, on the second floor, had occasionally passed the apartment of what she assumed was a family, although of indeterminate size. There was almost always at least one child, sometimes two or three, in the hall or on the landing near the stairwell. They all looked related – very blond and very pale – and seemed, to Kendra, to be relatively normal children. That is, they were sometimes crying, sometimes laughing, sometimes yelling, sometimes playing. Normal. There was also a younger lady on the second floor, an African American woman who had a job that required her to wear very formal, business-y clothes. The few times Kendra had seen her she'd been wearing sneakers with her suit and talking on her cell phone. But she'd smiled hello as they'd passed on the stairs.

If there were other tenants on the third floor, Kendra had never seen them. For all she knew, Dr. Lyonne had the entire floor to herself. Patients only saw the front office and the door you knocked on at the top of the stairs. She knocked, heard a muffled, "Come in," and opened the door.

The office wasn't big, but it didn't really need to be, Kendra always thought. It was for talking. You and Dr. Lyonne. She sits behind the desk, you sit in the chair, and you talk. If Dr. Lyonne had been a strict Freudian, there'd have been a couch, and maybe the room would have had to be bigger. As it was, it worked OK. A desk, a chair behind the desk, a chair in front of the desk. Two nondescript, impressionist paintings on the walls, white lace curtains, a shelf for some books, an end table for coffee.

Ba-da-bing, ba-da-shrink, she thought as she walked in, swung the door shut, dropped her backpack on the floor and sat in the comfortable, tan, leather wing chair. There was no foot rest or ottoman or anything, though. When she'd asked about that once, Dr. Lyonne told her that it wasn't a good idea for patients to get too comfortable. It encouraged mental laziness. Kendra seemed to think that the point of the couch in Dr. Freud's version of the psychiatric world was that it made patients comfortable on purpose, so that they'd relax and reveal more truth to the doctor. *Oh, well. Different strokes.*

"How are you feeling today," Dr. Lyonne asked as Kendra sat down.

"OK."

Dr. Lyonne looked up from her notepad. No tape recorder for Dr. Lyonne. She was old school. Kendra had even noticed once that her notes were in what she assumed were short-hand. It wasn't in English, anyway.

"Can you be more detailed?" the doctor asked. She was not that old, Kendra thought. And kind of pretty. Dark hair pulled back in a neat pony-tail. She sometimes wore glasses, sometimes contacts. Usually slacks and a nice silk blouse or sweater. Not really formal, but she always looked nice. Her skin was dark, but not tanned-dark. If Kendra'd had to guess, she'd have said Dr. Lyonne had at least one South American grandparent.

She'd been distracted. Dr. Lyonne repeated, "More details? How are you feeling?"

Kendra nodded and tried to look out the window. The lace curtains, though thin enough to let in lots of light, didn't let in much detail themselves. She could sense the movement of tree branches in the slight breeze. There was some blue peeking in around the edges. Not much more than that.

"I don't know," she finally replied. "I feel OK. Neck's a bit stiff from the gardening."

Dr. Lyonne nodded. "I'd like to hear more about your summer job. But I was specifically wondering about your new medication. Are you having fewer problems with side effects."

Fewer problems. Kendra thought. *What she means is, "Are you able to take them without becoming a complete zombie? Can you now think in complete sentences? Do you still seem to feel everything through a layer of thick, wool? Do your friends wonder if you're stoned all the time?"*

"Yeah," is what she said out-loud. "Nowhere near as bad as the old stuff. It makes me a bit fuzzy around the edges for an hour or two after I take it, but that wears off by, like, 10am or so."

Dr. Lyonne nodded. "Great. Nothing else?"

Kendra shrugged. "I've noticed I'm thirstier in the morning."

Dr. Lyonne nodded again. "Dry mouth." She made a note on her pad and then paused to reach down into a small refrigerator beneath her desk. She came back up with a bottled water which she handed to Kendra.

"Thanks," Kendra said, cracking open the protective seal on the bottle. She realized then that she'd had no breakfast and nothing even to drink. She really was thirsty, even though she hadn't taken her meds. But she had looked them up on the Internet. Which meant she knew what the major, expected side effects were. Some slight grogginess for a few hours after ingestion. "Do not operate heavy machinery" type stuff. Some people developed a rash. Kendra didn't want to fake that. About four symptoms down, she'd read "dry mouth" and looked it up. It wasn't quite the same as "thirsty," but she didn't want to get Dr. Lyonne's radar up by using the precise term from the medical materials.

She took a long pull on the cold water and wondered if she could get one "to go" from Dr. Lyonne. Probably. She didn't smile much, but she seemed OK. For a shrink.

"No other side-effects, then?" Dr. Lyonne asked.

Kendra shrugged. "None I've noticed. You might want to ask mom."

"I talk with your mother about every-other month. Since you've been on this new prescription about three weeks, I'll ask her next time we chat about it. Good idea. She may have noticed behavior changes that you wouldn't catch."

Fat chance, thought Kendra. *Mom might notice if I actually brought somebody home to live with me or walked around on fire, but short of that… not very likely.*

Dr. Lyonne seemed to settle down in her chair a bit, getting comfortable, arranging her pad and pen neatly in front of her. "I'd like to try something different today, Kendra," she said. "I wonder," she asked, "If you've ever heard of the Rorschach test."

Kendra nodded. "Ink blots. Sure. Sounds like fun."

Which, compared to most of her sessions with Dr. Lyonne, wasn't that far from the truth. Kendra had to see an actual psychiatrist in order to get the high-powered meds that controlled her schizophrenia. You couldn't get those from a psychologist or social worker. You needed a fresh scrip every two months. Kendra had several friends on drugs for ADHD or similar behavioral disorders, and they got their scrips either from their family docs or, in one case, by mail. Kendra's stuff, though, needed a dyed-in-the-wool shrink. Who, besides prescribing medicine, also made you talk about your feelings. And how you felt about your feelings. And how you felt about other people's feelings. And what you did about how you felt with your feelings.

Kendra could see how this kind of treatment would make sense for an adult. If she'd had twenty or thirty years' worth of experiences to screw her up, talking about them couldn't hurt. If she had been confused and manipulated by a string of bosses, lovers, family members, colleagues, friends… whatever. Sure. But her problems went way back. So far back that talking hadn't even been an option.

Anyway. Looking at blobs of ink. Comparatively… fun.

"Great," responded Dr. Lyonne, who smiled slightly. She reached into a drawer in her desk and pulled out a stack of thick, square cards, about ten inches on a side. The blobs must have been facing her, because all Kendra could see was a code of some kind on the back of the one nearest her. "K40901."

"I'm going to turn over a card," began Dr. Lyonne, "and show you a shape. I want you to look at it for as long as you need to, until you see an image of something in the shape. Don't force anything. If, after awhile, it really just looks like spilled ink to you, tell me that and we'll move on to the next one. OK?"

"OK," said Kendra. *But I do wonder how much my mom is paying for this…*

Dr. Lyonne flipped the first card over to face Kendra and it made a slight "tap" as it connected with the desk. The shape was almost insultingly easy and jumped out at her at almost the same instant the card hit the desk.

"It's a boat," Kendra said.

Dr. Lyonne didn't nod or smile or anything. She just let that card fall quietly, face-down on the desk, and then she flipped the next one over with a tap.

"Butterfly."

Tap. "A parade."

Tap. "Three cats."

Tap. "Water lilies."

Kendra wondered if it was supposed to be this easy. These weren't vague, strange shapes. They were like specific silhouettes. A little rough around the edges, maybe. But no real imagination necessary.

Tap. "A pinwheel."

Tap. "Ballerina."

Then they got a bit stranger. Or at least harder. More… stretched out. Or scattered.

Tap. A pause. "A Chinese fan?"

Dr. Lyonne paused for a moment. "There's no right or wrong answer, Kendra. This is a way for you to express your imagination without some of the usual barriers. Don't try to force a response. Just relax, take your time and wait until something comes naturally."

Tap. Pause. "Two dogs chasing each other."

Tap. Pause. "A pile of laundry next to a wheelbarrow."

It went on. Longer than Kendra would have expected. The deck of cards hadn't seemed that thick. And they kept getting weirder and, well, less "real." More like a Jackson Pollock painting. More spatters and random blips and blops. She took her time, but it still felt like a test.

Maybe that's because they call it a test, she thought.

Finally, they got to one where nothing was coming through. It was junk. Visual chaos. Random spatters of black. Kendra sat there, staring at it for awhile, and finally started to shake her head a bit.

"Take your time," Dr. Lyonne said softly, patiently.

Kendra was about to give up, when suddenly she saw it. Maybe the light outside the window shifted slightly. Or perhaps a cloud had gone over the sun, or a branch had moved in the breeze. Maybe that wasn't it. Maybe Dr. Lyonne had tilted the card forward a bit, or maybe Kendra had just leaned back in her chair or simply changed her focus a little. Whatever the reason, the image in the picture was now as starkly clear as those in the first few had been. More so, even.

But the picture wasn't in the ink. It was in the spaces between the ink. It was like those "3D" pictures that you can't see until you stare at them just right, but after your eyes "get it," you can't see it the old way. Kendra had even seen a much simpler version of a "white space" picture years before in an art class. It was a black silhouette of two vases. But the white spaces in between the black images looked like women's faces. If you stared at the black, you saw vases. Stare at the white, faces. Vases, faces, vases, faces. It had seemed funny to her at the time.

The picture in front of her now, though, was incredibly complex. It was a still life of a table or altar with candles, a box of some sort, a wide-brimmed cup and a bottle on top. Flowers and vines grew up the side of the table. Leaves and petals were strewn around the bottom of the scene. Again, all this detail was in the "white space" between the black spots and drips of ink. It wasn't a hyper-realistic scene, certainly. It looked like a grainy pen-and-ink, but it was still startling to see in its complexity. All the other "positive" images she'd seen were simple, like shadows in a children's book.

Something must have shown on her face, because Dr. Lyonne was looking at her curiously.

"Kendra?" she asked. "What do you see, honey?"

Honey? Kendra thought. *She never calls me 'honey?'* That more than anything made her cautious. And caution had only one response in Kendra's life.

Lie.

"It looks like an underwater scene, kinda," she said, squinting at the picture and rotating her head a bit.

Dr. Lyonne frowned a little. *She never frowns,* Kendra thought. *It's inappropriate for the therapist to apply judgment to the patient's response. It clouds the process and impedes truthful reporting.* She'd read lots about psychotherapy over the years.

"What do you mean, 'kinda?'" asked Dr. Lyonne.

Kendra shrugged and tried to look bored and disinterested. "I don't know. They keep getting messier and messier. The earlier ones were easy. These last few have been just really… messy. There's a bit there that looks like an octopus, and that stuff kinda looks like seaweed, so it reminded me a bit of an underwater scene. You know, like a treasure ship or something."

"Do you see a treasure ship in the scene?"

"No. Not really. Just the octopus and the seaweed."

"Well, like I said," Dr. Lyonne was back into her standard doctor voice, "Don't force anything. If you don't see something, just tell me that. And if you see a little of something, tell me that, too. But don't make up something just to please me. This isn't a test."

Kendra chuckled.

"What?" asked Dr. Lyonne.

"Then they shouldn't call it a test should they?"

Dr. Lyonne actually grinned. "You're right. A test does imply right and wrong and people do like to please their teachers and test givers. I'll see if I can come up with a less… loaded name for the activity. Now…" she gathered the remainder of the cards together and rapped them on the desk with a firm, clacking noise, "We've only got a few more, and then we're almost done for the hour. OK?"

"Sure. Let 'er rip."

Tap. The card turned over and Kendra had to use every bit of self control not to let the surprise and horror she felt show on her face. Seeing the first "white space" picture must have bent some process in her eyes or prejudiced her perception or something. Because within seconds of seeing the card, the black ink faded into the background and the stark, white picture jumped out and forced itself into her mind.

The negative-image showed a man being ripped apart by snakes with huge heads and dripping fangs. The patterns of ink hid and revealed the reptilian coils and the long, flowing hair of the man as he lay on his back, dying, ropes of his blood curling out to combine with the bodies of his killers.

Kendra stared at the image, carefully keeping her face neutral, trying to look as if she was unable to see anything there.

Finally, after almost a minute; "A haystack?"

"Don't ask me, Kendra. Tell me. And only if that's what you see. Do you see a haystack."

"Not really. This one just looks pretty random to me."

"OK. Just a few more."

Tap. Women with harpoons trying to bring down the moon.

Tap. A man with a bird's head and a hollow chest letting a parade of frogs leap through him.

Tap. A boat filled with dismembered hands.

Tap. Children dancing around a burning telephone.

Each time, Kendra sat and stared, bewildered and afraid, but showing nothing. She could feel one, tiny drop of cold sweat working its way down her neck, over her shoulder, along her spine.

She didn't know what they meant, these strange images. Each one picked out in reversed, negative white. But she knew she didn't want Dr. Lyonne to know she knew.

If she knows that I know that I think it's bad for her to know that I know, then she might know that I know she knows I know, thought Kendra. Which made her laugh on the inside a bit. Which showed on her face.

Dr. Lyonne's eyebrow went up. "Something's funny?"

Kendra shook her head. "It's just that I always thought you were supposed to see sexy stuff in these things. The first bunch was all bears and birds and windmills and junk. And now it just looks like spaghetti and confetti and packing foam. Do I have to be 16 or something before you show me the ones with sex in them?"

Now it was Dr. Lyonne's turn to laugh. Not much, but a chuckle nonetheless. "The Rorschach tests… or, shall we say, 'activities' are standardized. If people want to see sex, they see sex."

"Oh," Kendra replied.

"You sound disappointed," Dr. Lyonne observed.

Kendra shrugged. "Maybe a little."

Dr. Lyonne replied, "Well, we can do them again in a few months. If you'd like, I can play some bad 70's funk music in the background and turn on a red light while we go over them."

Kendra's jaw almost hit her collar bone.

"What?" Dr. Lyonne asked, eyebrow up again. "I can't make a joke once in awhile?"

Kendra shook her head. "You can… you just never have."

Dr. Lyonne chuckled a bit. "My mentor is… was… a very stern man. He didn't believe in any levity during the psychiatric process. But he didn't work with young people, either. And he retired many years ago. Back then, where he came from, there was much less humor in the world. And much less pain, too, I think. Maybe we need more humor to deal with the pain."

That was as long a statement of her own beliefs as Kendra had heard from Dr. Lyonne in the three years she'd been coming to see her. It almost made Kendra begin to like her. Almost.

"Be that as it may, Kendra," the doctor continued, "we've got a bit of time left and I'd like to hear more about your summer job."

"Oh. Sure. What do you want to know."

"You're working in a garden, is that right?" Dr. Lyonne was taking notes now, no eye contact. Standard mode. Almost as if they'd never had a little moment of humor. *Oh, well,* Kendra thought. *Back to the couch.*

"Not just 'a' garden," Kendra answered. "A bunch of them."

"Can you explain?"

"My boss, Mr. Vernon, he's a master gardener. He designs, sets up and maintains special gardens all over the city. He hired me to help out. Do basic maintenance work. Weeding. Litter and critter control. Stuff like that."

"Do you like the work."

Kendra shrugged. "It's outside, which is nice. It's not heavy-duty manual labor. Not like I was toting sacks of peat moss or fertilizer at a regular nursery or anything. The money's pretty good. So, yeah. I guess I like it. Once I get used to the schedule and the route it'll be easier."

"There's a route?"

"When you have to check in on twelve gardens at least twice every week, you need a route."

Dr. Lyonne looked surprised. "I would guess so. What about watering? Don't they need to be watered more often than that in the summer?"

Kendra couldn't for the life of her figure out what this had to do with her psychological health, but what the heck. At least it wasn't more twisted, scary negative pictures.

"There are daily crews for that kind of stuff. Some of them are on site, some of them are services. It doesn't require any training and can be done by regular lawn jockeys."

Dr. Lyonne nodded. "But you have some training, right?"

"Yeah. Some. I spent two summers working in a greenhouse. Specialty flowers and plants. Some bonsai. Lots of very specific care and treatment. Mr. Vernon's clients have some very rare and interesting plants, and they pay him, and, I guess, me, to keep them healthy."

"So you're like a… plant doctor?"

Kendra grinned. "More like a plant nurse. Mr. Vernon's the surgeon. He's actually got clients all over the country. No way he can visit them all often enough to keep an eye on things. So he's got a few people like me in every city. I guess. He never said that, but I assume so."

"Sounds like a nice guy," Dr. Lyonne said, not looking up from her pad.

Kendra shrugged. "I wouldn't know."

That made the doctor look up. "Why not?"

"I've never met him," Kendra replied. "My mom works with his wife. When mom heard from Mrs. Vernon that her husband was a famous gardener, she mentioned that I'd worked in the greenhouse last year and the year before. So a few month ago, Mrs. Vernon said that maybe there'd be a summer job for me in the gardens. So it worked out."

Dr. Lyonne scowled a bit. "If you've never met him, how do you know what to do?"

"He sent me a list of addresses and a bunch of files by email. Each file contained the list of plants and flowers and what needed to be done and what kinds of things I need to look out for. I have to file a report on his Web site every week with a bunch of data and anything I notice that needs work. For emergencies, I have his phone number. I haven't had to use it yet."

Dr. Lyonne looked a bit puzzled. "Let me get this straight," she said. "You work in the dirt, right?"

"Yep."

"Messing around with plants and flowers. Right?"

"Yep."

"And then you go home and track all this on your computer."

"Technically, I use my computer to track it on his computer over the Internet. But that's the gist of it, yeah."

Dr. Lyonne shook her head. "The intersection of technology and horticulture. Amazing."

Kendra shrugged. "Mr. Vernon's clients have very beautiful, sometimes very odd gardens. He's a genius in a very specialized industry. He uses a bunch of part-timers to do his field work. That's me. The computer system lets him have, like, ten times as many clients as he could without it. I take soil samples, acid levels, all kinds of chemical stuff. I can make some measurements and take pictures with my phone, and those get uploaded automatically. There's an app for that. One time he asked me to snail-mail him a clipping, so I did."

Again, Dr. Lyonne shook her head. "It's amazing how technology gets into everything."

The clock on her desk pinged. It always pinged at ten minutes before the hour.

"That's our time for today, Kendra," the doctor said. That's what she always said.

Kendra nodded, grabbed her backpack, tipped a half-nod/half-wave to Dr. Lyonne on her way out the door and ran down the stairs. She was two blocks away before she reached for the second water bottle she'd forgotten to ask for.

* * * * *

Kendra averaged about five gardens a day. Today was a four garden day, but one of them was a doozy. A topiary. One of her favorites. It would be her last stop.

She hopped on the metro and rode two stations further uptown and then changed to go out along one of the commuter lines for her first garden. It was as far out as she'd go today. She'd work her way back downtown doing stops two and three, and then cross back over beyond where she and her mom lived for the last stop. Go long and work your way back. She preferred to get the longest train rides over early in the day.

Walking to the first garden, she thought about what she'd need to do. It was fairly small, and ran almost entirely to specialty flowers, some in climate-controlled, semi-enclosed areas. Not as much fun, but not as much dirty work, either. More bugs. Oh, well. Bugs didn't bother her. She didn't understand why some girls got all weird about bugs and guts and stuff that was just… natural.

She arrived at the gate to the garden and punched a code into the electronic combination lock. That was one of the things that most of Mr. Vernon's gardens had in common. Made it easier than having to get keys for everyone. And if an employee got fired, everyone got a text message with the new code. It had already happened twice just since Kendra had started work this summer.

Kendra stepped into the garden area and her phone buzzed to let her know that there were new notes to read today… notes about some replacement supplies in the shed, it turned out. That was another hallmark of Mr. Vernon's sites. The shed, the tools, supplies, chemicals, plant food, seeds, etc. were kept on site and tracked via her smartphone app. Stuff got restocked by one of his company vans whenever needed. The sheds were powered and recharged the various portable, handheld electric tools. The power also took care of a small computer and wireless connection that relayed messages and supply requests back-and-forth from the main office.

Kendra opened the shed and pulled down her pruning shears and a new can of specialized fertilizer, as per the day's text message. As each came out of its spot on the shelf, her app relayed the information back to headquarters. The gloves she put on came out of her backpack. Those she had been given as a "new hire" gift by Mrs. Vernon (via her mom). They were very nice gardening gloves.

As usual, there was no one in the garden for the hour or so that Kendra was there. She worked quietly and efficiently, checking the flowers and plants for signs of injury, sickness or insects. She took care of a few minor problems herself, clipping off a sickly bud here, pruning an unsightly leaf there. She noted that one of the flowerbeds seemed to be too moist, while the ones opposite were too dry. It may have just been the time of day, or the wind or some other factor. But these plants were very moisture sensitive, and so she noted it in on her phone.

Materials back in the shed. Shed locked. Gate open. Gate closed. Gate locked. Lock confirmed. That last was an important step. The guy who'd taken her around the first half-week had made sure she understood that you lock the gate and then enter the unlock code in backwards to confirm that it's locked.

"You can't endanger clients' property by failing to unlock a gate," he'd told her. "But you can do so by failing to lock it. That's why locking is more important than unlocking." He'd nodded sagely as if imparting arcane wisdom of the ages. She'd nodded back as if glad to be absorbing such wisdom. Either way, she always remembered to confirm the locking code on the way out.

It was getting warmer. Kendra picked up a bottled water from a vendor outside the metro on her way down. This was a short jump, just two stations, to the number two garden. She drank the whole water on the subway and wished for more.

The second and third jobs went much like the first. At the third she bumped into one of the teams who did the watering, brought in new mulch, stuff like that. They had some pizza and gave her a slice, so she figured she could skip lunch, do the last garden, and maybe even get home a little early.

She had to walk almost five blocks to the last garden from her subway stop. It was in an older, more gentrified area of town. More brick, smaller buildings, old-fashioned architecture. As she crossed the street onto the block with the garden, she was glad to be coming into a much shadier stretch of road. Lots of big, older trees hanging over the curbs. Dappled sunlight passing through branches that almost touched above the street, making a kind of shaded corridor.

There were no commercial buildings on this block. Just apartments. And, from the street, it looked like just that; apartments and town houses. But the gate Kendra stopped in front of only *looked* like the front of a three story building. Behind it lay a hidden oasis of strange, green shapes at once both artful and chaotic.

This was the only garden for which there was an actual, physical key. Kendra reached into the zippered front pouch of her backpack and pulled it out. It was large and made of iron and looked just like you'd expect the key for some treasure chest to look. It was heavy and cold in her hand and it took a few tries and shakes before she could get the key to turn and the barred, iron gate to open.

Once inside, she closed and relocked the gate. This job would take her an hour at least and she didn't want some street person wandering in looking for a handout or a place to crash. After returning the key to her backpack, she turned and went through the short tunnel-like archway that separated the street from the garden.

It was only her fourth time at this garden and it still amazed and surprised her. A sharp bend in the brickwork directly after the gate hid the rest of the grounds from anyone looking in from the street. But once she was inside the gate, Kendra sensed that she'd passed into a different place. A strange world. And the tunnel was the first real step inside.

It was a narrow, brick archway, about ten feet tall at its center, curving down to about three feet tall on each side, at which point the walls went straight to the ground. It felt a bit, to Kendra, as if she were standing inside a short, brick pipe. The shape itself was fairly out of the ordinary, but the decorative architectural touches were what made it truly odd.

At the base of each side wall were a series of six inset alcoves. Not large, each only about the size of a shoebox. Inside each was a small statue of a nude child, and each little person was engaged in a different domestic activity; spinning, cooking, weaving, etc. The apex of the arch also had a number of insets, but these contained recessed lights which Kendra had never seen turned on. She assumed there were lit at night.

The floor of this short tunnel was also of brick, and was a kind of spiraling checkerboard pattern worked in shades of red and grey. It was pretty, Kendra thought, but, like the whole place, rather odd.

At the end of the tunnel she came into sunlight and the garden. Enclosed on all sides by the walls of the apartments surrounding it, and completely hidden from the street, it was as secret and confined a space as a convent or prison. That it was so well concealed only added to its allure as far as Kendra was concerned.

The enclosure was a full, square city block in size with well manicured grass covering almost the entire area. A narrow path made of small white pebbles went around the outside of the garden, and two small, old-fashioned looking park benches sat in the far corners opposite the side where the tunnel entered the square.

The center of the garden was the main attraction, though. A very slight rise, not even enough to be called a hill, curved gently up in the middle of the enclosed space. At the top loomed a group of sculptured hedges so unusual, yet so clearly designed and crafted, that they defied description. Their shapes were like nothing from nature, but did not in any clear way resemble man-made structures either.

At times some of the shapes reminded Kendra of paisley; those patterns you see on ties and in drapes. Some of the hedges seemed to have arms or appendages that reached out to entwine with shapes that rose and wove between some of the other plants. It wasn't a maze, no. Not a topiary labyrinth, like in *The Shining*. You could see clear across the garden in some places. No, it looked more like abstract art made of bushes. Kendra had seen some modern blown-glass sculpture that these green shapes reminded her of. It wasn't an exact comparison, *but with art, what is?*

She spent a minute or two just looking at the group of shapes. *They deserve a better collective name than "group,"* thought Kendra. *A murder of crows, pride of lions, gaggle of geese, pod of whales. What was it you called a bunch of larks? I heard it on TLC just last week. An exaltation! What should we call a group of abstract topiary forms?*

She busied her mind with that question as she busied her hands with her job. Same style shed as at the other garden, different tools and materials. In some of the other gardens she was allowed to do some pruning. Not here. She wasn't sure if Mr. Nelson did it himself, or if he had a higher-level gardener come in. Didn't really matter to her. She still had a lot to do. Weeding, checking for insects, testing moisture levels at a few places, taking a soil sample… lots of little chores. There were some other, less sophisticated shrubs around the sides of the garden, too, and she did all the maintenance on those. It was, for some reason, taking longer than she had remembered. By the time she was done she was hot, tired, hungry and thirsty.

There was a neat little bagel shop on the way home. *I can stop and get a bagel sandwich and some vitamin water,* Kendra thought. She looked at her watch. 6:50. *If I wait a bit to hit the metro I won't get to the bagel shop until after 7:30. It'll be less crowded and I'll have less of a wait.* She finished putting away her tools and supplies, locked the shed, and went to have a quick rest on the lawn at the base of the hedges. The grass was lovely, thick and soft. Perfect for napping on. She put her backpack under her head, stared up at the clear, blue sky, and watched a few tiny clouds float sluggishly across her view.

Maybe we could call them a "frame of topiaries," she thought. *Since you use frames to help train the hedges to be a particular shape. These are pretty weird though. Maybe a "glyph" would be better for them. Or a "mold."*

She looked up through the leaves, branches and intertwining limbs of the strange, artful hedges. As she turned her head to see a bit more of them, she noticed for the first time that there were statues sitting on the roofs of the buildings that made up the sides of the garden enclosure. She squinted into the sun and saw that they were gargoyles. They looked a bit like squat, monstrous dogs. With wings. And maybe talons and lizard tails. Stuff like that. Which was, she supposed, normal for gargoyles.

Curiouser and curiouser, she thought.

Warm sun. Soft grass. Tired and a little light-headed on low blood sugar and dehydration, Kendra let her mind drift. Which was easy, since she really didn't have a reason to keep it tethered.

All the clouds gone. Just blue sky so bright it was almost white, like the most faded color that denim jeans can get. The dark, deep leaves and the shadows of leaves in the topiary making a stark, sharp contrast to the bright, pale sky. Light and dark. Nonsense shapes. Art and nature. Whorls and curves.

Kendra turned her head back and forth on her backpack pillow and saw the shapes of the branches frame and expose the non-shapes, the negative space of the sky. *Like the ink blots and paper.* But the paper was the sky and the leaves were the ink. And suddenly, a woman's outline appeared, one hand raised above her head, the other on her hip, legs shoulder's width apart.

Nature imitates shrink, Kendra thought, smiling. *It really does look like the silhouette of a woman.*

The thought amused her and she wondered what one would say to get a lady to come down out of the sky. Chuckling to herself, she began to sing quietly:

"Step to the rhythm step step to the ride
I've got an open mind so why don't you all get inside
Tune in turn on to my tune that's live
Ladies flock like fish to my line
Hey, hey, hey, hey. Hey ladies! Get funky! Hey ladies!"

Kendra wasn't a huge Beastie Boys fan, but Shama's brother was totally old-school and it just seemed an appropriate way to shout out to some chick made of inverted space.

As Kendra finished the chorus, the sky behind the hedges seemed to glow a darker, yet stronger shade of blue for a moment. And then the inverted silhouette of the sky woman stepped out of her frame of hedge and shadow and floated down to stand on the grass beneath the branches that had so recently defined her. She struck a pose just a little ways off from where Kendra was reclining.

Surprised and amused, but not afraid, Kendra stopped singing and took a good look at the figure. First of all, the size was wrong. The body was proportioned like a normal person, but was about eight feet tall. Not long-legged like a basketball player or burly like a giant or anything. This was just an over-sized person.

And, of course, she was bright blue. The only breaks in the hue being shadows cast as if she was a solid creature, painted like the sky. That and her eyes, which were dark and seemed very human. She had no nipples and no genitals, which Kendra only noticed because she also had no clothes.

Kendra leaned up on her elbows to get a better look at her hallucination.

"This makes three today," she said out-loud. "Or is it four? Oh yeah. The pink clouds. I guess you're number four."

"What nonsense is this?" said the woman in a harsh, cold voice. "Give me your word."

A bit of cloud began to drift across the woman's chest. It looked like it was a reflection from the sky. Kendra looked up. Sure enough, a little cloud just the same shape was passing above the garden.

"I will take my meds as soon as I get home," murmured Kendra. She closed her eyes and rubbed her palms into them, squeezing her eyeballs a bit and massaging her forehead.

When she looked up, the woman was gone. Kendra was relieved.

Until something grabbed her by one of the straps of her overalls and lifted her completely off the ground. She struggled, shaking and grabbing at whatever held her up, but couldn't get a decent purchase on anything. She swung her arms, but connected with nothing. The fabric of the overalls was digging into her armpits, the crotch was pulling up tight in a kind of hanging-wedgie, and she still couldn't see what was happening.

Finally, with a quick, twisting motion, Kendra was spun around in mid-air and found herself facing the sky woman again. This time, when she spoke, Kendra could see that she had very white, very pointy teeth.

Again, that harsh, cold voice spoke: "It is yet day. The sun high. The aspect is wrong. We have never hunted in the day. I ask again," and she gave Kendra a shake, "What is your word?"

"I don't know what the heck you're talking about." She tried to pry the blue fingers from around the strap where they held her up, but could barely even get a grip on the creature's hand. She managed to register that its skin was cool and smooth like marble or glass.

"You have no word?" She shook Kendra again. "You did not call me?"

"No!" Finally, Kendra got a little mad. She'd talked with some hallucinations before, but they'd never messed with her like this. *Time to take charge of my own subconscious fiction,* she thought. "Put me the hell down!"

The sky-woman dropped Kendra to the ground in a lump.

"Hey!" she complained, rubbing her knee. "That hurt."

The creature wasn't listening to her anymore and began speaking to itself. "Summoned to The Garden, but with no binding. This is better luck than I've had in a very long time. If only it had been the night sky filling your song…"

Might as well play along, she thought. "We don't work in the gardens at night."

"What? Why?" the creature demanded. She reached back down as if to grab for Kendra again.

Kendra scooted back closer to the knot of shrubbery and answered, "Why would we? That's when the owners come in, I guess. What's the big deal?"

The sky-woman turned from Kendra and walked around the garden, looking at the benches and stone path. Then she saw the alley and walked through it, out of Kendra's range of vision.

Everything was quiet for a moment, but then Kendra heard a sound like a curse, but in a language she didn't understand. It sounded like Russian or Klingon or something very guttural.

The creature strode back into the garden with a purpose and came to stand directly over Kendra.

"You have a key," she said. It was not a question.

"Yes."

"Give it to me."

Again, Kendra thought, *Why not? I've played along with the delusions before and only been amused or mildly startled. Let's see what Ms. Big Blue Thing has in mind.* Kendra shrugged, reached into her pack and took out the old, brass key. She held it out and the sky-woman bent over her, hand reaching down.

But just before the large, blue fingers could grasp the key, a shadow passed behind the woman. Kendra looked to the side, lowering her hand and moving the key out of reach. The sky-woman looked behind her to see what had distracted the girl.

In the very next moment, a grey, bulky shape moved between them, pushing Kendra backwards on the grass, rolling her over on her side so that when she finally got to her knees she was about ten feet away from the sky-woman. Standing on the grass between the two was a gargoyle. One of the ones, Kendra thought, that had been sitting on the roof. With a sound like a garage door opening, it stretched thick, rocky wings up in a shield between Kendra and the blue creature. Kendra could only see about half its face over its shoulder, but it was comic-hideous; scary in a way that was too exaggerated. It snarled, and little pieces of stone dropped like drool from its mouth.

The sky-woman held her hands out in front of her, fingers spread, but pointing at the beast.

"Do not interfere, golem."

"Hahhkh!" The gargoyle made a sound that was something between a bark, a laugh and gravel being poured down a tin funnel. "Try. I show you teeth."

"Stone-monkey. I will have the key."

Now the gargoyle barked, and it was a noise like slabs of marble being slapped together. Two others of his kind landed on either side of him. Each was different, yet they were clearly related. One had a crown of horns and the other's head looked like a cross between a puppy and a lizard.

"Back inside," muttered the one with horns. His skin was darker than the first's, and his wings were pointier, more like a pterodactyl's.

"I will not," the sky-woman said, crouching low, clearly ready for a fight.

This is messed up, thought Kendra. *But, actually, pretty entertaining.*

She wasn't really worried. A lifetime of dealing with a personal, imaginary world of imbalanced brain chemicals had left her hard to shock. But she did want a better view, so she began to edge back toward the hedges. She glanced upwards to see how close she was and saw another pale, blue shape hiding between the branches of the topiary. Another negative space. This time in the shape of a cat.

She called to it: "Hello, kitty."

She was ready for it this time, but it was still rather startling. The outline of the sky-cat flashed, then a solid version leaped from the air and landed directly on the back of one of the gargoyles, tearing chunks of rock from its back. One of the other gargoyles turned to help, batting at the cat with rocky paws.

Rather than become engaged herself, the sky-woman stepped around the brawl in three unnaturally long strides, headed right at Kendra.

"The key…" she hissed. "Now!"

Kendra was still holding it at her side. Before, she hadn't really cared. But now the mean cat thing was hurting the gargoyle dog thing. And that wasn't nice. The gargoyles were much cuter than the cat or this pushy, blue chick.

"Nope," Kendra said. "No key for you."

"I will take it from you," growled the sky-woman, "and whatever flaps of skin come with it."

One of the gargoyles scrambled away from the fight with the sky-cat and hurled itself on the sky-woman's back. Gracefully, almost like a dance move, she ducked down on one knee, grabbed the thing's foreleg in a judo-like hold and threw it against the brick wall of the garden with a crunch. Kendra watched as it slipped to the ground, broken into two main pieces – front and back – both of which continued to move.

"Not long until night," the sky-woman said to no one in particular. Then she turned and strode back to where Kendra was sitting on the grass. She bent down and, again, lifted Kendra by her overall strap. This time, though, she merely left Kendra standing in front of her. As she stood, Kendra got a glimpse of another gargoyle in pieces surrounded by a pool of blue ichor. *Poor doggy,* she thought.

Very deliberately, the blue woman used one hand to raise up Kendra's arm, and began to try to pry the key out of her grip. If anything, the woman's efforts were hampered by the size of her own hands. She didn't seem to be able to get a purchase under Kendra's fingers. While this was going on,

Kendra simply watched. It was what she did. One part of her brain was excited and maybe a little afraid. But the other, the part that had kept her from losing her mind for many years, acted almost like a narrator, explaining how she should just let go of the key and see what happened. Or hang on to it. *No big deal either way.*

But before she could make up her mind, a large, grey set of teeth closed on the sky-woman's arm and bit it clean in two. Bluish fluid sprayed on the ground and on Kendra's clothes. She looked down and saw another gargoyle. This one was quite a bit larger than the other three. If they were bulldogs, he was a mastiff. She also saw that the sky-blood-liquid on the ground looked just like it did on the lady; little pieces of cloud moving through blue like the reflection of summer on a still lake.

The sky-woman screamed and brought Kendra's attention back to the fight.

Looking down at the big gargoyle, one arm a stump at the elbow, the sky-woman hissed, "Stand off, icon. This is not your concern."

In a voice like a small earthquake, the gargoyle replied, "My garden."

"Hah!" the creature laughed, seemingly unconcerned by the loss of her arm. She gestured around her. "So small a kingdom for a carving of your caliber. And only three…" she looked at the struggling halves of the split-open gargoyle, "Excuse me… two… subjects at your beck. So sad a king."

He shook his head. "Not king. Warden."

If it was possible, the sky-woman looked even more angry. But now she was offended, too. "Warden? Of a prison? Do you claim me as your prisoner?"

"Not prison," he replied. "Zoo."

Ohhhhh no you didn't, thought Kendra. *That's gonna piss her off.*

"I am no pet!" roared the creature, bending forward and charging straight at the gargoyle.

The sky-woman fought with more fury than skill. She seemed very strong to Kendra, who took a moment to stand up and dust off the seat of her pants. But not really skilled. Like an oversized junior-high school boy who's been thrown into his first fight.

The gargoyle simply hunkered down as the blue creature slapped and hit it on its shoulders, wings and head. Truthfully, the stone creature seemed more annoyed than afraid, and didn't react at all until the sky-woman reared back with her remaining arm above her head to strike downward at the dog-like creature.

At that moment, what had seemed a slothful pile of rocks jumped up with amazing speed and tore at the sky-woman's throat. It wasn't a killing blow, but what seemed to be gallons of cyan liquid spewed from a ragged tear in her shoulder. She screamed again and fell to her knees, clutching the wound with her one good hand.

"I will crush you for that," she spat.

The gargoyle sat patiently, panting a little, looking for all the world like he was waiting for someone to throw him a ball. *Or maybe a stone Frisbee,* Kendra thought. *Or a man-hole cover?*

The sky-woman tried to stand up but seemed too weak. She slid further onto the ground, leaning on her one good arm. When the gargoyle stood and trotted over to her she simply stared at him.

"Back in hole," the stone monster said.

The blue woman nodded, tried to stand, but clearly wasn't able.

"Grumph?" murmured the gargoyle, making a, "go on now" gesture with his snout.

"She," the sky-woman pointed at Kendra, "She must bid me leave."

Both of the fantastic creatures looked at Kendra. She had no idea what to say, so just shrugged.

"Well?" growled the gargoyle.

"I'm not sure how she got here. I sure as heck don't know how to send her back."

Although missing one arm and a large chunk of a shoulder, this seemed to amuse the sky-woman. She looked at both Kendra and the gargoyle the way a clever criminal might regard the bumbling detective who has, through sheer, ludicrous luck, managed to trap a prey much smarter than he.

The gargoyle broke the silence. "Kaolyn comes. He will know what to do."

Kendra nodded. *Why not? Wait for somebody else.* She sat down on the grass and was about to lean back and have a bit of a lie down when the gargoyle whuffed: "You. Sit on bench. Benches for a reason. No problems when people sit on bench."

Kendra nodded, got up, and went to sit on the bench. The gargoyle and the sky-woman continued to stare at each other.

After a few uneventful minutes, the gargoyle growled, "Don't move," and went over to one of the piles of rocks. He began pushing the big pieces closer together with his nose, nudging small rocks and bits of grit into piles with his over-sized, taloned paws. The sky-woman watched him, shaking her head gently, still lounging on the ground like a broken, blue manikin.

At one point, the gargoyle spied a largish pool of what Kendra was now thinking of as "sky blood" and went over to look at it more carefully. After sniffing it, he hopped into the pool and jumped around in it, looking to Kendra like a strange, stone puppy playing happily in a puddle. When there was nothing left of the blue puddle, the gargoyle went back to arranging the piles of his former comrades' chunks.

The gate rattled. All three of them looked up. "Mirkir!" a voice called from the shadow.

"Whuff." answered the gargoyle. He trotted over to stand next to the sky-woman.

A man with long, black hair came into the garden from the short tunnel. At least, from a distance, he looked like a man to Kendra. As he got closer, though, she noticed some very strange details. His hair, for example, seemed to be a tangle of waist-length dreadlocks. But as he approached, she saw that they appeared more like many narrow, plaited leather strands. Growing out of his head, yes, but not quite hair. And his "hair" started very far back on his head. It reminded her of pictures of Chinese immigrant laborers working on the railroad.

His face wasn't quite the right shape, either. It was a bit too long, and the chin was too square. He was wearing wrap-around silver sunglasses that totally hid his eyes, and he wore long, silver earrings in both ears. Chains of charms and symbols it looked like.

When he was within twenty feet or so, Kendra stood up and moved toward the gargoyle. She sensed they needed to get this business resolved and done with. Why? She didn't know. But although the fight was over, she felt ill-at-ease all of a sudden. And it wasn't the presence of this very strange-looking man. At least she didn't think it was. There was a heaviness in the air there hadn't been before.

The man spoke. "You are Rain's helper."

Kendra nodded and said, "Yeah. Mr. Vernon. Rain Vernon. He hired me. I'm Kendra White. I guess you're Kaolyn?"

He nodded back at her and held out his hand for her to shake. She held out hers without really thinking and looked down at the last instant before they touched. As they grasped hands, she realized that he seemed to have an extra set of knuckles on each finger. They were long, long fingers, too.

He had a firm, no-nonsense grip but didn't try to get all macho or anything, and as they shook Kendra felt a cool sensation up the back of her spine as if she'd just been tickled.

Kaolyn nodded, releasing her hand. "Rain would need someone with a touch of grace. But not a true Reckoner. He has had… trouble… with assistants before."

Kendra shook her head. Weird is weird, and that's fine. But she was getting hungry.

"Look," she said, "I'm sorry for whatever trouble my daydreaming caused, but I've got to get going. I've barely eaten anything all day and I've got…"

Kaolyn raised his long-fingered hand as if to say, "Hush." He took off his sunglasses and she saw that his eyes were shaped like diamonds. Yellow diamonds with green at their centers. They looked a bit like snake eyes, but less threatening.

He stared straight into her own green eyes and said, "Tell me about the voices."

None of her hallucinations had ever done that; referred to other hallucinations. That was new.

"Look," she repeated. "I have to get going. I've got…"

But somehow, the golden eyes stopped her words mid-thought. She felt… compelled to answer his question. She didn't know why. It didn't seem important. But she wanted to talk. And so she talked, and he listened, as did the gargoyle and the sky-woman, who sat with ill-concealed impatience and scorn, occasionally glancing up and over her shoulder at the garden wall behind her.

"When I was six I had tea parties with my imaginary friends. I told my mom about it. She said all little girls have tea with imaginary friends. So I didn't think it was a big deal that one was a little boy whose skin was blue like dark ink is blue and who could sing to me in four part harmony. One of them was a girl with parrot wings who brought us all cookies made from sunlight. When I ate them, I felt warmer. There were others. But Ink Boy and Parrot Girl were there most often.

"I was about eight when I started telling mom the stories that they told me. And I told her that they sometimes pushed me on the swing when nobody else was there. She thought I was being funny and telling stories to get attention. When Parrot Girl started teaching me the words to songs that nobody else had heard of, she got a bit scared and took me to a doctor. He seemed very nice and talked to me for a long time about Ink Boy and Parrot Girl and the Bear Clown and Miss Tin. All my friends.

"Then he talked to my mom and I had to go to the hospital for six months. They gave me lots of medicine and my friends went away."

Kaolyn's face looked very sad. "Ah, medicine. To mask the mask. Schizoid delusions? With auditory hallucinations? Right?"

Kendra nodded.

Kaolyn asked quietly, "You stopped taking your medicine recently, eh?"

Again she nodded.

"Is this the first time?"

She shook her head. "No. About three years ago. I stopped cold turkey because the meds made me feel like I couldn't breathe. Like I was always underwater or being choked or held down. I'd been on this stuff for four years straight. When I dropped it, I crashed, hard, and woke up in a hospital bed with tubes in my arm and an angel standing next to the bed."

"An angel?" Kaolyn looked puzzled.

Kendra nodded again. "A beautiful lady with wings and a light behind her head. I know she wasn't real. But she was looking at me like she wanted me to be OK. Like she was my friend. And then she disappeared."

"And you went back on your medicine?"

"Yeah." She was looking away now, over the strange man's shoulder. Out at nothing. In at memory.

"The new stuff is lots better. It doesn't creep me out or make me feel crappy. But I still just wanted to be… well… just me. It's weird when you look at your friends and you wonder if they'd be your friends if you weren't on your meds. So this time I tapered off slowly. Skipped one every three days, then every two. Then one of my eight pills a day, you know. Got down to none. Been real careful. Mom hasn't caught me yet."

Kaolyn nodded and patted her on the arm. She seemed to refocus, shake her head and realize that there were other people there.

"What was I saying?" she asked Kaolyn.

"It doesn't matter," he replied. He stood up next to the bench and looked around the garden. The sun was disappearing behind the buildings, and he looked up at the empty gargoyle-pillars in the corners of the roof. "You won't remember any of this."

He reached toward her with two of his long, long fingers. Kendra saw that he had a ring on his index finger that looked like a snake curling around and around his finger several times. It was silver and had green stones for eyes. He put his hand on the side of her face and she could feel the cool metal of the ring against the line of her jaw.

There was a blink of light, like when the sun reflects off a camera lens. And for just a moment Kaolyn looked to Kendra like a normal guy with long, greasy black hair. His eyes were brown, not yellow, and roundish like everyone else's eyes. The shape of his face wasn't strange anymore, either. She heard a small, "Whuff." And there at the foot of the bench was a bulldog. Not a gargoyle. Just a plain, ugly ol' bulldog. Cute, in its gruff, wheezing way. Where the sky-woman had been was a blue-grey hawk with a broken wing.

That's puzzling, thought Kendra. *I could have sworn they looked…*

At just that moment the moon, up early in the evening this time of the year, raised a shining sliver of her face above the far garden wall.

The sky-woman reappeared. And as if she'd heard a bell rung in the distance, she turned and smiled.

The sky had begun to darken. So had her skin. There was some red and orange at the horizon, and deep blue at the apex of the sky. Kendra saw this —the range of colors spreading across the woman — and thought it was quite beautiful.

Then the woman raised the ragged stump of her severed arm to the sky, a look of joy on her strange, blue face. And silver flowed from her shoulder up into the arm, over the elbow and into the space where her wrist and fingers would have been. The arm reformed itself, as smooth and silent as the moon rise.

Kaolyn sensed Kendra's attention and looked behind him. As he turned, the sky-woman pulled a piece of her own flesh from the side of her head and hurled it at him with brutal force. He ducked, and the material splashed the brick wall behind them, making a sizzling noise against the stone. A spatter of this darker, harsher, sky-blood caught Kendra in its spray and struck her across her chest near her collar bone.

For Kendra, time froze.

There was nothing in her world but pain. Like fire, like acid, yes. That kind of pain. It felt as if someone had branded her flesh with tiny coils of electricity. She couldn't get away from it. She scratched at the skin but there was nothing there; no fluid, no scar, no scab, not even a bump or a blister. She could feel it burning, but couldn't touch it with her hand. She could feel it eating its way through to the other side of her body.

Her body jerked and clenched so hard that she fell off the bench and onto the ground. Without thinking, she tore out a handful of grass and tried rubbing it into the pain. It did not help. She couldn't breathe enough to scream, though she thought she'd like to. She felt as if she would faint and welcomed it. *Yes, please,* she begged in her mind. *Please, I'd like to pass out now and wake up somewhere else.*

The sky-woman raised her hand to be fully in the moonlight and smiled, as much as she could, through the ruin she'd made of her own face. The she plunged her hand into her body, under her ribcage, digging for something inside. Her skin around that area was deep red, like the horizon at sunset, but with shafts of yellow and orange and blue running throughout.

Insanely, even through the terrible pain, Kendra couldn't stop marveling at how lovely the colors were.

Kaolyn, already ducked down to one knee, reached to the ground and pulled up a fistful of grass in each hand. He quickly rolled them together, like you would with dough or clay, into a small shaft of woven green. Looking up, he saw that the sky-woman had completely pressed her hand into her own torso, reaching for some substance deep inside herself. The rest of her body glowed with silver highlights and had begun to be edged by a deep, sharp black. She pressed harder, gasping and smiling at the same time, as her arm pushed further into her body.

In Kaolyn's hands, the little roll of grass had become longer, impossibly longer, growing to the size of a javelin. The bits of grass, the ragged blades that bent out near the tip, had come to resemble the barbs on a harpoon.

The sky-woman grunted, and it was a sound like a woman giving birth or being punched hard. But the look on her face was one of wonder and anticipation. She looked down at Kendra, the girl's hand still clutching the key to the garden, smiled, and began to walk toward her, one arm still buried elbow-deep in her abdomen, still clutching at something inside her own body.

Kendra could not move. The pain was paralyzing. It pinned her to the ground. All she could do was watch as the enormous, beautiful woman, painted all the colors of the dying sky, came at her.

Behind the sky-woman, Kaolyn stood up, placed the tip of his spear against his mouth and spat on the barbs. With a small sound like, "Hy-key-ah," he pulled the spear back over his shoulder, then lunged forward and threw the shaft at the sky-woman from behind.

It looked to Kendra as if the spear went through the center of the sky-woman's back, right between her shoulders. It came out just below her throat, and sent another shower of black-blue-red-silver fluid spewing toward Kendra.

She managed to roll out of the way as the blood-liquid rained down. The giant woman pulled her hand from inside her body, releasing whatever fey organ she'd meant to dislodge, and grasped at the spikes of the spear protruding from her throat instead. She could not seem to get a grip on it, her hands slipping and pulling uselessly at the blades of slick, shiny grass.

The woman fell to her knees, eyes wide but unseeing. With a last gasp, she fell sideways onto the ground near the bench, the shaft of the spear breaking in two beneath her. Wet, sloshing sounds continued to emanate from the dead, blue body for several moments, and then it was still and quiet.

The gargoyle, Mirkir, trotted over to sit next to Kaolyn on the grass.

"Pesky things," the gargoyle muttered. Kaolyn nodded.

Kendra stood up, unsteadily, and touched the spot on her neck. It didn't hurt anymore. There was a numbness there; a place where she couldn't feel anything. But at least it didn't hurt. She looked over at the two friends. One looked vaguely alien, complete with leather hair and reptilian eyes. The other looked like a gargoyle. The gargoyle had, indeed, just spoken. She glanced over her shoulder. The broken, blue body of the sky-woman lay spread out in the dim evening light, her skin growing darker as the sky above her did. Her sightless eyes were open and black, and her chin was tilted up at a strange angle, resting on the tip of the grass spear that poked through her throat.

It may have been the relief from pain, low blood sugar, dehydration or shock. Whatever the reason, Kendra slumped down on the bench, and then slid onto her side, passed out cold.

The man and the gargoyle stood looking at the girl and the dead woman-thing. The sky still held some light, but it would be full dark soon. There was a mess to clean up, and gargoyles to reassemble or replace. But that would wait for a moment.

"She's marked," muttered Kaolyn. The gargoyle lifted one grey, stony eyebrow.

"She may remember everything after all," he continued. The gargoyle said nothing.

"Well?" Kaolyn asked. "What do you think?"

The gargoyle looked up into the sky. "I think it's gonna rain," he said.

The light faded as Kaolyn tucked the brass key into Kendra's backpack.

Chapter 2. Labyrinth

When the greenman and the gargoyle brought the girl to the Library, Mr. Monday thought she was dead at first. Sometimes simpler creatures believe a sacrifice will earn power or influence. Which may be true in other domains, but not in the Library. As Monday's mentor had told him, a very long time ago, "The truth of a sacrifice is only as powerful as its effects."

Watching them via one of his simplest Ways, Monday murmured, "Take your blood and broken bodies to a master of change. I only see what is."

He felt them before he saw them, when they set foot on the concrete steps outside the Library. The Mundanes would see only a tall, thin man with a blue laundry bag on his shoulder and a bulldog by his side. An ugly bulldog. A short, fat, slobbery, cross-eyes, ugly bulldog. Monday immediately saw across their Seeming and knew the man wasn't human, the bag was a dead girl and the dog a minor gargoyle.

The two stone lions that guarded the steps didn't even bother to stop them. Very few Reckoners ever brought anything like a challenge into the Library. None who did emerged whole. The lions were there as a warning. Stated simply, they declared:

Mr. Monday does not tolerate foolishness.

Why didn't he know immediately that she wasn't dead? Because he didn't take the time to look. He could have read her line or focused on her condition as soon as she was brought inside. But he assumed the greenman simply wanted, as did all his visitors, information of some sort. A book or lineage, a map, recipe, tale or history. Monday didn't care for the new digital forms as much, but he had them available for the technophiles. Most of his serious clients still preferred paper. Or clay. Or a variety of other, highly unique media.

The body, the greenman, the gargoyle... all inconsequential. Mr. Monday went back to his reading; "Musical Architecture," by Whynne Breedie. His copy being only one of three that hadn't been lost to time and trouble.

A few minutes later, though, he sensed the greenman again as he stepped across the first Seeming in the atrium. Monday only noticed it as you might a car horn in the traffic outside, or the shifting of cloud shadow on your window. The Library was frequented by a great number of Reckoners as well as Mundanes. Something for everyone, eh? That's what a library is for, after all.

When the greenman began to move against the second Seeming, though, Monday looked up from his reading and cocked his head for a closer listen. Those who had been to the Library before – and especially regular clients – knew how to request a meeting. You ask a lesser clerk to see if the Librarian is available. They either know his schedule well enough to answer directly, or they call for details. Mostly they know which patrons he'd be willing to see immediately and which needed to be calendared.

You don't just start pushing into the core of the Library uninvited. That's rude. It would be like someone walking into your bathroom and chatting you up while you showered. Bad form, at least. Possibly even hostile.

So Mr. Monday stood up, saved his place with a page from his "Dilbert" calendar, walked out of his private office and into the administrative area.

Depending on how well you knew the Library, whom you wanted to see, and how well you reckoned, it could have looked eight different ways. Monday, of course, saw them all at once.

He was the Librarian, after all.

As he walked down the hallway, several employees and patrons waved or nodded or murmured a word of greeting. He smiled back and wove between the various people, carts, okulae and shelves to the door at the end of the hall and went out into the atrium.

The greenman was struggling with the second Seeming. He thought he was moving into a place that looked vaguely like the stacks, but with taller shelves and books made out of stone. There was less light, more shadow; a Seeming laid on to do exactly what it was doing to him; prevent his entering further without assistance.

Monday, though, was a curious person, as you'd expect. So rather than move out and confront the intruder as he struggled, he opened the second Seeming entirely and let him pass into the next Way of the domain. Not the center, where he had his office, but closer to the administration Way.

Have you ever been in a library and felt the presence of the books—a quiet, musty sense of being watched? Because, of course, books read people, too. Most dedicated bibliophiles, even Mundanes, can feel the pressure of all those words, pages, stories and lore. The part of your mind that breathes language feels as if it's either underwater or in the mountains. The mental pressure is different in a library. And it isn't entirely benign, is it? It's not always comfortable there, alone, among the stacks.

The greenman plunged through the Seeming and into the next Way like a horse tripping into the ocean. He went down on one knee and swung the body around in front of him so it wouldn't tip him backwards. The gargoyle went a few steps beyond that point but stopped when he sensed his companion's trouble.

It had been so long since Monday had apprenticed to his original master the he could barely recall the first time he'd been pushed into a true sanctuary of Sight. The place where real work is done. He vaguely recalled feeling as if he'd suddenly seen through a thousand pairs of eyes and heard a hundred conversations at one time. A rushing and pouring out of pictures, thoughts, sounds, light and shadow. A jungle of meaning. For one who is untrained and unaccompanied, it was quite nightmarish.

The greenman let the girl's body roll out of his arms and onto the stone floor. He wrapped his arms around his head and tried to fold in on himself. Trying to keep out the flood of images and sounds. What some of Monday's younger staff had taken to calling "content."

The gargoyle seemed to be having an easier time. He looked confused – *Most of his kind would be confused by a pinwheel*, Monday thought – but not troubled. *Closer to a true Natural than many*. He made a slow circle around the greenman, stopping to sniff the air a few times, before looking right at the Librarian.

Monday spoke: "I'll give you this; you found me quicker than most have"

The creature growled, "Why this?" His grey skin was streaked with white. *Pigeon guano, if I don't miss my guess.* He had wings, folded up like a bedroll on his back. *Ornamental, probably.*

The Librarian applied enough control over the Seeming to tone down the rush of images and sounds. The greenman must have perceived the change as a profound relief, as his arms came down from around his head and he leaned his hands on the floor.

Monday knew what the greenman was going to do before his hands left the floor. Long dreadlocks trailing behind him like black smoke, he surged to his feet and charged right at the older-seeming man. His green, diamond-shaped eyes bright and wide with anger.

The greenman climbed three steps to the top of the atrium, within about a yard of the Librarian, before Monday raised one finger slightly, letting the full effect of the Way of Erasure wash across the intruder.

At which point the greenman stopped as if he'd slammed into a wall. And held himself very, very still.

What did he feel? Hard to describe, but... Imagine you could sense all your memories, all your thoughts, feelings, emotions and skills as a limb. An extra arm or leg or maybe... an eye. Yes. An eyeball is a better analogy. And imagine that as you were running, you suddenly saw that someone had an ice-pick waiting at just the right place to plunge into that third eye and destroy every thought you'd ever had, every feeling, every memory and ability.

"Not a nice feeling, is it?" Monday asked. "But," he continued in low, slow tones, "I don't like being attacked in my own Library."

"Why," Monday continued, "Do you people think that because we're bookish we're slow? There's this almost inbred notion that academics, professors, teachers, librarians and researchers are plodding, sloth-like creatures. Maybe when we're out under the sun. But not here. Not in our realm."

Monday sighed. "So easy to predict. So easy to control."

48

The greenman shifted his eyes to try to look for some way out.

"If you move," the Librarian said to him quietly, "my word will gut your soul. Do you understand?"

He managed to nod without moving his head and Monday eased back a bit. The greenman sensed he had enough room to breathe, and just barely managed to do that without falling down.

Then Monday felt a slight pressure on his leg. When he looked down, he saw that the gargoyle had his pointy, stone teeth wrapped gently around his shin. He looked up with those simple, animal eyes and managed to convey a look of both apology and threat.

As clearly as if he had spoken, Monday knew what he meant was, *I'm sorry to have to do this. But if you hurt my friend, I'm going to bite your leg clean off.*

Monday laughed and released the Way entirely. Not because he was afraid, but because the creature was just so obvious and straightforward. And yet he had managed to come farther into the Librarian's domain than his supposedly craftier and more intelligent friend. *There's a lesson there for us all*, Monday thought.

The greenman visibly deflated and looked at the Librarian with suspicion and fear.

"Good. That's more like it," Monday said. "Now...What do you want?"

Monday stood absolutely motionless, sensing that his own stillness made the greenman even more uncomfortable. Greenmen are horribly good at reading body language. In his Library, Monday did not speak in any unintended fashion.

The intruder gestured with his hand at the body on the floor. "She has seen things," he said quietly, "that she does not understand."

"She's not dead?" Monday assumed not, but sometimes we ask to be sure.

He shook his head. "Just in shock. She was sprayed with skyblood."

"Then she should be dead," Monday replied. "Contact with an aethereal humor is almost always fatal for Mundanes. It usually presents as a heart attack or aneurysm."

"Yes. I know," the greenman said. "But she opened a shadow Way."

"You mean a mold. She filled a transition mold."

The greenman shrugged. "Yes. If you say so. See... she is not in the Domain of the garden's owner. The topiary garden. Where it happened. Because of what happened... because of how... the Law isn't clear. But if I left her in the street and leaned her up against a bench or something, somebody would've gashed her.

"Look," he stepped backward and rolled the girl from her side onto her back. He moved her arm from across her chest so that Monday could see her collar-bone. There were several spotty, iridescent blue marks on her skin. Skyblood.

"You're right," the Librarian said. "Someone would have, as you so succinctly put it, 'gashed' her. Aethereals don't have many friends. And fewer servants. Any of the gangs would have thought her a tag."

The greenman just nodded, still staring at the girl's shoulder. Now that Monday looked closely, he could see that she was still breathing.

The gargoyle broke the silence with a noise that sounded, to Monday, like, "Burf?"

The greenman stood. "I have to go," he mumbled. "Do you think... I don't know... I just thought I should bring her... somewhere. She has no House. Not that I know of. The garden might still kill her. Or claim her. The Law is unclear. But you answer questions. You... know things." He shrugged again. "This place? I didn't know what to do. I thought you could find out more."

Monday waved away his comment, shaking his head. "I'll take care of it," he said. Which is all the intruder had ever wanted the Librarian to say to begin with. "You can go now."

They both turned to go, but before they reached the door to the foyer Monday said, "Don't come in here again without asking."

They didn't slow or nod or show any sign they'd heard as they left.

Monday crouched down on the stone floor to have a better look at her. They wouldn't be bothered, as the atrium was a place in between other places, and only open to the Librarian and some of the senior clerks. And they knew well enough not to bother Monday while he was inside.

As he'd often said, "Good staff is the heart of a great library"

She seemed like a standard Mundane to Monday. *A "chronic,"* he thought to himself, *is, I believe, the slang term the young folk are using these days.* A girl. Small for fifteen; Monday, of course, could tell her age to the day from the briefest glimpse. Her brown hair was cut shorter in back than in front, so the bangs fell over her cheek. She was lying on her side, and he could see that the knees of her jeans were dirty – not grubby, but actually dirty, as if she'd been kneeling in soil. There was dirt under her fingernails, too.

The greenman has said something about a garden. Maybe she worked there? Or was hiding?

Her skin was pale, which could have been from shock or injury. *Pleasant enough to look at,* Monday thought.. *If you don't mind spending time with Mundanes, that is.*

He spoke to her, then, in a soft voice. Almost a whisper. "There's something so unnerving about you all sometimes. I can clench my teeth and be a nice host if I must, but it's like being around the truly blind. Or children who won't behave. Some part of me always wants to simply get up and leave."

But the shimmering, blue blotches near her shoulder hinted at a story. And what kind of Librarian can ignore that? Monday didn't believe that curiosity killed the cat. His theory was that she had been the victim of bad planning. And he hadn't lived... well... a very, very long time without getting quite good at planning for the possible effects of his curiosity.

He called for a clerk – whomever was nearest, he didn't care – to come assist him. Wallace Bradstreet quietly approached. *No real aptitude for serious research*, Monday thought. *But stout enough for today's needs.*

He was reaching down to touch her on the shoulder, near the blue patch, when he was interrupted from behind.

"Sir?" the young clerk said softly.

"Please bring this person to my office directly," Monday said, rising from a crouch.

He would later think, *How much would have been different had Wallace been just a moment later… had I touched her skin at that moment.*

Turning to walk back to his office himself, he saw that Wallace had made no move to comply.

"Wallace?" he asked, one eyebrow up. "Is there a problem?"

"Sir," he whispered. "She's… not… you know. Awake."

"I know that, Wallace," Monday replied. "That's why I called you. Please carry her to my office and put her on the rug in front of the fireplace."

He still looked unsure.

"Pick her up. In your arms, Wallace. Carry her into my office. Place her, gently, on the rug by the fireplace."

"I understand that, sir," he said, clearly uncomfortable. "But she's a… you know…"

"I think," the Librarian replied, "That I know what she is. And I know what I want. Please do as I've asked."

"Yes, sir," he mumbled, bending to pick her up.

Monday supposed Wallace was worried that she'd wake up in his office – his sanctum sanctorum – and become disoriented. Some of the inner workings of the Library had that effect on Mundanes. As long as Monday was with her, though, he could mitigate the effects of his Ways. What would happen after that was anyone's guess.

Wallace carried her in front of him, like a groom would carry a bride across the threshold, and followed Monday through the administration area and back into his office. He put her down, very gently, on the thick, patterned hearth rug, and stood up, stretching his back muscles a little bit.

Perhaps not as stout as I'd thought, mused Monday.

"Anything else, sir?"

"Not at this time, no. Thank you for your help, Wallace."

The young man nodded and left the office. Most of Monday's staff, especially at the lower levels, understood that he rarely engaged in idle chatter or gossip. A very few senior clerks, and of course Mrs. McKey, his assistant, took the liberty of engaging him in conversation occasionally. Which was to be expected. One of the rewards of long, devoted service is more personal access to one's superiors. Some of them even had something worthwhile to say once in a great while.

Monday sat down to read, picking up where he'd left off and didn't really think of the girl again until he heard her stir. It had been at least an hour since Wallace had deposited her there. She moaned very slightly and took a deep, loud breath. The Librarian turned his chair around to watch as she regained consciousness.

She levered herself up on her hip with one arm, the other hand rubbing her eyes. When she pulled her hand away, he could see that her eyes were very bright green. *Rather lovely, actually,* he thought. Her brown hair seemed to have a bit of red in it not evident earlier in the dim atmosphere of the atrium.

She looked around the room, as if trying to place it. What she saw was a rather large office with tall, narrow windows on one side, a fireplace opposite, and bookcases everywhere else—the shelves even went around the door and fireplace. There was also a large, antique roll-top desk covered in papers and books and other office paraphernalia. Against one wall was a gray, rather drab couch with standing floor lamps at each end. A stuffed, taxidermy crow sat on a wrought-iron perch. And in an old-style office chair on rollers sat an old-style librarian.

Monday resolved simply to kill her outright if the first words out of her mouth were, "Where am I?" Her death was certainly a possibility no matter what, but Monday hated to be bored.

Instead, she shook her head a bit, rubbed her eyes some more, looked up at Monday, squinting as if into a bright light, and asked, "Is the gargoyle OK?"

Well... Not totally wearisome after all.

He put down his book, steepled his hands in front of his chin and replied, "He seemed fit when he and the greenman dropped you off."

She nodded, not looking directly at Monday. "Good," she said. She still seemed quite foggy. Monday didn't press, letting her come around at her own pace.

After a few more deep breaths, she sat back on the rug, legs crossed, and looked right at Monday.

"You remind me of Mr. Vernon," she said simply.

"How is that?" the older man asked.

"You both look old at first," she explained. "But there's an energy to you. As if you've got extra batteries or something."

Monday nodded sagely. He had no idea what she was talking about.

"Why don't we," he said reasonably, "Start with your name." *Mundanes*, he thought, *often won't do or say much until their labels are taken care of. Which is certainly understandable when you consider how little they know.*

"I'm Kendra," she said. "Kendra White."

"Well Kendra, why do you think you're here?"

She frowned and rubbed her head with one hand, clearly still a bit puzzled. "The last thing I remember was the tall, alien-looking guy with the dreadlocks spearing the sky woman with a huge blade of grass. It's blood was blue and when some of it splashed on me it hurt like heck."

She looked down at her shoulder and saw the spots. "Doesn't hurt anymore, though," she commented.

Which wasn't really an answer to Monday's question. *I must remember to keep it basic with these people.*

"Where were you when this happened?" he asked.

"In one of Mr. Vernon's gardens. The topiary."

And then she laughed. Now, Monday was not much of a laugher himself, but he thought that hers was very fine and deep, especially for a young girl. He was often peeved when women giggled like birds or yipped like little dogs. Kendra had a full, honest laugh and for the first time he began to consider that she might live through the day. He had no idea what he would do with her, but was intrigued by the depth and character of her laugh. It almost reminded him of true speech, as opposed to the limited doggerel he was forced to use with Mundanes.

Monday allowed a small, half-smile. "And what," he asked, "is so funny, young lady?"

She shrugged. "This," she pointed at the blue marks on her skin. "You," she pointed at Mr. Monday. "Aliens. Gargoyles. Crazy, nude, blue women. I really shouldn't have gone off my meds."

Ah. Drugs, Monday thought. *When Mundanes come into contact with the real world they often blame their new perceptions on pharmacological effects. Apparently the lack of drugs could also be blamed. That's a new piece of information. Two points for the little girl.*

"Be that as it may," he continued, laboring to return to the subject, "Do you have any idea where you are or how you came to be here?"

She shook her head. "No," she replied. "I'm totally in the dark there."

He nodded, watching as she began to rotate her head as if to get some stiffness worked out of her neck. Then, quite suddenly, she stood up and said, "I appreciate you letting me... nap... or whatever... on your rug, Mr... Sir... But I've got to get home. I was going to be late before I passed out and freaked out and passed out again, I guess. So now I'm gonna have some 'splainin' to do, too."

She was smiling politely, waiting for Monday to dismiss her so that she could turn around, go out to the street, and, presumably, find a taxi or subway home. The Librarian was dampening many of the effects of his Ways that would most discomfit a Mundane, but not all of them. One can't completely hide the truth, merely cover it over a bit. And yet, there she stood, polite and confident, waiting for permission to leave.

He did not give it. He simply stood and waited.

"I have to get going now, Mister," she said. Her tone was wary, but her eyes were steady. *Many children in this era,* Monday thought, *grow up very quickly and become hardened early on. I'm not sure if this is always good. She looks as if she has been taught a thing or two about men who keep young girls back in their offices overlong.*

"Not yet," he said softly. "First, I want you to tell me what you first saw when you went to the topiary garden this afternoon."

She looked puzzled, and he knew she wouldn't actually answer his question with words. He didn't expect her to, and it didn't matter that she wouldn't. Simply asking the question generated the response he needed. The slightest thought about her morning provided the bookmark. You need to start somewhere, after all.

For her, he knew, the entrance of the Way would feel like going to sleep. Her eyes glazed over and she backed up one step, bumping into and then slipping down on the drab, gray couch. He sat beside her, and read a small chapter of her life. To walk his Way through and around the events that had led her to his Library.

Monday saw the garden, then. Heard the creak of the gate. Smelled the grass and the mulch. He was there because she was there.

It took the Librarian less than a minute to review the event in extreme detail. Had anyone asked him the color of the bus that had passed her as she stopped to find the key, he could have told them, even though Kendra could not have. He could have told Kendra what song she'd been humming to herself as she'd worked in the garden. In many ways, he'd lived the events more completely than had she.

But as he often told his staff, *Experience itself is no substitute for good editing.* It was his ability to edit and sort, store and retrieve information that made him so effective in his role. And Kendra's experience, all of it, went into a Way that he stored in what looked like note pad in his jacket pocket. Later, he'd take it out and transfer the important parts to a more permanent Way of preservation.

The Library closed to Mundanes at ten in the evening, and that time was approaching. The girl, Kendra, was sleeping on the couch as Monday's Way faded from her mind. The Librarian ignored her, continuing to read, occasionally making notes in the margin with a very sharp fountain pen. The ink he used was invisible to all but his own eyes.

A bit before midnight, there was a soft knock on the door. Monday knew it was Mrs. McKey. She knew where he was, and knew that he was aware of everyone's location in all the Libraries at all times. She couldn't have entered his office without permission, and knew that, too. But knocking is such a lovely, polite auditory cue. And she was, at most times, a lovely, polite person.

"Come in, Mrs. McKey," Monday said quietly, marking his place and putting the book down in his lap.

She only opened the door half-way, just enough to poke her head in. As always, she was dressed in shades of brown and grey, a little too warmly for the time of year. Her hair was cut short in a style currently popular among many older women. Fifty years before or so, it might have been called a "bob" or a "pageboy." Monday recalled the decades when she'd worn it in a very severe bun. If he'd suggested, then, that she cut it in a "bob," she'd have blushed to her roots and scolded him like a naughty schoolboy.

"I'll be going home now, Mr. Monday," she said quietly, her eyes sliding for a moment to rest on the body of the girl on the couch. He didn't take the bait.

"That's fine, Mrs. McKey," he replied.

"Will you be needing anything else before I leave?" Again, her eyes wandered to the couch. It had been quite some time since Monday had tested anyone in the center of his realm. Mrs. McKey had been a younger woman then, of course. Though she'd never been squeamish. *You can't work for a Master*, Monday thought, *and be all weak-kneed and squirrely.* To the Mundanes, she looked as if a stiff wind might knock her over—like someone's kindly, spinster aunt. But Monday had seen her kill a man with a fireplace poker and escape a burning building by jumping out a fifth story window.

"No, Mrs. McKey. Thank you, though." She turned to leave, clearly disappointed that he wouldn't be sharing any information. People who work in research hate to be kept in the dark. Monday decided to let a little light in.

"This is Kendra, Mrs. McKey," he said, gesturing at the sleeping girl. "There is a chance that she'll still be wandering through the Library when you return tomorrow morning to open up. There is a chance that she will be… not wandering. There is a very slight chance you may find her on the steps outside. In any event, you know what action to take. I will be in my rooms until 10am or so. Please don't disturb me unless it's urgent."

The silver-haired woman smiled and nodded. The particular event or incident was insignificant. But to be trusted by one's superiors is of great importance to one's self esteem.

"Of course Mr. Monday," she replied. The door clicked closed behind her and he could hear her sensible shoes making their precise little "clop, clop" noises as she made her way down the administration hallway.

Monday turned to regard the girl. *The tasks of discernment*, he thought, *are so much more complicated for many of my brothers and sisters.* In his case, though, the environment would provide the test. Survive the environment, pass the test. For those undergoing Monday's exam, it was very much like swimming… or drowning; once you're in the water, the element itself provides both the exam and the final grade.

Monday didn't even need to watch the proceedings, of course. But he'd taken a curious interest in the girl. She looked so fragile and… generic…

laying there on the couch. But she had some spirit. And she'd survived a skyblood mark. Perhaps keeping an eye on her would prove additionally entertaining.

He walked to the couch, crouched down and put a hand on her shoulder. She might otherwise simply have slept the night through, and that wouldn't have done at all. One way or another, her test would be over by dawn, and that would give Mrs. McKey an hour or two to get the girl back on her feet, or to get things cleaned up before the Mundanes appeared on the steps as the Library opened for business. *Say what you will about their limited abilities,* Monday thought, *but some of them do love their libraries.*

"Young lady," he said, as he stood to go. He said it firmly, but not too loudly. It could have been a whisper, in his office, and sufficed.

She sat up on the couch, looked around through squinting, sleepy eyes and said, "I'm still in your office."

Monday nodded and asked, "You didn't expect to be?"

She shook her head. "No. It reminded me too much of things I've imagined. Things that disappeared when I've gone to sleep and then woken up. Sorry to have crashed on your couch." She stretched her arms out a bit, yawned, and stood up.

The Librarian backed up two steps, as he had been crouching very near the couch. She looked up at him and said, "I've really got to be going now. My mom's going to be… well, maybe she won't be, but I should still get going."

She looked around for her book bag and spied it on the floor by the desk. She went over and picked it up, slinging it across her shoulder with that casual ease that all young people seem to have with their things. As if the objects that they use the most are part of them; tails or horns or manes.

"Yes," Monday said to her, and she turned back to look at him.

"Yes, what?" she asked.

"Yes, it's time for you to leave," he explained.

She looked, for a moment, very young and lost and he almost pitied her.

"I'm sorry, Mr…" she began.

"Monday," he informed her.

"Mr. Monday," she said, actually looking sorry. "I still don't know what the heck's been going on. I really do appreciate the nap. And I'm sorry if I've been a bother. If you need to call my mom to… I don't know… if there's anything you need from me?"

He nodded, wondering how he appeared to her. Unlike many Reckoners Monday rarely used a Seeming to appear different to Mundanes. He looked, within the Ways, more-or-less, like what they saw.

I suppose I actually look a bit grim, he thought. Tall, lanky, white hair thinning on top. Dark grey suit over black shirt and black tie and dark brown skin. Black shoes, of course. Why any man would wear brown shoes was beyond Monday's understanding.

 "It is time for you to leave, Kendra," he explained, "but whether or not you do leave will depend on you."

She looked confused. He didn't let her ask the obvious question. He simply explained all that he was prepared to explain, and nothing more.

"You have stumbled into my world," he said, walking around the front of his desk to collect his book. "You have been brought here when, really, you should not have been. And you have seen things you oughtn't have."

She looked ready to protest, and he held up his hand. She remained silent. Point for Kendra.

"It is not your fault, no. But that doesn't matter. Much of what transpires for good or ill is not of our choosing nor of our doing. Nevertheless, we must play the hand we are dealt."

He walked to the door, opened it, and turned to face her one last time.

"When I leave this room, you will be alone in my office," he said quietly and calmly. "There is no lock on this door. Nor are there any locks anywhere within my Library. At least none as you understand the concept. I am going upstairs, to my apartment, to eat, read a little, and then to bed.

"It is," he checked his watch, "12:39 am. You have until dawn to make your way out of this office, out of the Library and to the front steps of the building. I suggest, if you do so, that you wait there for Mrs. McKey. She will get you a nice breakfast and explain a few things. Do you understand?

Kendra shook her head. "No," she said. "If there are no locks, why on earth would it take me, what? Five or six hours to get out of the building?"

He shrugged. "No. It might not take you that long at all. That's as may be. But if you are still inside my institution when the sun rises, you will die."

Her mouth opened wide at that, and Monday knew she would say something foolish or ask for greater explanations, none of which would be of any value whatsoever. So he simply smiled, spun on his heel and shut the door behind himself.

The feel of Monday's Way expanding in his wake was always something he savored. He had been holding it in check for quite some time in order to give the girl a chance to rest and now it opened like a warm cascade of light behind him; a waterfall of images and memory and power. It was, to him, the natural, pure ambiance of the universe. The shining, beautiful layers of meaning that overlay the crudity of simple objects and base actions when they are truly Seen.

Through the office door, Monday heard the girl inhale a gasp, and then begin to scream.

There was no carpet in the administration hall. The heat and air all came in through small openings at the top of the doors. Sound carries very well in museums and libraries, for some strange reason. Her screaming, ragged and desperate, followed him all the way through the administration wing and he could even hear it, faintly, as he opened the door that led to his private quarters.

It sounds, he thought to himself, *as if she is on fire.*

Monday did not think himself a cruel man. And so he was glad when the door to his room, swinging shut behind him, finally cut off the sound of her shrieking. *Not a hopeful sign, all that yelling, I suppose,* he thought.

Chapter 3. Perception

The moment the door shut behind Mr. Monday, Kendra's universe became something...else.

She had one split second of confusion, and then--

light white pressure black and checkerboard ice hands ice eyes where white not white spinning all the eyes red falling red waterfall red river white moon yellow teeth teeth teeth choking my name my name long long word stopped point poke stab impale pierce shatter scatter dust stretch falling stretch sleeping stretch dream no dream red moon red teeth hands claws cold cold picking stacking dust fire needle pin poke stab NO, thank you, thank, you, no no no no redwhiteteethhandmoonfallwindwhip --

her mind and body interpreted what she was experiencing as points of pain up and down her arms and legs. Nausea, as if she were about to vomit everything she'd ever eaten. Dizziness and vertigo so bad she was sure she was falling. Extreme cold. All at once.

She shut her eyes, gasped for air, fell to the floor, and screamed because there was nothing else to do. Nothing to do besides let some of the terror out. So much was flowing into her, somehow she had to force some of it to leave her head. And screaming was all that was left.

Every color, every sound, every smell… every perception entering her mind was burdened with a thousand, thousand meanings and a hundred feelings. She couldn't move on the floor without it speaking to her, yelling at her, questioning her in languages she didn't understand. She couldn't breathe without the air itself trying to yell at her about subway art and bakery oven technology, the way urine smells if someone has liver disease, rock quarry physics and childbirth statistics, neon sculpture and bookbinding, the history of the orders of Catholic nuns and how fire spreads in hallways.

She struggled to her knees, arms wrapped tight around herself. Dimly aware of the shape of objects around her, even with her eyes closed, she fell and managed to land half-on, half-off the couch. It, too, had stories to tell. Insistent stories, complete with over-sharp sensations. Her inner-eye was alive with a million shades of brown for some reason. She remembered the couch as being more of a gray, but in her brain it was now a thing of brown history. And the sounds… they filled her mind with words… some she could understand, some she couldn't. Pieces of songs, snatches of conversations, so many voices. So many touches. Intimate touches, glancing fingers, bumps and pokes, the scrape of a vacuum cleaner across the back of her eyes.

Her mind was filled again. Filled to breaking, and so she screamed again. Screaming was perfectly logical. It also wasn't painful. Not like with a headache, when screaming would only make it worse. The noise was blissfully pure and... singular. There were no echoes. Her scream was one voice. Just one. That was good. She already knew everything about that voice. It was hers. It didn't come with a thousand other associations and marks.

So she concentrated on that, the screaming, trying to fight off another wave of nausea. Kendra pushed herself further up onto the couch and screamed again. Yes! That felt really, really nice! And if she concentrated on the sound – on a sensation that she was uniquely responsible for – it seemed to take the edge off some of the... other.

For the next few minutes she screamed like a mad woman. Up and down the scales, no words, just various tones. Different pitches, different volumes. She barely breathed and feared she'd pass out from lack of oxygen. Then she thought that passing out wasn't such a bad idea, and stopped worrying about it.

Each scream seemed to tear one layer of the madness away... seemed to snap her own mind in place on top of one set of images or sounds. Shriek! Away went the Galapagos turtles. Shout! And the guns of the Boer War were silenced. More screams and some of the voices in foreign tongues became quiet.

The pain began to subside. The nausea retreated to something manageable.

She was hugging her knees, now, rocking back and forth at one end of the couch like a severely autistic child, eyes shut as tightly as possible. She let the volume of the screams die down a bit, until it sounded more like she was calling out for something in a language without words. Raw, inarticulate noise, but not quite as loud and desperate as before. Moaning, yes. That's the word. Moaning. It still seemed to help.

Finally, she felt able to open her eyes.

The office was awash in visual echoes, ghost images of people appearing and disappearing. Fragments of sights and pieces of color flashing across her view like psychedelic comets.

She was still moaning. Long, low sounds like someone trying to push something foreign from a wound. But the pain was almost gone. Dying away like a toothache after the tooth's been pulled, so she gradually lowered her voice until she was silent.

If she held very still and focused on one particular spot – like the doorknob, for example – the riot of colors and images was much less frightening. She felt like she was balanced on top of an avalanche of sensation, and that the slightest movement would tip her over the edge.

In the front pocket of her pants, her cell phone rang. The sound and vibration sent a fresh wave of pain and nausea up her leg, hip and side.

She fell backward on the couch, biting her lip and trying like mad to get her hand inside her pocket in order to make it stop, make the shaking and the screeching of the little device stop. It pulsed with images and words with every ring and threatened to push her back into the sea of madness she'd just now crawled from.

Without thinking, she pulled it out of her pants and answered it. As soon as the ringing ceased, the pain and vertigo stopped, too.

She couldn't think clearly enough to say anything, but could hear someone talking at the other end of the connection: "Kendra?"

It was her mom. She barely managed to whisper, "Mom…"

"Kendra? Where are you? At Shama's house? Honey, it's fine if you want to spend the night, but you should really tell me." Her mother's voice sounded tinny and distant, like she was calling from another planet, not just a few miles away.

"Not at Shama's…" she could only whisper.

"What? What was that? I can't hear you Kendra."

For some reason, the sound of her mother's voice wasn't causing Kendra any pain. She was alert enough that that seemed strange to her.

"Not at Shama's," she repeated.

"OK. Well, so you worked late. Do you need a ride? Where are you?"

Do I need a ride? Good question… It was a normal question. A question that mothers asked kids all the time. But she didn't know where she was. In the Library.

She remembered: "If you are still inside my institution when the sun rises, you will die."

Who had said that? What an odd thing to say. What a non-normal thing to say. Who talks like that?

"Yes," Kendra was able to talk now, a bit louder than whispering. "Yes, mom. I'll need a ride. Let me… let me finish up something here and I'll give you a call back. In five minutes."

She checked her watch. 8:14 pm. That couldn't be right? It had been later than that when all the crazy stuff happened back in the garden. The sky lady. The… what did that guy call him? The green man? And he'd told her... she'd done the math... six hours or so...

"OK, Kendra. Talk to you in a bit." Her mom hung up.

Kendra put the phone back in her pocket. The room seemed almost normal now. Maybe she was a little dizzy, but that was all. She looked around and spotted her backpack on the floor near the end of the couch. She stood up, a little wobbly, but not too bad, and grabbed the backpack by one of the shoulder straps.

So far, so good, she thought. *My head's clearing up. I can see the… what was I looking for?*

She looked around the room one last time and couldn't remember if she'd lost something, or had come in looking for something or someone. She shrugged. No big deal.

Slinging the backpack over one shoulder she put her hand on the doorknob, turned it, and opened the door.

She was at the end of a long corridor. It looked like an office suite or the administration wing in a school or something. All the doors had those mottled glass tops that usually had somebody's name or department or title stenciled on them. Here, though, no stencils. Just the glass. Three doors on each side of the hall. An old fashioned bulb light in a conical, brass hood was providing the only dim illumination. No fluorescent light here.

It looks like something from the 50's, she thought, starting down the hallway.

For some reason, Kendra felt frightened. There was nothing overtly scary about the place. It was quiet and deserted, and that was weird. But she was used to weird. She even liked it. No, it was more as if she felt she should be afraid, but wasn't.

That just doesn't make sense. If I'm not afraid, I'm not. I'll just get out of here, figure out where I am, and call Mom for a ride.

The linoleum creaked a bit under her shoes, but that wasn't what was creeping her out. It was something that she wasn't seeing or hearing. Something beyond the range of her senses. Until it came close enough to touch, though, there just wasn't anything she could do about it.

There was another door at the end of the hallway, opposite the one she'd come out of. She was afraid of that door. That's what was scaring her. There was something behind that door. Something ominous and deadly. Towering and ancient. She could feel it; poised and balanced, waiting only for her hand on the knob to send it crashing down around her, drowning her in pain and nausea again.

She got close enough to it so that her breath fogged the glass. It was dark on the other side, perfectly dark. She could see nothing through the glass. She put her hands up on it. Still nothing. It was cool, but only like glass should be. She felt no weird vibration or trembling, no heartbeat or…

On impulse, she put her hand to the doorknob and opened the door with a jerk.

Nothing happened. The room on the other side was dark, but there was a light switch just inside the door on the left, exactly where you'd expect a light switch to be. She turned it on and another overhead light in a conical, brass hood shed a bright, yellowish glow on what appeared to be a waiting room of some kind. There were four chairs, two on each wall to her left and right, with a small end table between each pair. There was a couch, low and lumpy, against the wall opposite her. The whole room was done in shades of pale green, rusty orange and brown. It wasn't ugly so much as it was… not attractive. Frumpy. There were books piled on the end tables and more books piled on the floor between the couch and the corner. There were art prints on the wall and several framed pictures. All in all, about what you'd expect in the waiting room of an academic office.

The next door was right across from her. Same door. Glass above, wood below. Nothing to be seen. Darkness on the other side. Again the feeling of terror began to build inside her and…

Screw this! she thought. *I'm not going to cringe in fright every single time I come to a door! It's a… library? Right. He said that, didn't he? A library, for crying out loud! What's going to jump out and attack me? A diorama? A 'Read' poster? Forget it!*

With that, she stomped across the room, inadvertently knocking over a stack of magazines with her swinging backpack, and opened the door leading out of the waiting room.

She was in a hall of some kind. It was dark here, too, and the only light came from behind her in the room she'd just left. She felt along the wall, but no luck this time.

OK. There's enough light to start out. And after that, I'll just feel along the wall. Like in a labyrinth. All you have to do is keep your hand on one wall, and eventually you'll make it out. She remembered having read that somewhere. Or perhaps she'd heard it recently.

Kendra put her left hand on the wall and began to work her way away from the waiting room and the offices, and out into the library proper. The shadows of tall shelves and displays loomed over her, and as she moved farther from the light, she stepped closer and closer into true darkness until she was well and truly blind.

Keeping her left hand on the wall, she felt forward with her right hand, swinging it in gentle arcs as she slid her feet slowly along. She didn't know if there were stairs, or even other levels to this building. But her preference was not to find out by falling down them.

The wall she was following turned to the left, and, after awhile to the right, to the right again, and then to the left. Shortly after which, she entered a part of the library where tall windows let some little light in from the street and she was able to see again. Not much, but enough to be grateful for.

She could tell that she was in some kind of atrium. There weren't any big displays or anything, just many low tables with heavy, wood chairs surrounding them. *Maybe a study area,* she thought. She walked past the tables, sliding her fingers across the smooth, worn wood.

There was an archway at the far end of the study area, as she thought of it, and she headed toward it.

As she passed under the open arch, she got an even better view of the nighttime facility, as more light came in from a skylight above. Three sets of steps led down from a semi-circular platform under the archway where she stood. To the left and right, it looked as if there might be other wings of the building; at the end of the steps was a small area with several potted plants, and then heavy wooden doors with very large pull-handles. Directly in front of her, at the bottom of the third set of stairs, was a set of four very large, heavy looking doors, over which hung the sign she'd been looking for – "EXIT."

Kendra jogged down the steps and headed right for the exit doors. She assumed they'd be locked, but had to give them a try anyway. But, when she examined the door carefully, she found that the old-fashioned locking mechanism wasn't something that needed a key; only someone on the inside to turn a handle. The handle then pulled a set of bolts out of the top and bottom frame of the door, and…

She pushed, and the door opened easily. *Must be counterbalanced,* she thought, walking out into the cool night air. She let the door shut softly behind her, feeling slightly guilty about leaving the door unlocked at night.

Not my fault. They left me in there. And something about not being around at "dawn" or I'd be in trouble. "Be out by dawn or you're in trouble." Who talks like that?

Kendra checked her watch. 8:32 pm. *Really, still that early?* Now all she had to do was find some landmark – she had no idea where the heck this library was in town – and call her mom for a ride. She turned left past one of the stone lions and walked down the block, checking the street sign and not recognizing it.

Though it was night, summer was far enough along that it wasn't totally dark. In fact, the sky had a funny grey tint to it. Kendra had no trouble reading street signs until she came to an intersection that she remembered. She sat down on a bus stop bench and called her mom on her cell phone.

"Kendra," her mom said before she even identified herself. "Where are you?"

"I'm at the bus stop near the corner of Allbright and Peach," she replied. "It's right near the coffee shop with the big bowler hat on the sign out in front."

"Right," her mom said. "I'll be there in about fifteen minutes." And she hung up.

Just like mom, thought Kendra. *Only the facts, and nothing but.*

Her shoulders and neck were sore for some reason, so she put her backpack on the bench and did some stretching exercises, rotating her neck and head around and around. After a minute, the soreness was gone.

She sat down again, and noticed that a large bulldog was watching her from across the street. He wasn't on a leash, and she hoped he wasn't mean. She didn't like big dogs. He wasn't tall, but he was big. And ugly. But he wasn't moving, just sitting and panting, tongue all drippy and hanging out one side of his mouth.

It was very quiet. This wasn't a part of town she was overly familiar with, but it seemed much quieter than the parts she knew. No street noise. No cars, no horns. No trucks backing up.

Where is everybody? I don't think I've seen a single person since…

Kendra's mom drove up in her minivan.

Kendra grabbed her backpack, opened the passenger side door and slid in.

"Thanks for picking me up, Mom," she said. "That was a quick fifteen minutes."

"No problem."

Her mom put the car back into gear and pulled away from the curb. Two or three turns later and they were on a main street and there was traffic.

She may not be the most interesting mom on the planet, Kendra thought, *but she also doesn't ever get pissed. That's something, anyway.*

She wondered if her mom would even ask about where she'd been. Or why she'd been out past midnight on…

But it's not past midnight. It's not even nine. She just came to get me because the subway only runs on the hour after eight o'clock.

The lights of cars and shops and houses blurred by through her windows. The glass tinting seemed to turn them all grey and wishy-washy. She breathed on the glass and made a tic-tac-toe pattern with her finger in the moisture. She never won. Always a tie. That made her smile.

Kendra turned to look at her mom. In profile, her elegant, finely sculpted features were even more perfectly defined. Everyone was always telling her that: "Your mother is so beautiful." Kendra didn't see it. OK, in a text-book kind of way, maybe. But how could someone as purely rational, so deeply uninteresting and shallow be beautiful? At most, Kendra thought of her as "striking." Like a statue, maybe.

They turned onto Kendra's street and she leaned back to look up and out of the window at the brownstone condos that lined her block. They were all very tasteful and appropriate and there was even a private security company to augment the local police presence. The little bit of lawns they had were managed by someone other than Mr. Vernon. It was way too simple a job for someone of his stature in the industry.

There were trees in big boxes of dirt on both sides of the road. Their branches seemed black against the summer sky.

Her mom parked the car in their designated space in front of their condo and they both got out and walked up the front steps. A locked gate into a narrow alley led around the right side of the building to a small, fenced yard out back. There was enough room there for a patio table and four chairs and a small grill. Sometimes Kendra ate out back at the table, but she could never recall her mother doing so or anyone having ever used the grill.

The condo was three stories tall plus a basement, which was just storage and a laundry room. The ground floor had a kitchen, half-bath and combined living-room/dining-room area. The second floor was her mom's bedroom and study, and the third floor was Kendra's room and a storage area where her mom kept lots of old paperwork and stuff in filing cabinets. They each also had a full bath, which was nice.

At the top of the front steps, Kendra turned around to look out at their street, Wicking Cross. It was fully night, now, and the streetlights had come on. The red-brown of the brick buildings had paled to a dark grey and even the green of the potted trees seemed to have faded. There was no wind and no traffic noise and the only sound she heard was her mom's key in the lock.

Something about a key. Had mom lost a key? Kendra was puzzled.

"Mom?" she asked. "Did you lose a key?"

Her mom turned to face her, one hand on the doorknob, and for a moment her face looked very strange. Almost translucent, as if Kendra could see through her. But she wasn't seeing what would have been on the other side of her mom's head – their front door – but another place. A room. A room with books and... a stuffed crow?

"No, I didn't," her mom replied, and the strange vision was gone.

Kendra shrugged. Visions were nothing new. Her mom opened the door and they went inside.

They were both neat people, Lane White and her daughter, Kendra. Not in an obsessive way, but simply the type of people who clean up after themselves. Had unexpected guests arrived, they would have needed about 30 seconds to make the house presentable. Lane made a good living as the senior editor and talent scout for a major publishing house that put out a number of successful magazines, among them some of the most widely read travel magazines in the world. Lane White did not travel, but she had a sense for editing the work of those who did.

Their house was furnished rather sparsely. A small, oval dining room table with six chairs. A living room set with a couch and two rather uncomfortable yet stylish chairs. An entertainment center and TV. A few paintings. Nothing in any way remarkable. Kendra was always struck by the amount of personality that other people's houses had when she went visiting. Other people had odd, mismatched furniture and pictures made by their children on the wall. Other people had knick-knacks on small shelves above the toilet. Other people had… all sorts of interesting things. She and her mom had everything they needed. But not much else.

The lights were off in the dining room/living room area. And in the kitchen. In fact, the whole first floor was pretty dim. Just the one light over the sink in the kitchen was on.

"I didn't wake you up, did I?" asked Kendra.

Lane shook her head. "No. Honey, it's not even nine. But I was upstairs working. Are you going to read? Or watch some TV?"

Kendra shrugged. "I don't know. Not TV at the moment. I'm… tired. Pretty tired. I'll go up to my room, but I don't know if I'll sleep yet."

"OK."

And with that, her mom turned and went up the stairs to her study.

Kendra left her backpack by the front door and went up the stairs behind her mom, but kept on going when her mom turned off at the second floor landing. The stairs were fairly steep, since the house didn't have a large footprint and the designers hadn't wanted to take up any more room than necessary with the staircase. The stairs were carpeted in a nice, dark grey. A fairly deep pile for stairs. They made no noise as she walked up two flights to her room.

The third floor landing faced the front of the house and there was a round, chest-high window looking out onto the street. Kendra turned to the right and into her room. It wasn't a large bedroom, but it was her own space. Her mom never bugged her there and she was deeply glad, in this one particular, for Lane's indifference. The idea of a mother who barged into your room or wanted to help design your "look for the day" or anything like that made Kendra's stomach go sour.

If you hadn't known for sure, you might have thought it was a boy's room. There were very few "girly" affectations. They had mostly been put away well before Kendra turned thirteen. There were still some nice, very feminine clothes in the closet and shoes under the bed. And she did wear make-up to school. You could see some few bottles and tubes near the mirror on her dresser. But that was about it. No posters of bands or actors. No frilly or lacy pinkness or purple. Just shelves with books and CDs and a desk with a really nice, top-of-the-line computer and stereo. The bed cover and pillow-cases were light grey, as were the curtains. She had window views on both the front and back yards of the house.

She moved an armload of clothes and a few books and CDs off her low, comfortable reading chair and sat down to think about what she should do until she was ready to sleep. She wasn't in the middle of a book. She didn't have anything new on the "waiting to be read" list. Maybe re-read an old favorite?

That sounded comforting. Especially after such a… such a…

What kind of day was today? I'm tired, but, why? It was just a… normal day.

She stood up and went to her bookshelf to find something to keep her mind occupied for an hour or so. Maybe even something that would put her to sleep faster.

History? No. Too boring. Little kids' books? Didn't even know they were still here.

She had lots of books on her floor-to-ceiling shelves, stacked two-deep at times, one row behind the other. On a whim, she knelt down and reached behind the front row on the bottom shelf and pulled out a random book.

"The Magician's Nephew." First book in the Narnia series by C.S. Lewis. *I didn't even know I had a copy of that.*

It was a small, but nice hardcover edition. She'd read the books back in the fourth grade, but in a larger, paperback format she'd taken out of the school library. How had she missed owning a copy? Did she have the whole series around somewhere?

She reached back and started pulling more books out. Nope. Nothing else by Lewis. Apparently just the one.

She opened the book to the inside cover and found a handwritten inscription: "To Kendra, on her fourth birthday, though you're too young to understand why. Love, Dad."

The words were written in bright blue ink. A blue so intense it made her eyes hurt, almost like a strobe in a darkened room. And as she read them, she realized that those words were the only spot of color in the room. She looked up, suddenly panicked, heart beating fast, and scanned her entire bedroom. Everything.. every piece of furniture, every book, the walls, the bed, the curtains, the windows, the trees she could see outside… was rendered in shades of gray.

Her curtains were yellow. They were supposed to be yellow. She'd picked them out herself. A pale, summery yellow that made the room look like dawn almost all the time. But they were gray. And the carpet was supposed to be tan.

With a dreadful suspicion she stood up off the floor and went to stand in front of her dresser mirror. She, too, was reflected in shades of black-and-white. Her brown hair was gray. Her skin was light gray. Everything. Like an old movie. Strangely, being devoid of color, she seemed to resemble her mother even more than normal. Maybe it was because her mom's hair wasn't reddish brown anymore, but a dark, dark gray. And her skin was paler than Kendra's, too. The girl she saw in the mirror looked very much like one who would grow up to be another Lane White.

Am I sick? Did I go color-blind? Why can't I see any color at all?

But then she remembered the book in her hand.

She opened it up and looked at the inscription again. The words hadn't really registered before. Just the piercing bright color, which was still shining out from the page like neon. Now that she was over the initial shock of that, she realized what it said.

Love… Dad?

She had never had anything – no word, no letter, no message, no picture – from her father. Her mom refused to speak of him. The few times Kendra had asked, Lane had shut her down with a remark along the lines of, "We're better off without him," or "You don't want to know. Trust me."

She sat down on the stool she used when brushing her hair and (rarely) putting on make-up. She put the book down, still open, on the dresser. She looked at the shining blue words and couldn't understand how the book had appeared on her shelf.

Mom wouldn't have given it to me, that's for sure.

While one hand held the book open, she reached out and ran her fingers gently over the glowing, blue letters.

The instant she touched the ink, a stabbing pain pierced her shoulder. It felt as if someone had pushed a large, hot needle into her flesh, through her muscle and into the bone. Instinctively, she pulled her hands away from the book and it fell shut, the fresh, tight binding pulling it closed.

The pain stopped, but an aftertaste of it remained. A small ache, as if she'd been punched the day before.

Rotating her shoulder a bit to try to work out the last of the discomfort, Kendra pulled down the neck of her shirt and looked down at her shoulder to try and see what had caused the sharp, stabbing pain. There was a blue, almost shiny stain on her skin. An uneven splotch the shape of a small puddle.

Kendra couldn't get a very good look at it, as she was trying to stare almost straight down at her collar bone. She pulled the collar of her shirt down farther and leaned forward to look at the mark in the mirror instead. For a moment she was able to concentrate on the strange stain; it was the same blue as the ink in the book. A shiny, almost electric color. The only color left in her room.

But, after only a second or two, she became aware of something else in the reflected surface of the mirror and turned her eyes upward to look at her face. Confused, she leaned in very close and put a hand up to the glass as if touching its smooth surface would help confirm what she was seeing.

The face in the glass – her face – was not completely solid. It was partially transparent. And, stranger still, what she saw through it was not the image of her bedroom wall and door behind her, but, apparently, the pattern of an oriental rug or something similar. And, though she could only see it faintly, she could see this carpet in color. The image of her face that overlay the complex design still appeared in shades of gray. Her clothes and the rest of her room was mirrored in faded black and white. But the sinuous shapes, the complex knots and geometric patterns that she could barely make out behind – no, showing through! – her face, were visible in a multitude of colors.

Her hand on the mirror began to shake, so she put it in her lap instead.

I haven't taken my meds today. That's what it is. This is just a different kind of hallucination. I haven't taken my meds in… I don't remember. But it's been a few days at least. Right?

She looked in the top drawer of her dresser. There was the bottle. Half full.

Fumbling a bit with the child-proof cap, she shook two of the big, oblong pills out onto the surface of her dresser. They were white, but they had always been white. She got up and went out of her room and into the storage room next door where there was a small "college" fridge in which she kept bottled water and yogurt. She grabbed some Evian and went back to her room, sat down on the stool by her dresser, and stared at the two big pills.

They'll make this weirdness go away, she thought. Isn't that what I want?

Kendra looked down at the book, "The Magician's Nephew." With a shaky hand, she opened the cover up and looked down at the writing again. Still blue, still glowing like it was powered from within.

She kept the book open with one hand, pressing down on the binding to crack it loose a bit. With her other hand, she pulled her arm completely out of the neck-hole of her shirt so that she could clearly see the blue stain that marked her chest. It was still there, and when she glanced back and forth from it to the writing on the book, they looked as if they were made of the same material.

Hesitantly, slowly, she moved the hand holding the book open closer to the message written in the book.

Love, Dad.

Not thinking about it at all, she touched the fingers of her left hand to the mark on her collarbone just as she slid her right hand to cover the inscription in the book.

This time, though, when she made contact with the ink, although there was pain, there was also clarity. She felt as if she'd dived into a freezing cold or boiling hot pool of water, she wasn't sure which. But, either way, it was cleansing... stripping some kind of... filth from her. She felt as if layers of cobwebs or dust or grime were being pulled away from her, possibly taking her skin with them.

She didn't scream, though, not like last time. Not like the time...

in the library

She opened her eyes and stared at herself in the mirror. The color behind and through her reflected face was brighter now, sharper. She got up off her stool and leaned as far forward as she could, almost touching the surface of the mirror with her forehead. She peered into her own eyes but couldn't see anything but the pattern of threads and colors, shapes and woven cloth.

Kendra slipped her arm back into her shirt. With one hand in the book, folded around her palm as if she was marking her place, and the other hooked under her collar, casually touching the now hidden mark on her skin, she went down to her mother's floor of the house.

"Mom?" she called.

"Yes? I'm in the study," Lane replied.

Kendra stood in the doorway to her mother's work area. It was as sparsely decorated as a room could be and still be said to be decorated. You could even have been forgiven if you'd thought that someone was in the process of moving out of it. There was a desk, a chair for the desk, a lamp, and shelves. And though there were books on the shelves, they were all reference works.

"Mom. I need to go back to the library," Kendra said. She rocked back and forth from one foot to the other, which was something she often did when nervous. Her mom picked up on it, and stared at her feet until she stopped, mildly chagrined.

"Did you leave something there?" Lane asked. She didn't look angry. She didn't look irritated. She just didn't look... anything. Very neutral.

"Yeah," answered Kendra. "I did. And I... need it for my job tomorrow morning. I need to go over some stuff tonight on the computer for Mr. Vernon. I'm really sorry. The... night guard will let me in, I'm pretty sure."

Lane looked at her with a totally blank, totally passionless stare. And for a moment, again, Kendra could see color through her face, too. Not clearly enough to make out the details, but it was a stark contrast to the world of black and white that surrounded them both.

For some reason, her mom's empty stare made her a little afraid, and, without thinking about it, she pressed down harder on her shoulder. The mark there seemed to pulse beneath her fingers, sending a sharp twinge of pain along her arm and up into her neck, and for a moment, the world around her became even more transparent. Just like her own face in the mirror and her mom's face, she could see something… something with color… a world more seemingly solid than that in which she stood.

Her mom just sat there looking at her. She was saying something, but her mouth was moving very slowly. Too slowly. Kendra moved toward her and it seemed as if she was floating or skating more than walking. And when she reached her mother, she could see that her eyes were still focused on where Kendra had been, not on the spot where she was standing now.

Kendra turned and raced back to the windows at the front of the house and looked out into the street. There were a few people – random walkers – passing by, but they all seemed frozen and had the same, semi-transparent quality to them. She turned and looked back at her mom. Her lips weren't moving at all now.

What the hell is going on here?

She ran back into her room to look at herself in the mirror again. Yes, she was becoming as transparent as everything else. More so when she pressed down on the blue spot on her shoulder.

And what about the blue ink in the book? she thought.

Thinking of the book reminded her of the library.

"If you are still inside my institution when the sun rises, you will die."

But I'm not inside the library! I'm home! I made it out long before…

It had been night when she'd left the museum. Had there been a sunrise? Between when she'd gotten up and gone to see Dr. Lyonne and the fight with the sky woman and…

She remembered. All of it. The topiary, the green guy, the gargoyle, the fight. Waking up in the old guy's office. But all of that must have been a long, drawn out hallucination. Right?

There were her pills on the dresser.

There were clearly two worlds in her view now. The black-and-white one which her body inhabited and another world, the room in the library. She recognized it now. That was where the color was coming from. The rug on the floor, the fireplace, the stuffed crow, the roll-top desk. She could make out some details, but mostly what she saw was color bleeding through.

What time is it back in the museum? Does it matter? Was I imagining that? Where did this book come from? And the inscription? The only thing I've ever seen with the word "Dad" on it.

Her head spun and she reached out for her medication. The bottled water was there on her dresser now, too. She'd have to let go of the book in order to open the bottle.

"What is real?" she asked out loud, not expecting an answer.

Without any good reason, and not knowing why, she put down the pills and pulled the top of her shirt down again to expose the blue mark on her shoulder. Then she opened the book and read the inscription once more. It still meant nothing to her, but seemed more important than anything she'd ever read before.

Feeling somewhat foolish, and expecting it to hurt like hell for some reason, she pressed the shining, blue ink of her father's message onto the spot where the same color blue marred her skin.

But there was no pain. Only a bright flare of electric blue light, as if she were somehow inside a bolt of lightning. No sound, no smell, no sensation of movement. Just a blinding blue explosion that forced her to close her eyes.

When she opened them, she was curled up on the oriental rug of the library office. She felt stiff and cold, but otherwise unhurt. She sat up and stretched a bit, and realized that she wasn't in pain. The overwhelming barrage of images that had threatened to drown her before was somehow being held back. She could sense them all around her; like a lake on the other side of a dam. She was also vaguely sure that she herself could release the flood, if only she understood how to use the key. She heard the faintest of whisperings at the edge of her awareness. As if she were on one side of a door and a crowd of people were talking very softly on the other.

Kendra stood up and looked around the room. It was as she remembered. A vaguely cluttered, bookish office. In no way remarkable. Except for the fact that she'd just had one of the weirdest mind-trips of her life while passed out in it. She bent over and picked up her backpack from off the floor.

I am really going to have to start taking my meds all nice and regular like, she thought. *Imaginary friends are one thing, but today's freak out... too weird.*

She shook her head and even chuckled a bit to herself. It had been a long day, even if all the strangest stuff had been made up. Time to go get something substantial to eat. Crazy or not, she was hungry.

As she walked to the door, her foot hit something. It was a book, lying face-down on the oriental carpet. She bent over to pick it up.

"The Magician's Nephew," she read the title out loud.

She didn't want to look inside the front cover to see if there was an inscription. She also didn't want to pull down the top of her shirt and see if there was a blue, irregular, blotchy mark on her skin. She dropped the book back on the rug and headed for the door.

This is all crap. I'm going to go right to Dr. Lyonne. I'm going to...

But when she tried to put her hand on the doorknob, it instead struck a solid wall. She looked down. It looked like a door. It looked like a doorknob. It really, really... *really* looked like a door and doorknob. But it was only two-dimensional.

"Trompe-l'œil," they call it in art class, she thought to herself. *Art that's so real it "fools the eye."*

Even knowing it wasn't real, her eye was fooled. She tried to touch the doorknob again. Nope. It was a solid wall. Felt like stone or dry-wall maybe.

She turned to her left and looked at the wall with the desk and the stuffed crow. Now a bit panicked, she took two steps toward it and reached out to touch the crow. Smack! Her hand whacked into another plain, flat surface long before her brain said there should be anything there.

Truly frightened now, she began to race around the room, feeling the wall as she went. Nothing there. Nothing. It looked just like it did when she'd woken up, when she'd been there before, with the old guy. The couch was still "real" – she climbed on it as she felt the wall behind it – a wall that looked like it should have been a shelf full of books. And so was the floor lamp and the light socket and the hole for the fireplace. But everything else was simply a brilliant fake.

Kendra made two circuits of the room just to be sure. No. No door. No window. No desk, no desk chair. No mantel, no coat rack, no knick-knacks, no papers, no nothing. It was like being inside a 360-degree photograph.

She leaned back against where the door should have been and tried to think. *How did the old guy get out? He used the door. I saw him use the door. Just like everybody else uses a door. No big deal. He'll be back soon. He can let me out. I'll just wait for…*

"…if you are still inside my institution when the sun rises, you will die."

Such a formal way to put it. So cold.

She looked at her watch. It was 4:37 am. She'd been asleep or hallucinating or whatever for about four hours. She didn't know exactly what time sunrise was, but it wasn't real late. It was summer. Maybe 5:30. Maybe 6:00. Not a whole lot later than that, for sure.

"One hour. Maybe a bit more," she whispered out loud.

The soft, murmuring voices that bled from the edges of her perception seemed to echo her own. She thought she heard them whispering the word, "Maybe, maybe, maybe," over and over again.

I should be afraid, Kendra thought. That was all she could think. That she should be afraid. But what she was, instead, was angry.

Angry at the librarian guy for leaving her in this room. Angry at the green man and the gargoyle dog for bringing her here. Angry at the sky woman for getting the blue junk on her. Angry at Mr. Vernon for giving her the job in the first place.

Angry at her mom and Dr. Lyonne for either making her take her medicine or letting her get away with skipping it.

I don't even know how much of this crap is real. Like, where am I now? At home in bed? In the topiary garden, lying on the grass? In a hospital somewhere?

Kendra turned a full circle, looking around the office. Everything still appeared to be fully formed, fully "real," as if she could reach out and pull a book off the bookcase or touch the crow...

As soon as she thought of the crow, she heard a small voice in a vaguely "European" accent, in the back of her mind, say, "Fireplace."

The fireplace. When she'd traversed the room before, feeling the "flatness" of the illusory furniture and walls, the fireplace had still been there. She hadn't noticed it because... well, because it had been normal.

It was a pretty big fireplace, and so she didn't have to crawl to get under the mantel, just duck down a bit. She went to grab the mantel with one hand for balance, only to be reminded that it wasn't real... just "painted on." She leaned on the wall instead, and peered up into the chimney.

There was no damper or flu, just a straight column of bricks going up into darkness. Enough light wandered in from the office for her to see that the bricking was irregular; not particularly smooth or even.

"Good for climbing," the European voice whispered in the back of her mind.

She ducked back in, grabbed her backpack off the floor and headed back toward the fireplace. Stopped, turned, and looked down at the book she'd left on the carpet. "The Magician's Nephew." After about three seconds of consideration, she picked up the book and stowed it in the main compartment of the pack.

Before going back into the fireplace, she reached in and clicked one of the three carabineers off of the inside loop of the backpack where she kept them. Then she made the waist strap of the backpack as long as possible, and used the carabineer to clip the strap to one of her belt loops. Satisfied that it was attached firmly, and that her pants wouldn't slide down because of the extra weight, she ducked back into the fireplace.

She'd only been rock-climbing twice since that summer camp experience two years before. Both times had been with full-on adult supervision, belaying teams... the whole "safety first" gig. Kendra peered up into the dark, vertical tunnel above her and wished for a flashlight. She couldn't even see light at the top.

Is there a cap on the top of this sucker? Or a grating? Maybe it's just still dark out.

Maybe… Maybe… Maybe… she heard the whispered word again, climbing into the fireplace like spiders from the office beyond.

Maybe. Right. Ready or not…

She began to climb.

It was easier, in many ways, than the climbing wall at the sports complex she'd been to most recently. First of all, there were bricks to grip on all four walls, which she could reach easily. Also, she could lean on one side while searching for a good hold on the other walls. So, technically, it wasn't anywhere near as hard a climb.

But, of course, there were no adults above or below her and no belaying line with three kids attached to it down below shouting, "Belay on!" when you were safe to climb. And the walls of the chimney were slippery with ash residue. And it was dark.

Kendra climbed for what seemed like a very long time to her. After a while, she chanced a look down, which, she knew, is often a bad idea when rock-climbing. She couldn't see the bottom of the chimney. No light at all. She was either up too high, or too little light got in from the office. She looked up again. Still nothing from above.

She kept climbing.

Her shoulders were the first parts to feel the ache. Her legs and feet were in good shape from all the walking and stair climbing she did. And her fingers had been calloused from the work in the gardens. But, for whatever reason, climbing a chimney was really making her shoulders hurt. She tried to do more of the work with her legs, but her brain kept telling he that she needed to press back with her shoulders, too.

Then her calves started to feel it. The burning sensation that means you should rest. She tried to press herself into a more comfortable position, but when her calves got a break, it only made her shoulders hurt more. She decided to simply press on, since stopping wasn't helping much.

The darkness was getting to her, too. Climbing by feel alone in an enclosed, smoky-smelling, gritty tunnel. No sounds but her own breathing, the scrape of her fingers and sneakers and knees on the brick, the occasional bump of her backpack thudding against the wall. The sound of her breathing getting louder and hoarser.

It occurred to her at one point that she did not have enough strength to climb back down. She had passed some "point of no return." It was either climb up and out... or fall.

How tall can this chimney be? She thought. *I should have been counting bricks or something.*

But she knew that wouldn't help. It would have, maybe, staved off her fear in an obsessive compulsive way. But knowing how far you've come doesn't matter when you don't know how far you need to go.

Bump.

Finally!

Her head smacked into something above her. The pain was nothing compared to the joy she felt that the climb was over. She groped upwards with one hand and found what seemed to be a wooden board. After exploring around its edge, she found a handle of some kind and pushed. It moved a bit, but she didn't have the right angle to shove it more than a couple inches. She rotated carefully around the chimney—her arms and legs were very sore – until she was directly under the handle and had also moved up a little closer to it.

This time she pushed as hard as she could and the door above her swung all the way open and didn't come back down. Gentle, grey light poured down on her, making her squint and blink.

Not able to see anything yet, eyes still watering and adjusting to the change, Kendra pulled herself out of the chimney. She collapsed on her side, backpack still hanging down into the chimney. She lay there, grateful to do so, breathing heavily and stretching her arms and legs slightly to try and get the soreness out of them.

Finally, the pain receding to a dull ache, she sat up, pulled her backpack out of the chimney hole beside her, and took a look around.

Kendra was not on a roof, which is where she had assumed she'd end up. It appeared to her as if she was in the middle of a forest meadow at night. The soft light that had seemed so bright to her at first was coming from a sea of stars undiminished by city lights, and by a sickle moon, hovering near the horizon.

She looked down at the chimney opening. It was, indeed, a brick lined hole... but it was a hole in the middle of a grassy bit of ground. She could see the wooden door that she'd opened laying in the grass.

She stood up and walked around the hole, stretching out her legs and rotating her shoulders in their sockets, turning her head and neck, too, to try and relieve some of the stiffness there. She did some stretching exercises, and when she was feeling OK about the state of her limbs, she knelt back down and looked over the edge of the hole into the chimney.

Nothing. She could see the first two dozen or so rows of bricks, but that was about it. After that, darkness.

Am I really here? she thought. *I wasn't actually home when I thought I was. Or was I?*

Instantly, she was angry again. The climb had sure felt real. Her arms and legs and fingers still hurt. She had grit and soot all over her... everything. She absentmindedly started dusting herself off as she got madder and madder.

I'm not closer to... anything... than I was before! I'm just lost in a different picture! At least Alice had a Cheshire Cat and a rabbit and... a caterpillar! All I get is some enigmatic old librarian making threats!

Thinking about books reminded her about the one in her backpack. She pulled it out and looked at the inside, front cover again. The inscription still glowed blue. She pulled the neck of her shirt down and looked for the marking on her collarbone. Still there, too.

If you can't beat the weirdness, join it, she thought, and pressed the ink of the inscription to the mark on her skin. At the same time hollering, as loudly as she could, "I could really use a hand, here!"

There was a brief flash of pain, like the headache you get when you drink your milkshake too fast. Then she felt a faint breeze blow past her, but couldn't tell if it had anything to do with the book or her "blue-mark," as she was coming to think of it.

It seemed as if nothing had changed.

She turned around to look back at the chimney hole again, and standing between her and it was a short, bearded man wearing a sleek fur coat.

Kendra was so surprised that she took a stumbling step backwards, tripped on her backpack, and sat down, hard, on the grassy ground.

The man smiled a bit, looking half amused, half tolerant, and leaned down to offer her a hand up. Without thinking, she took it.

He didn't just help her to her feet – he hauled her up entirely. He was much stronger than he looked. She almost felt as if she were levitating he pulled so hard, and she swore her feet left the ground for a second. But he didn't jar or yank at her joints. Not a tug; a strong, sustained pull. Like an elevator.

When she'd regained her balance, she took a step back and looked at the man a bit more closely. He really was quite short. Kendra was only about five-foot-two, and he couldn't have been more than a couple inches taller than that.

His coat was made from patches of many types of fur; different colors, thicknesses and sizes. It almost looked planned, like a quilt… but not quite. There was a specific randomness to it, like stained glass. Some sort of pattern that Kendra couldn't quite pick up. The coat concealed him from neck to mid calf, where his feet were covered by black, cloth boots. The only parts of his skin that were visible were his hands, which were small and dainty, almost like a girl's, and his face, where it showed through his neatly trimmed beard.

He was still smiling at her, and she took that as the first good omen of the day.

"Girl," he said in a soft, smooth voice, "When you call for help, you don't do it half-way, do you?"

He seemed genuinely pleased, not mad, so Kendra grinned back up at him and shook her head. He stuck his hand back out at her, clearly meaning for her to shake. So she did, and noticed that his hand, though small, was very strong and hard. She'd expected it to be smooth and soft.

"Bran Alix, missy. Call me Bran," he said, releasing her hand and turning to look around.

"Where are we then that you need help getting out of?" he continued. He bent down on one knee to peer into the chimney hole as he spoke, and then stood back up, looking at the trees, the sky, the moon, all around, as if taking a measure of the place.

"I have no idea," said Kendra. "And my name is Kendra, by the way."

He turned back to face her again. "Of course it is. You couldn't have very well called someone in who didn't know you, could you?"

Curiouser and curiouser... thought Kendra.

Out loud she said, "I really have no idea what you're talking about."

Now it was Bran's turn to look puzzled. His narrow, red-brown eyebrows came down in the middle, and his mouth was paralleled by his neat mustache as he scowled. "What do you mean by that, girl? What don't you know?"

"When I asked for help, I didn't know what would happen," she replied. "Not in the least."

That seemed to surprise him.

"You called me all the way from San Francisco, out into this Otherwhere, without knowing what you were doing?" His eyebrows went up so high they became lost behind long, straight bangs that fell forward over his forehead.

"I guess," Kendra replied. "But since I don't know what that means, I'll have to take your word for it."

Bran nodded thoughtfully, putting his hands into the pockets of his fur coat. "Well, wherever we are, you're in need of my variety of help, or I wouldn't have been pulled by your call, that's for sure. And being your uncle and all, I'm obliged to be of assistance, of course, so…"

"What?" she stepped toward him again, causing him to back up, almost to the edge of the chimney hole. When she saw that, she put a hand out on his arm to warn him, pointing with the other hand at what he'd almost stepped into. He glanced back, made a, "Yikes!" face and quickly trotted a few steps away, pulling her with him.

When they were a good ten yards from the hole, Kendra stopped and held onto his arm, keeping him from going any further.

"You're my uncle?" she asked, dubious and clearly showing it.

"Sure. Yeah." He nodded as if it was obvious. "Your mom's brother Bran. Half-brother, anyway. Your mother never…"

And then realization came over his face and he nodded, remembering something. "No. She wouldn't... No. She wouldn't have mentioned me."

"Why not? That's crazy. Why wouldn't my mom mention having a brother?"

Bran held up his hands, surrendering. "Long story. And I don't get involved in family stuff," he said. "I came here to help you get out of a jam. Leastwise, that's what the calling felt like. You're stuck here, right? Somehow? You tell me what's up, and let Uncle Bran help out, then I'll scoot and it's none of my business anyhow. All right?"

She nodded. "Sure. I guess. Thanks."

He nodded back. "So. Where are we?"

"I have no idea."

He shrugged. "Makes it a bit harder to escape, but not so much. Who put you here?"

"Some librarian. I think he said his name was 'Monday.'"

All the joviality and easy, good humor left Bran's face. Suddenly he looked very, very serious. And more than a little angry. He reached out and grabbed her arm with that small, strong hand and pulled her, with a jerk, a bit closer to him.

"And just what in the names of the Seven Gates are you doing trapped in the Way of a Master?" He leaned in even closer to her, bending his head to look directly into her eyes. Up close he seemed much older than she had initially thought. There were lines around his mouth and eyes that she hadn't seen before.

"I told you," she replied a bit hesitantly, "I have no idea what's going on. The last time my day seemed any kind of normal was when I was working in one of Mr. Vernon's gardens…"

She proceeded to give him a very quick overview of what had happened since then. The sky woman and the fight with the green man and the gargoyle. She showed him the blue-mark on her shoulder. She described waking up in the library and Mr. Monday's challenge.

When she got to that point, Bran interrupted, grabbing her arm a little too hard for her comfort.

"He put a hard limit on it? If you're not out of his Way by dawn, you'll die? And you dragged me in here?" He closed his eyes for a moment and took a deep breath. "Do you know what that means, girl?"

She shook her head.

"I can't leave without you. And if I'm still here when the walls come down, your death will take me, too!"

He looked angry and scared both. His face had gone a little red and he was trembling slightly. For a moment she thought he might hit her, but he took a deep breath and managed to calm down a bit.

"All right," he finally said, letting go of her arm and pushing his hair back out of his eyes. "How much time have we got. Give me a moment."

He stepped back away from her, closed his eyes and murmured something under his breath.

There was a sound like paper ripping, and to Kendra it seemed as if a small section of the sky above Bran's head opened, like a window in the background of night, letting in a quick burst of radiance.

Bran shook his head, inhaled sharply, like a hiss, and said, "We've only got about twenty minutes left."

He looked around wildly, as if searching for something. "What's down there?" he asked, pointing at the hole in the ground.

"Monday's office," Kendra replied. "It had a fireplace. I climbed out of it and got to here."

He nodded. "Good girl. This is already further from the center of his Way. Now we just have to find the exit."

"Right. Find the exit."

She still had no idea what he was talking about, but at least he had a plan.

Without another word, Bran got down on the ground and pulled up a handful of grass. He went over to the chimney hole and dropped the green blades over the opening and watched them fall slowly toward the opening in the ground. A few of them blew sideways, but most of them wafted up, carried on an air current. Some seemed to float more to one side than the other of the hole...

"This way," he said, taking her arm and pulling her along on the direction that the grass had indicated.

"Wait!" she called. "My backpack." She pulled out of his grip and ran back for her pack, slinging it over one shoulder. She also picked the book up off the ground and tucked it inside as she trotted back to Bran who was waiting for her with unconcealed impatience.

He clearly believed in the direction he'd chosen, and Kendra had no idea what to do, so she followed him. He wasn't running so much as jogging, but she had to nearly run to keep up. The terrain they were passing through was generally even ground, lightly forested with white birch and some kind of bushes that Kendra couldn't identify. There wasn't any ground vegetation to speak of, and so running, even in the near darkness, wasn't too difficult.

After about five minutes, they came to the edge of the forest and stepped out onto an open, plain-like area that seemed to stretch for miles into the distance. Bran looked left and right, but there was nothing to be seen but the forest they'd just come through.

"I'm sure we're further from the center here," he said, more to himself than to her.

Kendra said nothing. *This whole day, from the sky woman on, is probably a hallucination brought on by low blood-sugar and being off my meds*, she thought.

"What?" Bran turned quickly to look down at her. "What did you say?"

Had she said that out loud? She hadn't meant to.

"Uh... Nothing. Sorry."

"No. Really. It's important. Are you that unaware of where you are? You really have no idea of how you got here, who put you here, how you called me? Any of it?"

She was back to being mad again. "Damn it, no! I have no idea about any of this! For all I know you're a figment of my imagination. I could still be passed out on my back in the garden or in a hospital bed in the loony ward. I'm sorry, I don't mean to hurt your feelings, but that's just how weird all of this is to me."

Kendra thought he'd be angry. Instead he looked even more scared. Calm, but scared.

Bran put one hand on each of her shoulders and addressed her in a calm, even, gentle tone.

"If you don't believe this is happening to you, we can't escape. Every path will lead to a new path, every door to a new room, every gate to a new wall."

Kendra sighed. "How can I believe in this stuff? I've been on meds to make things like this go away since I was a little kid. Imaginary friends, invisible voices, stairways to secret houses in the air… all of it. When I take the drugs, no… this," she waved her hand at the scene surrounding them.

Bran nodded sympathetically. He even looked a bit sad.

"Let me ask you something," he said. "When you sleep, does the world go away?"

"Of course not," she said.

"Right," he agreed. "The drugs they make you take are like sleep. They make part of your mind… still. Quiet. But just because you don't see the friends or hear the voices, doesn't mean they are not there."

He stood up and pointed. "Just because that horizon is not the one that your mother will see when she wakes up, doesn't mean it isn't real."

Kendra shook her head. "I don't understand."

"You will," he replied. "You're a Reckoner now. I assumed from the way you summoned me that you'd always been one. I forgot, though. You were raised by your mother. Not in a Domain."

"Of course I was raised by my mother? Why wouldn't I have been?"

"Never mind. Not important now. But you've made some kind of transition. Mostly Mundanes who are exposed to the Ways go mad."

Kendra thought back to what had happened when Mr. Monday had left her alone in his office. To the flood of sights, sounds, memories and pain that had washed over her. That had been very close to madness. She understood what Bran meant.

She stood there at the edge of a forest in a land that didn't exist, as far as she understood it, on the planet Earth. Where did it exist? She had no idea. Inside the librarian's office? In his mind? In a magic ball?

"Kendra?" Bran was shaking her shoulder gently. She must have been zoning out a bit.

"Yeah. What?"

"We only have about ten minutes left."

She nodded, still thinking about belief and madness. About her imaginary childhood friends and how, maybe, they were still out there. Were they older now, too? They'd have to be, if what Bran said was true.

"What did you call Mr. Monday?" she asked Bran, following a trail in her mind that seemed to lead somewhere.

"A Master," he replied. "In the Mundane world he's known as Solomon Monday. He is the Master of the Domain of Sight."

Kendra smiled a bit, thinking of the old man in his grey suit and black shirt and tie. "Out of sight, out of mind."

"What? Kendra," Bran said, pulling at her arm again, "We have to get moving. Somewhere. We've only got a few minutes until dawn."

He seemed very agitated.

"Out of mind… out of sight?" She was talking to herself again. But this time she knew it.

He was about to say something, but she stopped him by holding up a hand.

"Bran. Uncle Bran. What is your…Domain? What do you do?"

He looked puzzled. "The House of Release, of course. Why else would I have come when you called for help to get out of a trap?"

He keeps forgetting that I know nothing, Kendra thought.

"So," she asked, "what can you do?"

He still looked confused. "I can get out of many enclosed spaces," he replied. "Most Mundane locks will yield to my touch. Most doors will open at my command. I am a master of knots, their tying and untying. Once I know a place, I can always find my way back. Things like that."

"Are you the Master of Release?" she asked.

He laughed. "Oh, no. Just a Reckoner. More apt than some, less than others..."

But then he remembered where he was, and the time. Kendra knew from the look on his face what he was thinking of. Dawn. It would be only a minute or two away now. He was afraid, but not angry. He simply looked... sad. And maybe a little tired.

Kendra looked up at the moon. It seemed like "her" moon. And the stars were the same. And the air. And the ground and her aching muscles and the strap of her backpack on her shoulder. And the faint, musty smell of her dirty hair.

Suddenly she realized that she believed it all. The fight, the blue mark, the inscription, the library, this place, all of it. The years inside the drugs' embrace had been a lie. All of this simply felt more... true. It rang in her head like an alarm clock going off, as if, like Bran had said, she'd been asleep.

It was like being washed in clean, cold water after years of being covered in a fine film of dust and cobwebs. She gasped, a little afraid of how much more... unafraid... she was than ever before.

She took one of Bran's hands in both of hers and said, "Uncle Bran. I don't understand what's going on. And I don't know how I got here. But I don't question it anymore. I believe in this place, and you. I really do."

He nodded and smiled a bit, and patted her two hands with his free one. "That's a good girl," he said. "Let's walk while we wait." He stood up and they headed out away from the forest toward the horizon.

She'd hoped that her belief would shatter the sky and open a doorway for them to escape through. She'd thought that maybe, somehow, it would be the only key they'd need; her simple faith. Like the prince's kiss or sunlight on a vampire or something.

On the wind, came the whispered voice she'd heard before. "Maybe... maybe... maybe..." The words seemed to float down from the gray clouds above.

She turned and looked back toward the forest.

"What is it, girl?" Bran asked.

She thought about the office and the Trompe-l'œil walls. And about the climb up the impossibly long chimney. And Bran coming at her call. And the grass that had wafted up and away from the chimney hole. Not just away to one side. But up. Which was also away.

"Put me on your shoulders," she said suddenly.

"What?"

"Do it! Just do it!"

He shrugged and reached down to pick her up around the waist, slinging her easily up to sit on his shoulders. She reached up as high as she could. Nothing.

"Hold onto my ankles. I'm going to stand on you," she said.

What choice did he have. "All right, go ahead," he called up.

One knee, two knees. One foot, two feet. First squatting, then, balancing with a hand in his soft hair, she stood up slowly...

And bumped her head on the sky.

Chapter 4: Flight

When Monday came down from his private wing a bit after 10am, he found Mrs. McKey waiting at the bottom of the stairway looking agitated. Which was unusual for her. It took quite a bit of agitating before it ever reflected in her demeanor.

"Good morning, Mrs. McKey. I trust you slept well?"

"Very well, thank you, Mr. Monday. And you?" She knew he wouldn't be hurried.

"Also very well. Thank you. Now. What can I do for you? Is there something you wish to discuss?"

She was relieved, he could tell, that he didn't linger over additional polite conversation. With some of the other staff he might have, just to make the point. But Mrs. McKey was as well trained and perfectly behaved an assistant as anyone could possibly hope for. If she was agitated, clearly something required her superior's attention.

"Yes, Mr. Monday. The girl. Kendra White. The one from your office last night. She made it out, you know."

He nodded. "Of course I know. I assume she met you on the front steps as instructed after dawn."

He had felt her escape in his sleep, but didn't bother waking fully, knowing that Mrs. McKey would tend to the girl's needs and send her home.

Mrs. McKey nodded back at her employer. "Yes, Mr. Monday. Indeed. She had been waiting a little while. And, as you'd told her to wait for me, she did so. She said she would indeed like whatever help I could give and some breakfast. So I took her to the Waffle House down the block and bought her some hot chocolate -- it was all she'd order -- and answered a few questions. She's very curious, you know, and her situation is… somewhat unique. But I assume you know that."

Monday nodded. "Yes. Go on."

"Well, when we were finished, I paid for the chocolate and said that I hoped she had a good day and left her sitting at the booth. But half way up the library steps, I found that she was following right behind me."

The Librarian let a little surprise show on his face, as this was clearly what Mrs. McKey was expecting from him at this point in her tale.

"Indeed. Please continue," he invited.

"Well, I said to her, 'What do you want, Kendra?' And she said, 'I'd like to talk to Mr. Monday some more, please.' And I told her that wouldn't be possible."

Monday nodded. No reason for the girl to talk to him; they had nothing to say to each other. She had survived the test, which meant she could survive as a Reckoner in the real world. A late blooming Reckoner--a Mundane that made it into the world--was quite odd, but not particularly interesting. It had happened dozens of times in history that he knew of. It was interesting in the way that some very rare diseases were... but that was all he needed to know about her. Anything else would be superfluous.

"Quite correct, Mrs. McKey. Did she make a fuss?"

"Oh, no. She said, 'Oh. OK.' And sat down on the library steps. And I turned and came back inside. But by the time I'd reached the administration wing, I felt as if..."

He held up a hand. "Let me guess. She was there behind you again."

Mrs. McKey nodded and Monday now understood why she was so upset. *She knows how much I dislike having uninvited visitors in the administration wing,* he thought. *Since I'd been asleep when the girl came in, and since she had been, technically, a guest of mine the night before, my Way hadn't intruded on my sleep to warn me that my home had been invaded.*

He smiled reassuringly and patted Mrs. McKey on the shoulder in what he hoped was a comforting manner.

"Don't worry," he said softly. "I certainly don't blame you. And, as it turns out she's a Reckoner, it is no great shame or trouble to have had her for awhile in the atrium. I'll just..."

But Mrs. McKey was shaking her head. Monday cocked an eyebrow at her as if to say, *Go on...*

"She's not in the atrium, sir."

Mrs. McKey only called Monday "sir" when something dreadful had happened. It had been more than seventy years since she'd last called him "sir."

"Then," he assumed, "she snuck past you and is sitting and reading a magazine in the waiting room in the administration wing?"

She shook her head again. Very, very slightly.

"No, sir."

"Out with it, woman! Where is the girl?"

Mrs. McKey took a step back and turned her face away from Monday as she spoke.

"She is in your office, sir."

In my office? He thought, incredulous. *That is... well, essentially impossible.*

"Mrs. McKey?"

"Yes, sir?"

"Why didn't you put her out of my office?" he was quite calm again. No use getting flustered. The situation would be well in hand soon enough.

Now Mrs. McKey hung her head and studied her shoes. She looked, for all the world, like a sixty-year-old school girl. Monday lowered his head and tried to catch her gaze, but she avoided his eyes entirely. Generally, the Librarian did not repeat himself, so he simply waited for her answer. Eventually, he got it.

"She's locked herself in, sir."

This was too much.

As Monday stepped around Mrs. McKey, he drew his Way around him like a cloak. Various aspects clung to his mind like parts snapping into place to form an engine or machine. The rest of the library was intact. The grounds were immaculate. The assistants were at work helping clients, both Mundane and Reckoners. Everything was as it should be.

But when Monday cast his Way toward his office, there was a blank. It was, indeed, locked.

Only Monday should have been able to lock his office from the inside. If, somehow, some other little person had put something in front of the door or rigged a bolt or mechanism of some sort, Mrs. McKey would have been able to… take care of them... quite admirably. Taking care of problems was one of her job functions, after all.

Monday could hear her trailing behind him as he walked briskly through the Library toward the administration wing. Several of the assistants greeted him as they passed through. He merely nodded at them on the way by.

When he got to the atrium and the door to the administration wing, he turned and looked back at Mrs. McKey, who had to stop rather abruptly in order to keep from bumping into him.

"Mrs. McKey," he asked, "What steps did you take in attempting to extricate the girl from my office?"

She had pulled herself together again. *Good girl,* Monday thought. *The measure of a person's worth is how well they perform under pressure.*

"When I found that I couldn't open the door through ordinary means, Mr. Monday, I asked your office to disgorge itself." She spoke as if she were reading a report, which is exactly what he'd asked for.

"Good first step. And when that didn't work?"

"I spoke several words of Showing, all of which should have sent her screaming from the room."

He nodded. "That would have been my next play as well. And then?"

"Fearing that she had somehow blocked the door physically, I had Wallace and Mark try to force it."

He pursed his lips in thought, but finally nodded. Monday wasn't sure what a tiny little girl like Kendra could have done that would require the muscle of two burly young fellows to undo, but it wasn't an illogical choice.

"And then?" he asked.

"I… I'm sorry Mr. Monday," she muttered.

"Just tell me, Mrs. McKey," he said soothingly. Or in a way that he hoped was soothing. "I promise not to be angry."

She nodded, looked down at her shoes again, grimaced, and said, "I woke one of your personal Ways. Taking down all the seemings."

"You what?!?"

She drew back as if he'd struck her and began nodding very quickly, almost vibrating her head.

"I'm sorry, Mr. Monday. I thought that it might frighten the girl out." Mrs. McKey was clearly very agitated.

"But it did not."

"No, sir."

He didn't suppose it would have, after she'd survived it last night, completely bare to the power of his sanctum. Today? *If it was someone else's problem, I'd find it fascinating,* he thought. *But in my office?* For perhaps the millionth time in his life he reflected that the difference between "fascinating" and "irritating" was one of perspective and distance.

With an audibly irritated tone, he told Mrs. McKey, "Call the greenman. I believe his name is Kaolyn. The one who brought her here. Summon him immediately. When I get her out of my office I will want words with him. She has been more trouble than I thought possible. He will relieve me of this trouble or I will burden him… quite considerably more."

"Yes, Mr. Monday. At once, sir."

Monday opened the door to the administration wing and held it for her. She scurried past and up into her own office, shutting the door behind her. It wasn't really her fault. None of it was. Well, setting his Way loose was an error in judgment. But she'd clearly been desperate to get the girl out of her superior's office before he woke up.

I won't be too hard on her, he thought.

Monday strode down the administration corridor, past the visitors' area, past the outer offices, and straight up to the door to his office. He could tell without touching the doorknob that it had been locked, somehow, from the other side. He could also tell that it would open to his touch no matter what had been done to it.

"I don't care who or what is inside my Domain," he murmured. "At the center of my Way, I will not be bound."

Before he got to the door, however, it opened from the inside.

Monday's stride did not falter at all as he walked through the door and into the office. He saw at once that there had been some scuffling going on; a few books scattered on the floor, papers in disarray, etc. No major damage done, though. Which was a good sign.

The girl was sitting on his couch, feet tucked up underneath her in that way girls have. Monday's crow was sitting on the couch's arm rest, within about a foot of her. As he entered the room, both of their heads swiveled to watch him come in, almost as if they were on the same swing arm. It would have been amusing, had Monday been in any kind of mood to be amused.

And had the crow not been absolutely still and frozen for some hundreds of years before that moment.

"What… have you done… to my bird," he asked Kendra without preamble. For any Reckoner who knew him, the ice in his tone would have been enough to terrify.

"Thanks for the cocoa," the girl said, completely ignoring the threat in his voice. She reached up and absentmindedly stroked the feathers on the back of the crow's neck. The bird continued to stare at Monday.

"What? Cocoa?" The Librarian had been watching the crow and hadn't quite been paying attention.

"Thanks for the cocoa," she repeated. "Mrs. McKey told me that although she was there, it was you who'd paid. I asked her to thank you for me, but since you're here now… thank you."

She was being deliberately obtuse.

"I will ask you one more time," Monday said. "What have you done to my bird?"

For a moment, the two creatures' heads swiveled toward each other, locking eyes. Then both turned back to stare at the old man again.

"She's not your bird," Kendra said simply. "Not anymore."

In his office, it was almost impossible to hide anything from Monday. It was the place where mysteries came to shed their masks. And yet, he had no idea what had changed about the crow… except that instead of sitting on its iron perch, where it had been utterly motionless for as long as he'd had it, it was now on the couch, and preening its feathers.

"I assure you my dear," he replied. "It is, indeed, my bird."

Kendra shook her head. "First of all, it's not an 'it.' She's a 'she.' Second of all, if she wants to leave, she can come with me."

Monday was becoming increasingly angry. The crow had been a gift from another Master, and was quite a powerful research aid. It was a kind of magnifying glass for certain types of information and situations, and he used it as such, much to his pleasure, several times a month. While he was not a sentimental man, he was certainly one who valued a good tool, and this crow was one of the best.

"When, or should I say 'if,' you leave," he said, "we shall see what becomes of the bird. Until then... we will wait for the greenman to come and take you away. Permanently this time, one hopes."

She looked up at him with those lovely green eyes of hers and replied, "OK. But while we're waiting, I have some questions for you, Mr. Monday."

"Everyone here has questions," he said, turning to sit in his desk chair. "That's the whole point of a library."

He spun it around to look at her. She had to turn on the couch to face him and did so without getting up, simply shifting her torso and twisting, again in that way girls have that men can never seem to match.

Now the crow was between them, and the girl leaned on the armrest, her eyes on the same level as those of the bird.

"Will you answer mine?" she asked.

He shook his head. "No."

She looked puzzled. "Why not?"

He opened his hands in a gesture of disregard; "Why should I?"

She scowled as she replied, "Because you were kind of nasty last night and helping me out would be a nice thing to do." Then she grinned. "Also, you're a librarian. You're supposed to help young people learn stuff."

He shook his head again. "You really have no idea what you're up to, to whom you're speaking, where you are or the consequences of your actions. Because of that, and because, against great odds, you managed to survive my Way last night, I may let your rudeness go unpunished.

"I don't know how you got into my office, or blocked Mrs. McKey and my assistants from getting in, nor how you affected such a profound change in my bird. And," he held up a hand as she started to speak, "I frankly do not care." That last was not true, but she didn't need to know that.

"All I want from you, now, though," he continued, "is for you to leave. I have summoned back the greenman who brought you here. I will instruct him to answer your questions as best as he can. I, however, will not."

She seemed to consider the offer as if there was a serious chance she might refuse it or counter with one of her own. Finally, she nodded.

"OK," she said. "If he can help fill me in, that's fine. But I have one question that I think only you can answer."

Monday hated to repeat himself. "I am not prepared to answer any of your questions."

She leaned back in the couch, considered what he'd said, and nodded.

"If that's how you feel. Never mind, then."

He hadn't expected her to drop it that quickly. But then, she had been full of surprises all along.

And now, against his better judgment, he was curious. *A weakness of my Domain,* he thought. But he wouldn't give her the satisfaction of asking.

They sat there like that--the man, the bird, the girl--for about twenty minutes, unmoving except for the small shifts in posture everyone makes from time to time.

If I had any idea how Hahang had made that bird, Monday thought, *I'd try to reclaim it… Time for that later, I suppose.*

After a bit, the phone on Monday's desk rang. One quick, quiet purr. Again, the heads of the girl and the crow turned in unison toward the source of the sound.

He picked up the hand piece. "Yes."

"The greenman is waiting in the guest area, Mr. Monday."

"Thank you, Mrs. McKey. Send him in."

He hung up the phone and steepled his fingers in front of his face. Kendra seemed content to wait as well, twisting in the couch to observe the doorway.

In a minute the door opened and the greenman who had, less than a day before, deposited this troublesome girl on the atrium floor, entered Monday's office.

"Your name is Kaolyn, I believe?"

"Yes," he replied. He was clearly none too pleased to have been called here. *Good,* thought Monday.

"You brought this girl, Kendra, to me last night. She has passed my test. She is now a Reckoner. She has questions. She will leave here with you. And then you will answer them."

Kendra stood up from the couch in one fluid motion, and the bird jumped to sit on her shoulder. As Monday was about to say something about that situation, the girl stuck out her hand and, without thinking, the Librarian held out his own to shake it.

And in that touch, he knew who she was. He saw and smelled the beginning of her day – *apple blossoms* – and saw her wake and dress and prepare and then go down to the kitchen with her mother.

That one! I know her... I know her! She is that woman who fell from Release! But she did not have a child. She was made barren, we were told, when Morgan tried to draw her to Increase... Is this girl hers? Theirs? Or adopted? Or of a Mundane father?

Too many questions, too unexpected. Had he been prepared he could have prolonged the moment but it was so completely out of context. He felt... Distracted? Out of focus. *What was I asking her? What did she need?*

Their hands parted. The greenman nodded, silently, and gestured the girl out of Monday's office. He could hear their steps in the hall and feel them as they wended through the Library and out the door.

And that's fine. She's been an irritant. And I have things to do.

Monday was normally a very observant person. Perhaps, in fact, the most observant man on the planet. But at this moment, he was unable to really concentrate. He thought about the girl. Thought maybe her parents were important. Maybe not.

It would explain why she was an untrained Reckoner, he finally concluded. And that thought anchored him. It was a reasonable explanation. A good conclusion to the data at hand.

Fine. Fine, yes. That's it. Her mother had once been a Reckoner, and had had a child by a Mundane. The girl had just enough of us in her to make the difference when she was splashed with the skyblood. That makes sense.

He was glad. Monday didn't like being unsure. He liked to know. And now he did. He had an answer.

But it wasn't until he paused in his work, much later that morning, that he realized the crow had, indeed, left with the girl. He reprimanded Mrs. McKey for the loss--not overly harshly, but firmly, nonetheless. He was puzzled as to how the bird had slipped both his mind and his demesne so handily... but he could hardly blame McKey for that. Perhaps the whole evening had simply been too... oddly distracting.

Perhaps I'm getting old, he thought, and wondered how he might contact Flux to arrange for a replacement for the crow, or a similarly helpful artifact. Hahang had been bothering him for more than a century to come visit her, and maybe... maybe he could ask about the girl's mother. No, her mother was of Release. Father of Flux?. *White? Was that her name? Yes. Lane White. I can kill two birds, ha-ha, with one stone.*

Maybe next week. I'll arrange a visit.

No, he thought after a bit. *She can come here. Movement is easier for her.*

* * * * *

Kendra walked out of the library into the sunshine and into a world she... understood.

Finally. Finally.

The ordeal of the Librarian's Way had occupied her thoughts entirely, and then she had been so busy trying to worm any kind of useful information out of Mrs. McKey that she hadn't really taken a moment to stop and absorb her new understanding, her new senses, her new sight.

Kaolyn beside her, she stood quietly on the steps of the library, between the lion statues, and saw them for what they were. Lions. Golden and rippling with sleek muscle. Glowing in the late morning light, with gentle heat waves rising off their sides as they breathed. Turning their heads first to the left then to the right, sometimes looking up, sometimes down, stretching and shaking their manes. One of them turned to look at her, satisfied that neither she nor the greenman was a threat, went back to its--his?-- observations.

Across the street a flash of color caught Kendra's eye and she looked up to see a small boy skipping down the sidewalk in huge bounds, rising and falling slowly, like she'd seen astronauts do on the surface of the moon. The color she'd seen was a splash of rainbow light that seeped up from the concrete every time his foot struck. He had small, almost cherubic wings and was eating Peanut M&M's from a gallon Ziploc bag, grinning like a maniac. A moment later, a rather harried woman rushed out of a nearby doorway and raced to catch up with him, grabbing him by the elbow and almost pressing him back down to earth. She took the bag of candy from him and gave him a look that was half scold, half amusement. The boy licked his lips and smiled, and the two walked down the sidewalk, hand in hand. Kendra barely noticed that the woman had four arms, the other three of which were holding shopping bags.

She turned to face Kaolyn and said, "It finally makes sense."

He smiled and was about to say something when a muffled voice from her backpack exclaimed, "You can either let us out, or I can burst these seams. It's getting a might close in here."

Kendra muttered, "Whoops," and put her backpack on the step next to her, sitting down to unzip it. A moment after doing so, Bran appeared beside her, also sitting on the step, with the crow on his shoulder.

"Ah," he sighed, stretching his arms out and rolling his head on his neck. "Much better."

"I agree," said the crow, in a soft, vaguely accented contralto.

Kendra turned her head to look at them and said, "I'm sorry. It's just that this..." she gestured at the whole world... "is so new to me. It's... it doesn't... it makes me feel..."

"It feels right," suggested the crow.

"Yes," Kendra said. "It feels right. Everything used to feel like I was seeing it through wax paper, or trying to touch it through mittens. I finally feel... balanced."

Bran patted her on the shoulder. "Most Reckoners grow up with the Sight. Almost all, in fact. Not having Sight is a kind of blindness for us. Some have more than others, and an unlucky few never develop it or lose it through accident or disease. It almost always leads to death."

"Why?" Kendra asked.

"Without Sight, it is almost impossible to walk the Ways. If you are very powerful, or very desperate, you might still open a Way. But day-to-day life? Imagine being blind, deaf, dumb... losing your senses of touch and smell and taste. How would you know the world? For Reckoners, the difference between life and death is, in many ways, Sight."

Kendra nodded, suddenly angry. "And my mom has been drugging it away from me for all these years."

"Don't blame her," the crow said. "You should have been raised a Reckoner. The fact that you didn't go completely crazy or just wither and die is a testament to your strength. Part of which you got from her."

"Bah!" barked Bran. "What a bunch of feel-goody shite. For some reason, who knows why, your mom and your shrink set you on a dangerous path. Lane is my half-sister, yes... but had I known she'd a daughter after, well... her first husband left... I would have stepped in."

Kendra was about to ask about her father, but Bran pushed on, clearly uncomfortable with the subject and unwilling to pause. "Being an untrained, unaffiliated Reckoner," he continued, "is more perilous than being a Mundane. Whatever strength you have, it's yours. Don't waste another thought on your mother or any chronics you knew before."

"That's not a kind word, Bran," scolded the crow.

"Bah!" Bran repeated. "I'm not a kind man." And with that, he stood up, brushing off his knees and the seat of his pants.

Kendra stood up, too, and put a hand on his arm. The short, burly man looked at her suspiciously but didn't pull away.

"Please, Bran," she said. "I'm grateful for your help. Truly. But I don't know what any of this stuff about my mom or dad means."

Bran looked pained and made a face as if he'd bitten into something sour. Then he seemed to make a decision. His face softened, and he took Kendra's hand in both his own.

"I'll tell you this much, lass, as you deserve to at least know the right names. Your mother was born Elaynia Geary in the House of Release. We shared a mother in Release, but her Father was of Flux. So you have grandparents in at least two houses, which is itself a rarity. Growing up between two Domains, your mother was more... flexible... than many. That led her to meet and fall in love with a Reckoner of Increase, Morgan White."

Kendra piped up, "My father!?"

Bran shook his head. "No, girl. That would be impossible. They were married, and she took his name, but when she tried to change allegiance to his House... she lost her Reckoning and he, well... He disappeared."

My mom had what I have now, Kendra thought. *And lost it. That would be awful. And it explains a lot.*

"But why couldn't Morgan be my father?"

Bran kept shaking his head as he spoke, his voice low and gruff. "These are not things that are spoken of in our world, niece. To change Houses is, well... very rare. And it often results in a loss of power. Sometimes even a complete loss. Again, rare... but not unheard of. It's one reason why we keep to our own, and why having family in more than one Domain can be, well... dangerous. At some point you have to choose, and if you choose badly..." He shrugged.

"You lose some or all of your Reckoning," Kaolyn filled in.

"That's right," Bran said. "It's very rare. And it's not talked about, except as a cautionary tale. In the case of your mom, crossing Domains reduced her to a... to a Mundane. That kind of shock would have ended an unborn child."

"Which is why Morgan can't be my father?"

Bran nodded. "That, and the fact that, if he was, Increase would have claimed you long ago. As we live so much longer than Mundanes, Reckoners are not as fertile. Children are cherished. And anyone in the Houses would have been able to see your ability had it not been for the drugs you were on."

That made Kendra scowl. "So someone wanted to keep me from being a Reckoner?"

"Maybe," Bran made a weighing gesture with his hands, "maybe not. Your mother went into the Mundane world with no memory of the Ways. A child by another Mundane would have some touch of power, as you do... but that would seem, to her, like madness. Many of those judged mad in your world... well, your old world... are Mundanes with some Reckoner blood or a touch of power."

Kendra scowled and looked from her uncle to the greenman and back again. "But why didn't my mother's family, her Domain, look after her? And check in on me? To see if I was, well..."

"A half-breed bastard child of a broken traitor?" the crow chimed in.

Kendra gasped, and was about to protest, when Bran laid his hand back on her arm. "It's harsh, but the bird saved me from having to say it. When you cross out of your House... it's like turning your back not just on family, but on... everything. And her loss of Reckoning was seen, by many, as a just punishment for her treason."

For the first time in a while, the greenman spoke up. "The Ways are deeper than family and broader than the world," he said. Both Bran and the crow nodded, as if he'd said something from a book of proverbs.

"It is time for me to go, lass," Bran said. "I'm already late for... well... for several responsibilities of my own."

"What should I do now?" Kendra asked. "I don't have any idea where to go or..."

"Maybe I'll see you later, Kendra," Bran interrupted. He began making a gesture with his left hand in an odd, circular way. It looked to Kendra like he was spinning something around on a string, but with no string. And no something.

He kept doing that while he continued, "Maybe I won't. Either way, glad I could be of help. If you find yourself stuck in a Master's Way again... don't call. No offense."

"But, Bran," Kendra started to ask. "I've got so many questions I need..."

She got no further. A nice, expensive sports car pulled up near where they were sitting. A confused looking man got out of the driver's side, looked up and down the street, and then started jogging away, clearly agitated, leaving the car idling at the curb. Bran stopped twirling his hand and used it to wave at the girl, the greenman and the crow before getting into the car. Without another word, he gunned the engine and drove off.

"That was..." Kendra muttered.

"Rude?" Kaolyn finished.

"You can't expect Release to stay still for a moment. They're worse than children," the crow said.

"True," Kaolyn agreed. "But he's her uncle. He owes her... more than that."

"He helped us both escape from the Librarian," the crow said, settling more comfortably on Kendra's shoulder. "For that I will be grateful. Once the old lady activated the Librarian's Way, Bran could see the chains that have bound me for... a long time. And if he hadn't cast a Way of Attention just as Kendra shook his hand, Monday would probably have noticed me leaving and tried to keep me there."

"What's a Way of Attention?" Kendra asked.

"It makes something more noticeable," the crow answered. "Like shining a light on something or hanging a bell on it."

"How did that help you escape?"

"Well, Bran knew that he was in the center of the Domain of Sight. It would be very hard for him to hide anything from Monday in his own stronghold. So rather than try to, he just made it more likely that the Librarian would focus on something else. Then he made us small enough to fit into your backpack and... there you have it. Hiding by not being the most obvious thing in the room."

Kendra nodded. "Interesting. I've heard that called 'hiding in plain sight.' But I guess this is even a bit more... effective."

"It often is," Kaolyn agreed. "There are examples in nature of creatures that change their habitat to appear different to predators, making them look elsewhere. Sometimes changing your environment works better than changing yourself."

"Quite," said the crow. "And often easier."

Kendra turned to look at the black bird sitting on her shoulder. "I'm sorry," she said, "but I don't think I caught your name earlier. Things were a bit rushed in Monday's office, and I was glad to help you escape. But I don't know if you introduced yourself or not."

"I did," replied the crow. "But I'm not hurt that you don't remember. You were under great duress. I am Tess. Some called me 'Tess Corva' even before I assumed this shape."

"I don't understand," said Kendra. "Corva means..."

"It means 'crow,'" Tess explained. "For many years I was known as 'The Crow,' 'The She-Crow,' 'Lady Corvina,' and others. Many names, all the same bird."

"Why?"

Tess hesitated. "That is a dark story, and one for another day, girl. Today we are free, you and I, and you need to consider what you will do with that freedom."

Kendra looked around again. Everywhere she turned, a few fantastic people and creatures were carrying on, walking (or flying or crawling) around, surrounded by many more "regular" people. *Mundanes,* she thought, *is what the Reckoners call them. Or chronics.* Buildings sprouted strange and, in some cases, physically incongruous additions. For example, the Starbucks down the street had a candy-cane striped pipe, about a foot across, curling out of its roof, spiraling up into the sky, finally disappearing out of sight, hundreds of feet above. The street in front of the Barnes & Noble was paved in what seemed to be a kind of sponge. Everyone, Reckoners and Mundanes, bounced a little as they walked over it. Though none seemed to notice. She turned and looked up as a person passed her by and saw that it was a woman in a beautiful blue dress that shone like mother of pearl, shifting and changing depth and luminescence as she moved. And that the woman had the head of an eagle.

"I have no idea," Kendra said softly, "where to go or what to do."

Kaolyn put a hand on her shoulder. "You need to choose a Way," he said. "You need to ally yourself to a Domain and make it known. As long as you are detached, you are in danger."

"Danger? Why?"

"Because you are outside the Law," he replied.

Kendra looked confused. And a bit miffed.

"The Law," Tess explained, "governs the interactions between the Domains. It has been in effect since the end of the last Reckoner War, more than seven thousand years ago."

"How," asked Kendra, "can I be outside the law? I'm a Reckoner now, right?"

"True," agreed the crow. "But the Law adheres to the Way, not the Walker. It was crafted that way to... discourage... uh..."

"Gross and uncoordinated, independent action," filled in Kaolyn.

Tess nodded her beak. "That's a reasonable modern translation. Thank you, greenman."

Kaolyn tipped his head in recognition. Tess continued, "The Law says, basically, that the Domains may not prey on each other for power. That they may not do harm to one another in pursuit of gain. And that they may not conspire to upset the balance of power."

"That sounds very peaceful," Kendra said.

Both the crow and the greenman laughed. "Oh, no," Kaolyn said. "It just means that the mayhem goes on at a personal level, rather than being concerted by the Masters and their Ways. Individual Reckoners are as prone to violence as Mundanes."

Kendra scowled, confused. "But you said that the Law doesn't... how did you put it? 'Adhere to Walkers,' because it's supposed to discourage independent action. If the Law lets Reckoners go after each other, isn't that, well... bad?"

"It can be," said Kaolyn. "But it's 'bad' on a small scale. Same as with Mundanes."

"Think of it this way," said Tess. "Imagine that you could, without much effort, change the border between two countries. That you and a few of your friends could decide, 'New York state is now part of Canada.' That would be very confusing, yes?"

Kendra nodded.

"Now imagine, in addition, that you could also, at a whim, change the laws of Canada. Making it, say, illegal to drive a car at night. Or eat seafood. Or marry anyone with a different color hair than you."

"That," Kendra replied, "would also be confusing. Yes."

"It's the same way with the Law," continued Tess. "You, as one person, can certainly decide, 'I will not marry a man with red hair,' or 'I will move to Canada.' But forcing large scale changes on the rest of the world... that's very... upsetting."

"And that was what was happening before this last... Reckoners' War?"

Kaolyn and Tess both nodded. The greenman spoke up, saying, "It was bad. Many hundreds of thousands of Mundanes died, and hundreds of Reckoners. The earth itself was even touched, and, some say, if the war hadn't ended, that it could have destroyed everything. All people, all creatures. All life."

They were quiet for a moment, until Kendra spoke up.

"I guess I need a really, really basic introduction to Domains, then. If I have to join one, that is. I mean... I don't even know how many there are. Or anything other than that Monday is in the one of Sight or something, and Bran in... what did he call it? Release? And my mother was in... what did Bran call it?"

"Your mother left Release for Increase," Tess said.

"Right. And you, Kaolyn, are in... what?" Kendra asked.

"As a greenman," Kaolyn explained, "I couldn't be in any other House than Earth."

"He's a Natural," Tess explained.

"I have no idea what that means. What any of this means," Tess said. "But," she continued before they thought she was complaining, "I want to learn."

Kaolyn looked around. Foot traffic around the Library was medium heavy, as it was getting to be lunch time. "Why don't you and I get something to eat," he suggested, "and Tess can..."

"Tess," the crow said in a dreamy, faraway voice, "can fly in the open sky for the first time in a few hundred years or so."

Kaolyn nodded. "I understand your need. Will you be able to find us later?"

The bird nodded. "Unless you are masked or within a Greater Way. And even then..." she cocked her shiny, black head to one side. "I have some skills. When I have stretched my wings, I will find you."

And with that, the black bird rose into the sky with a cry of joy so pure that those nearest the trio turned, looked... and smiled.

Chapter 5. Sign

From above the plain, very little detail is visible to you at first. Your eyes would only be able to make out the billowing clouds of dust and a relatively empty space between two undulating masses of shadow and reflection. The sky is overcast but bright. One of those annoying days when the light hurts your eyes no matter which direction you look, but doesn't seem to penetrate the clouds.

Then, on the wings of some invisible bird, your view descends and you begin to make out some of the largest, most impressive details. The huge banners being held aloft by teams of ten or more men. The rolling war machines as big as castles, towers filled with archers and flashes of arcane fire. Beasts the size of elephants, but with spikes down their spines and horns dipped in gold. Giant man-like creatures with saddles on each shoulder carrying robed figures, completely hidden from the light of day beneath folds of black and red cloth.

Dropping down further, you see the masses of marching men and half-men and near-men and not-men. The officers astride giant cats and horses made of blue fire. The lines of pikes and spears and shields being borne toward each other with inexorable slowness.

Now you can hear it, too. The drums. The marching cadences. The piercing cry of the fey beasts being held back by enormous chains of bronze and smoke. The barked orders from atop the war machines. The ululations of berserkers, driving themselves to frenzy before the battle begins.

Your view turns, banking to the left and up the slope of a nearby hill to reveal a tent at the edge of a bluff. A group of men in colorful costumes, ropes of gold and silver glinting at throat and wrist, watch the armies move toward each other in the valley below. Surrounded by a moat of what looks to be liquid darkness, they stand, quietly, and observe the gathering hordes.

And again, your view wheels. You speed off and above the valley, above the armies, above the tent and the beasts and the growing noise and dust. Across the battlefield. Up another hill. Steeper this time. With a rocky crest and there... yes... two figures, almost invisible against the rust colored rock. Clad only in ochre robes and sandals. Caked with dust and squatting down low, presenting almost no silhouette above the rock line.

Your view dips and you are there.

Two men. One small and compact, ropy muscles beneath a robe, a short, black beard and close-cropped black hair. The other with a single bright-blue eye and a scar where the other should have been. The second man is very thin and taller, though it's hard to tell as he is bent over, trying to become as small as possible.

"Sayem," the shorter one says. "Have we waited too long?"

The taller one shakes his head. "No, Beniin. The battle is not meant to be a short one. It must last at least until dusk when the power of the Brothers will be at its height. If we move too soon, some of the Blood Warriors will escape. They must not be able to reach the shallows of the Tigris."

The shorter one looks surprised. "Surely even the great mounts cannot run so far so fast..."

The tall one shrugs. "I have seen them do so more than once."

The other bows, slightly, as if in deference. "If you have seen it, Sayem, it is surely so."

From this vantage, the two armies are only writhing bodies in the distance. No detail, no sound. But the distance between them is shrinking. Soon the vanguards will collide.

Time passes. Maybe an hour. It is hard to tell, but the shadows below the rocks have moved a few degrees. The sun is hotter, though the sky is still gray.

The taller of the two men, the one called Sayem, finally nods and speaks a quiet word into the wind.

Though you cannot hear the word, it seems to crack the air and fly away from the two men like an invisible arrow. You follow it, over the valley, over the armies, over the monsters and the great machines and the tent and the moat of darkness. You fly swiftly, very swiftly, almost riding the whispered word as it traverses a plain full of small farms, small towns, scratched out dirt roads. You follow alongside a wider road, now. Caravans of camels and mules slip by beneath you. Herds of sheep and goats being led East, the direction you fly, toward the walls of a city.

As you fly over the city, you see that its walls are wide, but not particularly tall. Maybe twenty feet or so. But topped by a path broad enough to accommodate columns of marchers four men wide. You speed over hundreds of men atop the wall in these files of four. Men with bows, men with spears, men with staffs.

The city is also not so tall, but wide and airy inside its walls. No buildings over three stories. All made of mud brick, but baked and whitewashed to a shining, almost painful white. Gardens and pools of water disappear beneath you. Barracks with more soldiers, yes... but also shops, a market, schools filled with children, studios of artisans, smiths, tinkers and potters.

And, in a blink, it is gone. Your whispered word returns you to flight above the plain. More caravans, these heading West, back toward the large, low city you've just left. More herds. More soldiers. More farms and fields.

The fields give way to scrubby, sparse woods. Skinny trees that barely hold the soil in place. Dry, hardy plants that house little life beyond their own bony stems. Then they are gone, too, replaced by brown grass. Then the grass is gone. And all that flows beneath you is the sand.

It doesn't take long, but it seems that the sand goes on forever. By the time you see the rise of land before you, there is nothing visible in any direction but the dunes and blowing, arid currents of desert sand and the occasional outcropping of rock. Nothing lives here. Nothing but a few very slow, very powerful wyrms who have slept beneath the hot sand for a thousand years or more. You can sense them in the lay of the land. The dunes, seemingly random in their placement, actually follow the lines of the dragons' backs. Their slow breathing--an inhale, maybe, once in a moon--guides the architecture of wind and sand.

There! At the edge of the desert, a rise. A great heap of sand where storms and wind and the breath of sleeping monsters has caused an enormous wall to build up over the centuries. A barrier as implacable and massive as a mountain, drawn across this narrowing of land at the edge of nothing.

The word you are riding comes to rest beside an old, old man who sits at the base of this wall of sand, his legs crossed, his eyes closed. He is nearly naked, wearing only a loincloth, a turban and a long, white beard. His skin is copper and his eyes are ink.

The word seems to rouse him from a kind of trance. He smiles, rotates his head a few times to loosen his neck, and stands.

Looking down at his feet, he takes a few strides up the initial slope of the enormous wall. Within twenty paces, the rise becomes so steep, and the sand so loose and shifty, that he is unable to move further. He stops and looks to the left for what seems a long, long time. Then to the right. Finally, he nods and takes a few, sliding steps to his right. There, he kneels and begins to dig with his hands.

The sand fills in the hole almost as quickly as he scoops it out, sliding down from the slope above. But he keeps at it. Sweat begins to stain the plain, white cloth on his head and then to trickle down his shoulders and arms. He breathes heavier, now, and glances occasionally upwards.

Finally, the sand that flows into the hole he is digging comes more quickly than he can move it aside and he allows himself to slide backwards a bit, pivoting gracefully on one foot and trotting down to where the sand is flat and hard. Dusting his hands off against each other, he begins to walk away from the mountainous wall of sand behind him.

As he walks, he hums a tune. It seems like something a child might sing while doing chores, or maybe a fisherman's ditty. He is no longer breathing hard, and swings his arms to the cadence of his song, marching in time to words only he can hear.

The whisper of noise behind him is so slight, at first, that you think it may just be the wind against sand or stone. But it is too regular. Too insistent. And now it is growing in volume. A shush that becomes a hiss and then a moan and, finally, a rumble.

Your view pivots and you see that behind the man, in the distance, a cloud of dust is rising. At first it is small, like something a horse would kick up while galloping across the desert. But it grows. Along with the noise that is now a thunder, the cloud swells and becomes dark.

It is not just sand, you realize. It doesn't move like dust. The particles that make it up are heavy and slow. And the noise that is now shaking the earth could not come from falling sand alone.

At first, the water is a trickle of darkening streaks in the sand, reaching out to turn the ground beneath the old man soft and moist. For a moment, he loses his stride and has to skip a little, speeding up a bit, to regain the cadence of his song. But he does so, simply humming faster and picking up the pace.

By the time the water begins to splash around his ankles, he has slowed down again. And then, as it begins to rise around his calves, he stops.

Another word reaches him on a wind from the West. This one you recognize. A name. "Aasher."

The old man nods, smiling again, and speaks one word in return. "Sayem."

The water is now at his knees and the sound coming from behind him is a roar. He does not turn to see the roiling, churning mass of water and mud, roaring toward him almost as fast as sound as it floods the narrow desert valley. He does not see it tower and curl, reaching higher than the walls of the city he faces across the desert. The city of his birth.

But he feels it, there, behind him. Feels what it has become, his destructive progeny. And in the moment before it crushes him utterly, he speaks again, sending out a last thought with his final breath:

"My son. So proud."

Your view is wrenched upward, pulled as if on a string or shot from a bow. You look down and see the great mass of earth and water as it grows and strengthens. It is brown and black and gray and juggles boulders the size of houses as if they were grains of rice. It slows, a bit where the desert widens but, soon, the force behind it grows, too, and the wall of destruction speeds onward.

The dragons stir in their sleep as the water rises above them, but do not wake.

The dark mass reaches the edge of the desert and flies across the plain, the noise of its passage a terrible roar. There is no time to see individual farms or flocks as they disappear beneath its thunder. Certainly no time to see the people as they are surprised in their fields, their beds and kitchens. At school, marching in the practice yards. At the wheel, the loom, the well. Most have no time for even a final thought as they are obliterated utterly in its passing.

Your view gallops faster than the seething waters, now. You fly before it, turning back to see its dark erasure of the landscape behind you. For just a moment, the city walls you flew over earlier are bright in contrast against its black power... then they are gone, too. Not swallowed nor drowned, but crushed. Bricks turned to rubble and flesh ground into paste in an instant.

The armies do not have time to turn, but some of the giant riders in black and red seem to sense their doom. They glance back and, barely, know that their world is about to end. But they cannot utter the words of power. Along with the brutes they ride and the men and other things that have begun the great battle, they are swept into nothingness, ground into meat and then scraps and then paste.

The water buries the great war machines as it did the shining city. One moment there, the next gone. Waves of water, rocks and trees sweep by beneath the view of the men on the cliff above. The wind of the flood's passing almost knocks them from their feet, but they have time to react. Time to strengthen the moat of darkness that surrounds them. The water reaches... reaches... but then falls back, never getting quite high enough to pull them down.

Both armies, though... obliterated. Wiped from the face of the earth.

Finally, the water begins to calm. It churns, yes, but now in all directions. Waves and counter-waves bumping against each other. They level, the flood drawing down from its height. By true night, it is nearly calm and nothing can be seen but the moonlight on gently lapping waves.

You wonder about the two men. The ones you'd heard speak earlier. The tall one and the one with a single bright, blue eye. But they are gone. At least from your view.

You take one more look and see that the richly clad men have built a boat out of fire and are sailing Northwest, in the direction the water itself had been flowing. Soon, they are out of sight.

* * * * *

The scene of flood, battle and destruction faded from her sight, and Kendra blinked slowly. A face came into focus. A young man's face. Framed by already thinning, dark hair. Cheeks maybe a little full, not quite chubby or fat. Eyes a standard, medium brown. Eyes that were frowning. Impatiently.

"That's my part of the bargain," the face said, and Kendra snapped a bit further into focus, seeing the mural of the Parthenon behind him. The cheap, framed print of an ancient statue that (she thought) was Roman, not Greek.

Looking around, slowly, still a bit out of it, she took in the table with its checked plastic cover, the napkin dispenser, the laminated menus. The glasses of water and small, pale salads still untouched.

"The Parthenon," she muttered.

"Yes, yes," the man's face said, and she looked back up at him.

"Now... you owe me..."

"Give her a minute, clerk," said a voice to Kendra's left. She turned, and saw that there was a black bird sitting on the back of a booth seat. Or it was a young woman in black leather and silver jewelry. Or it was both.

She shook her head and almost unconsciously reached for a sip of water.

"The agreement was..." the man continued.

"Shut it," interrupted the bird/girl again. "The value is not equal, not even close. You will continue to teach her until I judge that the balance is fair, and then you will get your 'data.'"

"But that wasn't..."

"Shut your mouth, Wallace," the bird interrupted again. "Or I will stitch it shut."

It was a bird. A crow? Yes. Blackbird. Crow. Corva. The girl was gone. Unless Kendra turned her head almost all the other way, and then she could still see the leather and pale skin out of the corner of her eye. *Things are still a bit fuzzy,* she thought.

Kendra turned her head back again to face the man opposite her in the booth.

Wallace? Wallace. Wallace... Bradstreet? Right. The guy from the Library.

He seemed... not angry. Maybe frustrated. Peeved. That was the word.

"You're peeved," she said.

At that, he smiled. Just a little. Before returning to his scowl.

"Not really," he mumbled, playing with his salad. "I just want to know more about that mark."

The crow... Tess, Kendra remembered now... hopped down to stand on the table between them.

"He's not a bad sort," the bird explained. "But a clerk of Sight with a new knowing nearly in his grasp is almost as bad as a young girl with a crush. Single-minded and, to others, obnoxiously oblivious to unrelated details. Such as a need for food."

Tess pecked at croutons and Kendra took another sip of water. The man waited. Patient, but barely so. When their meals came, he ate his gyro quietly while Kendra ploughed through a burger and cinnamon fries.

Part way through, Wallace asked, "You come to a Greek restaurant for a hamburger?"

Kendra shrugged. "It's a good burger. And the fries are excellent. I'd normally have just the salad, but I was too stressed out to eat breakfast with Monday's secretary, so..."

Kaolyn, back from bringing a plate of food to Mirkir on the street, sat down next to her.

"Monday's secretary?" he asked chuckling.

"What's funny?"

The man across from her was chuckling, too.

"I swear to God," Kendra said. "If you people don't stop treating me like an idiot child and just explain things to me without all the self-satisfied, amused editorial, I will..."

Tess interrupted, "The girl makes a good point. She's basically a day old. Just assume that she's a student in a class and you're her teachers. Behave professionally."

"Thanks, Tess."

Kaolyn nodded. "I'm sorry, girl. It's just... McKey may look like a secretary to you. But next time, turn whatever of the Sight you have on her and really try to see her. While she may perform some... administrative... duties as part of her function. She's no more a secretary than Mirkir is my pet."

"Then what is she?"

Wallace made an *I'm thinking* face while waggling his hand in a sort of *little of this, little of that* gesture.

"If I had to uses Mundane terms," he said. "I'd call her a combination consigliore, bodyguard and assassin."

Kendra's eyebrows shot up. "That nice looking old lady in frumpy shoes?"

Tess spoke up. "Remember, dear... That's the seeming put on for Mundanes."

"Well allrighty then," Kendra said. "I've never had an assassin buy me hot cocoa, but today's a day for firsts."

She went back to eating and then looked up, suspiciously, at Wallace.

"So... when you said you were a 'clerk' for Mr. Monday... does that mean that you are..."

"No," he replied. "I'm pretty much a clerk. There are other words for it in Reckoner. But the closest Mundane translation would also be 'clerk.' What I do is pretty much what I look like I'm doing."

"Which is?"

"Research for the Library's clients. Data entry. That sort of thing."

"So you're really a librarian."

Wallace shrugged, finishing his water and gesturing to the waitress for a refill. "Pretty much. I don't have an MLS, but since I started at the Library before that was a thing, I kind of got grandfathered in."

"MLS?"

"Master of Library Science. Most Mundane librarians have a graduate degree. I don't. Which means that, sometimes, I catch some crap from my Mundane friends in the business." He shrugged again. It seemed to be a regular gesture of his, Kendra thought.

"You have Mundane friends?" she asked. "Bran made it sound like hanging out with non-Reckoners was, I don't know... uncouth?"

Wallace waggled his hand again. "Depends. Release isn't much interested in Mundanes. There's not much a chronic can lose, break or lock up that they care about. Sight is different. All kinds of good information comes from outside our domain. I mean, if we were only interested in ourselves... how boring would that be? And some Mundane scholars are actually quite perceptive within narrow fields."

She nodded. The fact that what he'd just said made about 90% sense to her was comforting.

"So you hang out with regular librarians?"

He nodded. "I kind of have to. Our library has way more Mundane patrons than Reckoners. It's part of Mr. Monday's overall... strategy, I would call it. Mundanes handle most of the Mundane issues and vice versa for Reckoners, but there ends up being some overlap. And because I specialize in Mundane history, we end up together more than most."

Another shrug. "After a few decades, you get used to them. I think a lot of the prejudice is because most of us just don't spend enough time with them to appreciate some of their good points."

Kendra looked up, startled. "A few decades? Dude... you don't look that much older than me."

Wallace grinned. "How old do I look?"

It was Kendra's turn to shrug. "I don't know. Twenty-three, maybe? Twenty-five max."

Tess interrupted before either Kaolyn or Wallace could get half-way through another chuckle.

"Dear," she explained, "Reckoners age far, far slower than Mundanes in most cases. Aside from exceptions, most notably in Earth, we live many, many centuries."

Kendra dropped a cinnamon fry. "Centuries?"

"Yes, dear. Again... unless you're a Natural, like Kaolyn, here."

Kendra blinked and shook her head. "And how long with Kaolyn live?"

He answered for himself. "As you measure time, probably about seven years."

She dropped the same fry again.

"Wait. Wallace here will live for hundreds of years, but you'll be dead at seven?"

Tess answered, "Different domains, different Ways, girl. The lives of Earth are tied to seasons very differently than ours. As are their memories and perceptions. Some of what Kaolyn 'remembers' will have come from an earlier greenman."

Kendra shook her head. "Lots to learn."

"Right," answered Wallace, pulling about ten napkins out of the dispenser and wiping his hands. "And not just for you. I believe you owe me some information..."

A shadow fell, almost instantly, over their table, darkening both the light from the cheap fluorescents overhead and the daylight from the large windows at the front of the cafe. A chill also seemed to seep up from the floor, drawing the warmth from her hands and feet. The noises of the restaurant, too, faded further away.

"Final warning, boy..." said the crow." I will tell you when your side of the bargain is full. And then you can test her mark. Until then... behave."

Wallace swallowed quickly and then nodded.

For a moment, all was still. Then the shadow and its chill receded.

Kendra was about to ask Tess what that was all about when somebody's phone made a noise. Kaolyn reached into his pocket, pulled out a phone and read something on its screen. He looked up at Kendra, back to his phone and looked like he was about to say something when the door to the restaurant exploded inward.

With her newfound doubled senses, Kendra could tell that the explosion was a Way of some sort. In the Mundane world, seen to her as through a highly reflective window, it was just the door being opened so quickly that it slammed back into the frame with a loud, jangly crash. The waitress, the cook behind the counter, all the patrons, everyone at Kendra's table all turned to look at the same moment.

The cook, waitress and Mundane patrons saw four young men in jeans and t-shirts, tattooed and pierced, two of them holding pistols. The two with the guns came through the restaurant while the other two stood by the door keeping watch on the street.

Kendra saw this, too... but also saw four men wearing nothing but body paint and various tools that hung on chains around their waists, wrists and necks. Their nudity wasn't as shocking to her as the fact that their eyes were entirely black and yet still seemed to glow with some kind of fey, inner light.

"Put all the cash in a to-go bag, man," the one near the counter said to the cook, who also tended the register.

"Be cool, be cool," the cook said. "I got it. Look. Right here. I got it."

While he stuffed money into a plastic bag, the other one with a gun came to stand by Kendra's table. In her new vision, it was not a gun he was holding but a kind of mirror. It reflected the light from the cafe windows like a crystal prism, and he tilted it to shift the light onto Kaolyn first, then Wallace, and finally her.

As the light blinked in her eyes, making her squint, time seemed to slow for Kendra, yet every detail of her surroundings was shockingly clear.

She saw that Tess had lifted off the table and was poised to take flight, beak opened in the beginning of a harsh, high cry. Kaolyn was starting to stand, one hand on the table, one moving toward the intruder's mirror. Wallace had shrunk back in his seat and seemed to be staring right through her at something on the wall behind her head.

The man with the mirror had a shaved head, she realized. It was painted, too, with the same loops and whorls that wound around his body. They reminded her of the scary Rorschach Test from Dr. Lyonne's office.

The mirror seemed to grow larger in the man's hand and she could hardly keep her eyes open. The light it reflected was bright and getting brighter. Almost blinding, but somehow still making the world she could see even clearer. The details of his hand jumped into high definition. Tiny, delicate tracings painted around each finger. Snakes curling around his wrist.

She was about to fall into the mirror, she thought. Which was OK. Because the restaurant was filling with acrid smoke. Maybe. Or steam. Or... something. But the mirror was safe. That's where she should go to get away from... whatever. *It looks so nice and smooth and peaceful in the mirror.*

Just as she was about to lean forward into its bright, flickering surface, a small hand touched her on her knee. She looked away from the mirror for a moment (*I'll be right back*) and there was a blonde girl there in a blue, kind of frock-y dress, like something from another time. She looked to Kendra a bit like John Tenniel's illustrations of Alice. Sweet and innocent, but a bit of a scamp, too.

In a very bad, overdone Arnold Schwarzenegger-style Austrian accent, the girl said, "Come with me if you want to live."

Kendra was confused. But then the girl smiled and a pair of huge green wings spread behind her, obscuring the mirror and the painted man, the restaurant, the patrons and the mural of the Parthenon.

"Parrot Girl," Kendra whispered.

The little girl waggled her eyebrows roguishly and held out her hand.

Kendra took it and together they flew away.

Chapter 6. Journey

There was only one garden in the world in which Rain Vernon felt uncomfortable, and this was it.

To a Mundane or any Reckoner from a domain other than Earth, it would have seemed entirely beautiful. There was a harmony of light, of color... even of sound and movement that drew the eye ever deeper into more delightful details. The stretch of branches. Grasses left to grow long, but in waves that seemed, almost, patterned. Flowers growing by mossy rocks on the banks of a small stream. Butterflies and birds, ladybugs, blossoms... all grew in a profusion of beauty that seemed to straddle the line between the wild, untamed state of nature and the ability of an artistic mind to fathom deeper patterns from the chaotic twists of growth.

It was all a lie.

Its owner, Gareth Ezer, Warden of Increase, was easily the wealthiest man on the planet, though probably only a score of people understood the extent of his riches. As head of what many believed to be the most powerful of the Seven Domains, Gareth balanced the influence of his Mundane wealth and the power of his Ways in the same way that the garden seemed to balance between nature and art. He was charming and thoughtful, remembered everyone's name after the first meeting, gave fortunes away anonymously to charity every year and traveled with a staff that was so loyal to him they might as well have been golems created in thrall to the beating of his heart. He had never come close to anything even mildly smelling of scandal. The media loved him because he bought millions in advertising for his non-profit programs, said truly witty, quotable things and answered their calls personally. He often invited members of the press along with him on fact-finding junkets, opening up his initial brainstorming processes more completely and honestly than any inventor or entrepreneur had ever done before.

He was a widower. He had no children. It was rumored that he would leave his entire estate to be split among the orphanages he supported. It was rumored that he had invented fabulous machines and new technology that he kept secret because he believed the world wasn't ready for them yet. It was rumored he was working on a meta-cure for all diseases. Many rumors. All of them the kind you'd want to be true.

Gareth oversaw his empire from a house on Long Island that seemed, compared to others in the neighborhood, about average. It was large, of course. It was in the best part of town, of course. But it could have belonged to any of a hundred financiers, movie producers, pop stars, best-selling authors or international bankers. From the outside, it was what you'd expect: a mansion for a very, very rich man.

The garden, though, was unique.

It was beautiful, of course. But Rain knew it had been meticulously crafted, plant-by-plant, petal-by-petal, stone-by-stone to the exacting demands of a master who needed it to achieve an effect, not to truly be beautiful. True beauty, he knew, depended, as the Mundanes said, "On the eye of the beholder." Therefore, the garden was not allowed to be beautiful by any standard open to interpretation. It was, instead, engineered to appear as beautiful as possible to anyone, while doing nothing to distract the mind with questions of subtlety or interpretation. To a truly knowing eye, it was to "real" gardens what rayon is to silk.

Rain sat quietly on a garden chair and waited. He tried to ignore the garden, but in a way he could feel it crying, as it always did, to be... free.

He didn't wait long. Gareth, true to his nature, kept his word and his appointments. He would never make someone wait in order to see them sweat or to emphasize his power over them. That was inefficient. If he needed someone to sweat or to fear him, he would make that happen directly.

Rain stood as the older-seeming man strode through the gate and into the garden. Gareth waved a hand at him, a gracious host, motioning him to sit back down. Rain was taken a bit aback, as always, by how one man could seem both so handsome and wise, physically impressive and emotionally healthy all at once. He wondered, not for the first time, if a Reckoner from Sight might see that as a facade the same way he perceived the true shallowness of the garden.

Gareth unbuttoned his dark blue sports coat as he sat next to Rain. He wore no tie, as that was the fashion these days. His silver hair was thick and not too wavy... just interesting enough to make you think it was casually combed rather than meticulously groomed. His eyes were a pale gray that seemed interested in everything you had to say. Kind eyes that saw the best in everyone.

None of his clothing was absurdly expensive. Tailored, of course. Well cut. Good lines, finest cloth. But nothing ostentatious. Rain had met rich men and women who seemed to want to wear as much of their fortune in exotic animal skin, jewels and designer puffery as possible. Not Gareth Ezer. He wore the best of the least expensive or the least of the most expensive. Clothes that might inspire respect, but never envy.

Leaning back in his chair, looking around his garden, Gareth seemed to Rain like the world's most reliable family banker or lawyer. Someone you'd invest your life's savings with or quit jobs to work for. Someone who could have been president, had he been more politically inclined rather than technically and financially. Someone you could befriend, trust and love without fear.

All of which was true. Until you became a hindrance to his plans. At which point Gareth Ezer, through his army of retainers, would bankrupt, scandalize, ruin, harry and, if necessary, murder you with the same ease used to prune an errant branch in this falsely beautiful garden.

If charm got the job done, charm was the tool. Encouragement, inspiration, investment, promotion... all had their place. And if genocide was called for? Rain knew, personally, of at least four incidents in which Ezer had engineered the deaths of thousands of Mundanes.

Outside of a few very well placed Reckoners, no one knew how ruthless Ezer could be in the pursuit of his aims. Because, of course, secrecy was a tool, too. And a weapon.

"Rain," Ezer said, leaning forward, elbows on knees in a pose that suggested he was confiding in a friend, "I heard about what happened in your topiary."

Vernon nodded, waiting. Like Ezer, he wouldn't venture information without needing to.

"I assume," Ezer continued, "It was entirely an accident."

Rain nodded. "As far as I can tell, Gareth, she stopped taking her drugs a few weeks ago, but convinced Lyonne and her mother that she was still on them."

Ezer nodded. "And then she somehow unlocked a Way..."

"Yes. A transition mold that held a creature one of my clients sometimes..."

Ezer waved again. Still friendly, but dismissively. As if to say, No matter, my friend.

"And then she somehow ended up in the Library."

Rain nodded again. Hoping he wouldn't ask...

"How on earth did that happen, Rain?" Still friendly. Just a bit... perplexed. Concerned. Still the friendly uncle who wanted only your best.

"One of my greenmen took her there."

Ezer frowned a little. Just a bit. "Why?"

Rain paused and gestured at the pitcher of iced-tea on the table next to them. "May I?"

"Of course," Ezer said, smiling. "Help yourself. I know you like the raspberry recipe Darlene whips up, so I had her make us some."

"Thanks, much."

He needed a moment to think, so Rain took his time pouring two glasses, the second of which Gareth accepted with a nod of thanks.

How much to divulge? he wondered, his mind churning. He'd been agonizing over that question since Ezer had summoned him the day before. *If I don't tell him something that he already knows, he'll suspect me of keeping even more from him. But if I tell him something I don't need to...*

Best to wrap the truth in a lie, he decided.

Rain shrugged, trying to appear somewhat casual. "My greenman didn't know what else to do. Obviously I wouldn't have told him about the girl..."

Ezer nodded. "Of course not."

"When he found her in the garden, the greenman had no way to contact me. Not right at that time. And he didn't want someone else to come along and find her there. He knows that my garden is special, but not about..."

Ezer held up a hand. "Of course he didn't know. You already said that. Because no one but you and that human creature of yours know about the girl's condition. Correct? That so called 'doctor' you have under your spell?

The one who first alerted you to the girl and whom you assured me could be relied upon?"

Fighting the urge to babble, Rain simply answered, "No, sir. No one else knows. Just we two."

The silver-haired man leaned back, grinning. "'Sir?' My friend," he stood and gestured for Rain to follow. "We are not Mundanes. We are Reckoners. We are, all of us, equal. Different, of course... but equal."

That is a lie that you know is a lie, and it's a lie you know I don't believe... so why are you even saying it? wondered Rain. Everything you do is toward a purpose.

"So," Ezer continued, walking the path that wandered around his mansion, in his wake. "We have a seemingly... random... action on the part of the girl, combined with a very unlikely accident, topped off with another random action on the part of the greenman, all of which brings us to a strait that we have been endeavoring, expensively, to avoid for many years. Does that about sum things up?"

Rain just nodded.

"And do you truly think it was all accidental? All random? No... efforts put forth on the part of our competitors?"

By the Name of the Mother, Rain thought, *you do talk like a chronic sometimes.*

"I think that it was, as you say, a set of unlikely events. No hand behind them. No intention."

Ezer stopped suddenly, turning toward the other man. "Vernon. Listen to me. You need to stop being afraid of me, and start being afraid of whatever is happening out there." He waved his hand at the messy, disorganized world beyond his garden.

"You are, as the Mundanes say, 'on my team,' old friend. And, in terms of this circumstance, it is a very small team. I trust you implicitly and completely. I have no doubt that you would and will do right by me whenever given the choice. You are a wise and powerful friend. And I give you my word that until I see incontrovertible evidence that you have deliberately betrayed me, I will assume nothing but good intentions and hard work on your part. Do you understand?"

Ezer put a hand on Rain's shoulder, and the look in those gray eyes was so empathic, so friendly, so confident, that Rain simply nodded, knowing that he would, in fact, do everything in his power to keep from disappointing this man.

"Good," Ezer said, giving his shoulder a brief, firm, friendly squeeze. "You aren't wrong to be afraid. But, truly, we are brothers in this and your fear should be for our cause, not for your own safety or security."

They had circled the house entirely once as they talked and were back at the benches by the stream. Ezer reached into his coat pocket and took out a sealed envelope, handing it to Rain.

"I do not believe the events leading to the girl's awakening were an accident," he said. "But, at this point, the cause is somewhat irrelevant. What is important is how we use this new circumstance to our advantage."

Rain nodded and looked down at the envelope in his hand, confusion in his eyes.

"She will come to you," Ezer said. "She will have many questions, and you know how to answer most of them, and how to evade the ones you don't. You will invite her to Earth. She may be... unconvinced or disappointed in your invitation. When that moment comes, and she is ready to leave and seek another Domain, give her this. If we had more time, I could prepare something deeper, something more attractive and compelling. But this is all we have time for at the moment. A rather... blunt instrument."

"And that is?" Rain was almost afraid to ask.

"The truth," Ezer replied, turning to go back into the house.

Rain watched him go. Part way to the front door, Ezer bent to dust something off a white rose, spending a minute or so examining the flowers, blowing on them, even, to get the lay of the petals just-so. Ezer finished, dusted his hands against each other, and disappeared into the mansion.

Putting the envelope inside his own, much less expensive tweed coat, Rain fled the hateful place.

* * * * *

Two weeks after the fight in the Parthenon restaurant, and still no one had heard from Kendra.

Rain Vernon had called Lane White the day after Kendra's disappearance. The day before he was summoned to see Ezer. He told Lane that Kendra hadn't checked in for her gardening duties in two days. Lane told him that she was sorry Kendra hadn't let him know, but that she'd been offered a paid internship for the rest of the summer with a company that did something with computers that she, Lane, didn't really understand. The internship was in Chicago. Lane said that she thought Kendra had told him, because she'd said that everything was wrapped up and she was fine to leave.

Rain didn't push it. *Ah, yes,* he'd said. *I do recall that, now. Sorry to have bothered you.*

Three days after that, Dr. Lyonne called Lane. Much the same conversation. Lane assured her that Kendra had taken enough medication with her to last the rest of the summer. She'd seen the bottles. Made sure herself while helping Kendra to pack. She remembered having a chuckle with Kendra about how, hopefully, the TSA agents who scanned her bags wouldn't think she was a druggie.

"That's funny, isn't it?" asked Lane. "The idea of Kendra being a druggie."

Dr. Lyonne agreed that, yes, it was funny. Lane didn't sound quite... right... to her, but then again Lane had never sounded right to her.

"If you hear from Kendra," she said before hanging up, "Please have her give me a call. She asked me to find some articles for her and I can send them to her whenever it's convenient for her."

"She's checking her email. You should send them to her now," Lane said.

"You've heard from her?" Dr. Lyonne asked.

"No. But she always checks her email."

Dr. Lyonne didn't push it. *I'll do that.*

After four days, Rain had Kaolyn begin to activate some of the guardians in his various estates around the country. His creatures, whether made of stone, wood or water, picked up no scent. After seven days, he expanded his search to other countries, but didn't hope for any more success.

He began, at ten days, to receive requests from Gareth Ezer for daily progress reports.

At the two week mark, Kaolyn met Rain in the topiary garden to report on the total lack of success.

They sat on one of the benches near the brick tunnel. Rain ran his fingers through his hair and wished he'd had more sleep. Kaolyn, relaxed as most of his kind tended to be, ate a sandwich from a brown paper bag, washed down with Dr. Pepper.

"Nothing at all, then," repeated Rain.

"Nope," mumbled the greenman around a mouth of watercress and corned beef.

"And no idea who it was who took her? The female with wings?"

"Nope."

Mirkir landed on the ground next to the bench with a soft *whump* that was unexpectedly quiet for a creature of his mass and composition.

"And your kind?" Rain asked. "They've heard nothing, either?"

Mirkir shook his head with a slight grinding sound. "Nope."

Rain wasn't sure they weren't making fun of him. It was hard to tell with Naturals. Sometimes they were just odd. Other times their humor ran deeper and colder. Either way, he didn't really care at this point.

"If we don't find the girl soon," he told them both, "Ezer is going to be angry."

Mirkir grunted. "Angry. Err."

Again... Rain wasn't sure if the gargoyle was being flip, if he had really meant to say, "angrier," or was just repeating what had been said with a growly suffix.

Kaolyn tossed the last bite of the sandwich to Mirkir who tried to catch it, but managed only to flip it off his nose and onto his back. Watching the stone creature spin in tight circles trying to retrieve it from his back should have been amusing.

Almost, it was anyway. But not quite.

"You mean," the greenman said, "that he'll be angry with you. I don't think he gives the air in one breath about me or mine."

Rain stewed on that for a moment, fighting his frustration. It did no good to get angry at a Natural. They did what they did. Very little sentiment, either positive or negative. Almost no resentment or personal ego involved in their decisions. Nevertheless…

"I still do not understand why you took the girl to the Library, instead of coming to get me."

Kaolyn rolled his sandwich bag into a ball, passing it from hand to hand, watching the stone dog.

"I told you before. The Law was unclear. Lacking clarity, I took her to a place where someone could learn more and make a determination."

"Naturals and the law," Rain shook his head. "You precede the Law, yet seem to cling to it more fiercely than any of the Houses."

Kaolyn nodded, still playing with the paper ball. "We understand the consequences of lawlessness better than you. We are often the worst harmed by them."

Rain knew what he meant, and didn't even really disagree. He'd always known that naturals were… hard to read. He'd accepted that when he'd drawn up their original contracts. But it didn't help him feel any less angry.

The greenman sensed that and explained further, "Despite being in your garden, she did not belong to you. She did not belong to us. I thought of places that were… neutral. Where someone of the Houses could make a determination. If I had given her to the street, you might be even more angry now."

That's very true, Rain thought.

Finally, the last bit of sandwich having been dislodged and consumed, Mirkir lay down at Kaolyn's feet and fell immediately into a raspy, snoring sleep.

Kaolyn wiped his hands off on each other, crumpled the lunch bag, put it in a pocket, and leaned back.

"What now, Rain?"

Rain shrugged. "I honestly don't know. I'd ask Sight for help, but…"

Kaolyn nodded. "The eye, invited, sees more than asked."

"There are... complexities... of this business that do not bear that level of scrutiny."

"If I understood more, maybe I could help more," Kaolyn said. "If I'd understood that she meant something more to you than a hireling, I could have brought her to you when the Librarian called me to retrieve her the next day. I could have kept her out of sight. We could have avoided the Blood soldiers entirely, then."

Except I'm the one who sent the soldiers, thought Rain. *As soon as my other eyes told me about the garden. I thought if they grabbed her, you'd be none the wiser. I'd have Kendra back, you'd still have no idea how important she is, and Ezer wouldn't be...*

He sighed. *No use now.* "I can tell you a little," he went on. "But I'm not sure it will help."

Kaolyn waited. Patient as always.

"Ezer believes that Kendra is in danger, and has been for years."

Kaolyn frowned. "From who?"

"It's a bit unclear," Rain said, pacing back and forth in front of the bench. "There was... an incident... with her mother, Lane White, many years ago. Before Kendra was born."

"The loss of her Way," Kaolyn said.

Rain stopped, startled. "You know about it?"

"I didn't until last week when I started watching her as part of the search."

"And?"

"And what? If you spend any time at all really looking at her, you can tell that Lane White was once a Reckoner."

Maybe if you're a Natural, Rain thought.

"How?" he asked out loud.

Kaolyn shrugged again. "Hard to describe. Mundanes move through most Ways without touching them. It's like they're not there at all. Lane... she leaves a wake."

Rain shook his head. "I don't understand."

Scrunching up his face a bit, Kaolyn tried again. "Like the drain in a tub. It's not just 'not tub,' it's a... negative thing. The thing that empties the tub. The Ways don't move through her like she's not there. They part around her as if she was tacking through them like a sailing ship."

Mostly to himself, Rain said, "And nobody noticed this..."

"It's hard to notice," Kaolyn replied. "And who'd look? To us, she's a Mundane. Why bother? But I cast a few simple tracking Ways around Kendra's room in case she came back. Once, when Lane came in to put some clothes on the girl's bed, I was outside the window. She'd triggered one of them, and I wanted to see what was going on. That's when I saw."

"And you could tell from that that she'd once been a Reckoner?"

Kaolyn shook his head. "No. I could only tell that there was something going on. At first I thought it was another's Way, cast on her, leaving a trail. But as far as I could tell... nothing like that. She leaves no scent of any Domain."

"You sure you'd be able to tell that?"

Again with the shrug. It was starting to annoy Rain. "Yes. You should be, too. I mean, you're not a Natural, but you're still of Earth. The mark of any other House should ring true to you, even if only a little."

Rain nodded. "Yes, yes. It does. Usually. I guess I just don't pay attention much. And I don't get out around other Domains much."

Kaolyn poked Mirkir with his toe and the gargoyle grunted, softly, in his sleep.

"Rain," the greenman said, "what does this have to do with Kendra and Ezer?"

"He believes," replied Rain, "that whatever happened to Lane White was deliberate. Not an accident. And that someone may try to do it to Kendra, too."

Kaolyn nodded. "The girl told me she'd been on drugs since she was very small. Anti-psychotics. If you started young enough, and were raised by Mundanes... maybe someone has been hiding her all her life. And what happened here," he gestured at the garden, "was part of the plan to more permanently end her Way."

How much to tell him, Rain wondered. *Not too much. Not yet.*

"That sounds... plausible," the gardener replied.

Kaolyn stood up and booted Mirkir a bit harder. The stone creature opened one eye and stuck out his tongue.

"I'm going to go talk to that junior library clerk boy," the greenman said.

"Who?"

"The one who was with us when she was taken," Kaolyn said. "I think his name was Warren or Wally or something. He works in the Librarian's outer Way. I know where he eats lunch."

Rain reached out to put a hand on Kaolyn's arm. "We don't want to involve Sight."

"I understand," Kaolyn replied. "I think I can keep the boy's help off the books."

Rain chuckled. "So to speak."

Kaolyn smiled a little. "Yeah. So to speak."

As the greenman headed for the brick tunnel and out of the garden, Rain called after him, "You think he can help find her?"

Kaolyn turned back. "I think he knows more than he thinks he does."

Kaolyn left the garden, Mirkir trailing behind him, shaking his stone wings and stamping a bit. And Rain was left to wonder, *How can two creatures in the same Domain see the world so differently?*

Had Kaolyn heard the question, he would have answered, "You live in the world. I am the world."

* * * * *

For a moment, it didn't seem like flying to Kendra. She touched Parrot Girl's hand, and something changed and she wasn't in the restaurant and she was spinning and there were colors and a wind and flashes of light and darkness and it was very cold for a moment and then...

She was climbing into a bright blue sky, like diving off a diving board but in reverse. The air sped by her, whipping her hair and stinging her eyes, and she saw the clouds above her coming closer and she looked down to see the streets and buildings getting further away and Parrot Girl grinned at her and bent a bit to one side and the world turned and tipped again, only this time it was part of the flight and the sky leaned one way and they dove the other and picked up speed and were hurtling toward a park and a pond and--

Kendra threw up.

A lot.

She was looking down at the moment, which was, she supposed, a small blessing. And she just managed to see that she'd showered a flock of pigeons with vomit before Parrot Girl noticed, looked very scared and sorry and took both of her hands in hers and then there was another flash and--

They were sitting on a bench on the other side of the pond.

"Are you OK?" the young, blonde girl asked. Her wings were folded, now, or invisible or something and Kendra wiped her mouth on the back of her hand and managed a weak nod.

"Good," said Parrot Girl. "Because we can't stay here."

"I..." Kendra said, but Parrot Girl grabbed her hand and there was another flash. And another and another, and after each one Kendra felt as if she might throw up again, but they happened too quickly and there wasn't enough time to see anything except brief, freeze-frame images of--

a hillside overlooking the city; she vaguely recognized it from pictures

a roadside rest stop, with RVs and 18-wheeler trucks

a field of grain with a single, enormous tree in the middle of it

the deck of a large ship with containers and a crane

the shore of a cold beach, gray sky and white gulls above

the first class compartment of a jet liner

some kind of platform in the middle of the ocean

another beach, this one warmer but darker, with a couple sitting on blanket near the high-tide mark

an old, burned out building of some kind... maybe a mill or a barn

the silhouette of a castle.

That last one stuck.

Kendra felt stone beneath her feet, leaned forward to feel it under her hands, too. A low wall, about waist high. Rough stone. Old stone, soft with moss and time.

Parrot Girl put a hand on her shoulder and said, "We can stay here at least for..."

Kendra threw up again over the side of the wall and heard it splash on a surface some distance below.

It took a few minutes but the world, and her stomach, stopped spinning. Beyond vertigo, she'd felt as if her mind had been disconnected from her body and dragged along behind her like the tail of a kite. She slumped down on the stone floor of the... *wall? battlement? what do you call this?* and tucked her face down between her knees.

It was quiet there. Just the wind in the stones and a few peeping bugs. Nice and cool. A good, summer evening temperature. After a few minutes, Kendra was able to look up and notice that it was late afternoon, the sun hanging low in the sky over a flat line of gray that she thought must be the sea.

A small hand appeared in front of her with an unwrapped stick of gum. Without thinking she took it and began chewing.

In a little while, Kendra nodded, and said, "Ahh... Juicy Fruit."

Parrot Girl chuckled. "No, it's Double Mint. But that's funny. I get the reference."

"I figured... after your awful Arnold impression... you might."

Looking up, Kendra saw that Parrot Girl was mock-scowling at her. "My Arnold impression wins awards. I could have been a contender."

Kendra raised an eyebrow. "Now you're mixing references."

Parrot Girl shrugged and stood up, looming over Kendra as much as a four-foot tall girl who looked to weigh about seventy pounds can be said to "loom."

"You OK?" the girl asked.

Kendra made a kind of sour face. "We're in Europe, right?"

Parrot Girl nodded.

"Not sure 'OK' is how I'd put it. My stomach has calmed down. I don't feel like I'm going to have a seizure. But I'm confused and winded and, well... it's been a really, really long day."

She paused and frowned.

"What?" asked Parrot Girl.

"My mom... I'm worried that she's worried."

"I'll get her a message," the other girl said. "And I can impersonate you, too."

Kendra kept scowling.

"Trust me," she said. "And get some sleep." She gestured for Kendra to follow her. "I bet there's at least one room in here that's out of the wind and rain."

"It's not raining," Kendra replied, standing up, a bit shakily, to follow the girl.

"It will. It always does."

* * * * *

Kendra did sleep. Very soundly. Without dreams, without pause, without discomfort. Which, she realized as she stretched and popped her spine, was a bit odd... since she'd slept on a stone floor.

The sun was coming in through a small, high window and she looked around to see that Parrot Girl was still asleep, curled up in a nest of wings and blonde hair and lace.

I'm in a castle in Scotland with a fairy, she thought. And went to look around.

Parrot Girl had brought her food the night before; some soup, still hot, and crackers and a box of Pop Tarts and, most strange, a six-pack of some kind of chocolate drink in bottles that seemed left over from World War Two. It had been a bit fizzy, and tasty, and she assumed Parrot Girl wouldn't have saved her from the painted men if she'd been meaning to poison her. So she'd eaten the food, laid back to relax, and fallen asleep.

The first good sleep I've had... she couldn't remember. Her sleep had always been a bit buggered by her drugs. Or worry about mom. Or worry about school. Or just... Stuff. She'd never been a good sleeper. Until last night.

Probably all the excitement. The shock or whatever. Probably...

But she realized, somehow, that it wasn't that. It wasn't a recuperative sleep. It wasn't something her brain and body had done to help her recover from trauma or injury. It was... the way she was supposed to be. On a cold, stone floor, in a ruined Scottish castle, next to a blonde child with giant, green wings... she had found...

Peace.

It felt like being clean after a day sweating in the sun and dirt. It felt like the air conditioning in a dark movie theater. Like the moment she first juggled three balls successfully. Like finishing a good book in a long series and knowing there was so much more to come. Like bumping into a friend in a strange place.

Peaceful. I feel peaceful.

Part of her mind insisted she be afraid of everything that had happened to her. But it was an invented part. An imaginary part. Like when you purposefully make shadows seem scary after seeing a horror movie. You know it's just a coat rack.. but ooooohhhh.... ooogy-boogy. Fun to scare yourself.

That part of her brain, the conscious editor, was saying, "You should be afraid and upset."

But I'm not.

Kendra strolled out onto the walkway surrounding the tower room they'd slept in and looked at the sky. It was bright with blues and yellows and... other things. She saw some kind of glowing rope appear in a wave and settle back to earth. There were specks in the distance that made a kind of harmony that wasn't really made of sound. There was a... dragon? lizard? something? sleeping on top of a cloud and, somehow, she knew that it was part of the cloud.

The breeze brought her new scents, the stones told her stories through her bare feet and the trees in the distance spelled words that she now could read.

Soft footfalls behind her. She didn't turn. A tiny hand on her shoulder.

"Welcome home, sister," Parrot Girl whispered, and Kendra nodded as the tears began.

* * * * *

It was a good, long cry. The kind that emptied all the junk you couldn't say out loud. Curled up with her head on Parrot Girl's lap, Kendra sobbed for at least half an hour. The great, green wings petted her back and shoulders, the breeze from them drying her tears. And, finally, she sat up, chuckling a little.

"What's funny?" Parrot Girl asked, grinning.

"I was remembering your Austrian accent."

"My excellent Arnold impersonation, you mean."

Rubbing her eyes, Kendra nodded. "Yeah, that's exactly what I meant."

Parrot Girl patted her knee. "You ready for breakfast?"

Kendra shook her head. "No. First, some answers."

"OK by me," the other girl said. "But for answers, we should either go to the top or the bottom."

Kendra looked confused. "Of what? And why?"

Parrot Girl stood, held her hand, and helped Kendra to her feet. "Of here. Because it's important."

Kendra looked down at the little blonde girl, wings now invisible, and said, "Whatever you say. Your circus, your monkeys. Up or down."

"Heh. Good," Parrot Girl agreed with a nod. "We'll start with up."

She turned and took two steps across the stones, put one foot up, and began walking up the vertical wall of the castle. Kendra followed without thinking, still holding hands.

The world looks different sideways, she thought. *Not bad. Just... different.*

It was a short walk, when you removed the consideration of gravity and climbing. The tower was really only about eight stories tall or so above the wall they'd been on. At the top, Parrot Girl simply pivoted and hopped over the crenelated wall and Kendra followed.

Stone floor, stone wall, and a hole leading to what Kendra assumed had been a stairway. Weathered and broken in places. But with a marvelous view of a hilly, green countryside.

She turned in a full circle one way, then paused, and turned in the other, taking in all the sights and sounds and other senses she now had.

"OK," she finally said. "We're at the top. Question and answer time."

"Fair enough," Parrot Girl said, sitting down on the stone floor of the tower. Kendra, following suit, asked the first question that came to mind.

"What Domain are you from?"

Parrot Girl poked her in the knee with a bony little finger. "That," she exclaimed, "is both an excellent question and a stupid one."

Kendra stuck her tongue out.

"Fair enough, sister," Parrot Girl said. "You know nothing, and it's hard to remember that. Just like that crow thing said."

"You heard that? You were there?"

"No. You talk in your sleep."

"And I said..."

144

"You said, 'Corva is right. I'm not stupid. I just don't know anything.'"

"And you know who Tess Corva is?"

"No. But you talked more and I'm good at context."

Kendra clucked her tongue and cracked a knuckle against her jaw. "OK. Whatever. So just answer my question."

Parrot Girl stood, shook out her giant green wings to their full span, and curtsied.

"I, whom you call 'Parrot Girl,' am widely and famously known as 'Vannia Tacticus,' of House Chaotic, the Fluid Court."

"The 'House Chaotic?'"

Parrot Girl -- Vannia, Kendra supposed she should call her now -- dropped back onto the floor, her wings disappearing again behind her.

"Yes. The House Chaotic. The Domain of Chaos. Benders of rules, breakers of lines, the dance of dice, the cut of cards, the whimsy of weather the..."

"Abuser of alliteration?"

"Ha! Yes. Sure. Ha." And it was Vannia's turn to stick her tongue out.

"So there is a Domain of Chaos, OK," Kendra mused out loud. "And... Sight. And Uncle Bran mentioned Release. And I think I heard something about... Dirt?"

That made Vannia snort and laugh so hard she started choking.

"Domain of Dirt! I will remember that! Oh, that greenman will spit nettles... Ha!"

After about a minute of that, Kendra reached out and gave Vannia a flick on her earlobe.

"Hey! What's up with that?"

"This tutorial will take days, if not weeks, if everything I say that's stupid and ignorant sends you off into peals of derisive laughter," Kendra said. "It gets old. Fast."

Vannia sat up and brushed imaginary dust from her dress. "Point taken. I will aspire to an attitude of respect and professionalism while we abide within the Tutor Castle."

Kendra waited with a straight face, knowing that Parrot Girl wouldn't be able to resist laughing at her own pun. But, apparently, she didn't get it herself. So...

"Sight. Chaos. Release. And..."

"Right," Vannia said, counting off on her fingers as she recited a poem in a sing-songy voice:

> *Earth, the Mother, first and last,*
> *Bearing Blood, the eldest sign.*
> *Chaos leaves the patterned path,*
> *Draws out Sight to spy and find.*
> *Flux pulls power from the round.*
> *Increase seeks the gain of gain.*
> *Release opposes any bounds.*
> *Ever balanced, poised Domains.*
> *Each and every, all and one.*
> *Seven equal, seven done.*

It seemed to Kendra that she heard, and understood, the poem in several languages at once, and that it rhymed -- or at least had a kind of lyrical meter -- in each.

"So... seven Domains," she said, counting them as she went through the poem in her memory.

"Yup."

"And the poem defines them, basically?"

"It's not just a definition, it's our history," Vannia replied.

"Well... a short history."

Vannia turned her head to one side and regarded Kendra with a very serious, level stare. A stare that was way, way too mature for the small child she seemed.

"Listen again," she said softly, and repeated her recitation.

Earth, the Mother, first and last,

In the other, less familiar languages, Kendra heard the sounds of water and wind. Smelled the ash of volcanic clouds and the salt of shallow seas. Creatures moved upon the lands and waters and in the air and through the rock and within the wood and moss. They <u>were</u> the Earth. Not just "on the Earth," as were Mundane men and the animals she knew from childhood. They were "of the Earth." As much part of the landscape as a mountain or canyon. They were connected to its (*her* she felt herself corrected)... to her seasons and elements. These were the "Naturals," as she'd heard Tess call them. Creatures whose lives rose from the world itself and its... her... rhythms and depths.

Bearing Blood, the eldest sign.

The things she heard and saw next are closer to what she'd call "human." Creatures that seek to control their destiny more than accept it. Individuals who become aware of how their interactions can help or hinder each other. The value of hunting in groups. The uses of stone and stick and fire. The beginning of language, but not as Kendra understands it. The first language of intentional Ways rather than those that live and die with the shifting of seasons and continents. Tribes join together to harvest scarce resources, share lore and craft and, eventually, fight and kill others. Deliberate murder. But also deliberate mercy. The love of family and clan beyond simple survival. This is Blood. The ties of strength, honor and obligation that bind us to those who came before and gave us life and those we bear and raise.

Chaos leaves the patterned path,

For a very long time, only Earth and Blood. A very, very long time. Time for lands and seas to shift. And then, as tribe and clan began to form what humans would eventually call "civilization," a rejection of the patterns of Blood. Not just resentment over losing a mate or wealth or status, but a true hatred of the definitions of mate, wealth and status. A distrust of the systems necessary to maintain them. But also a rejection of the choice-less patterns of Earth. A desire for individual action. A love of surprise. Of personal definition. Into the relatively stable world of Earth and Blood, the rise of Chaos brings both confusion and even greater development. Freedom. For in breaking patterns, more are revealed.

Draws out Sight to spy and find.

The birth of Sight is an almost instantaneous reaction to that of Chaos. At least in terms of history; only ten or so generations after Chaos began to warp the Ways of Blood and Earth. One family -- a father, his two sons and one daughter -- found it much more rewarding to examine the effects of

Chaos and the reactions of Blood and Earth than to participate. Language as Kendra understands it, was born. And then, eventually, writing. When the world held only two Houses -- Earth and Blood -- their interactions were largely predictable, universal and repetitious. The introduction of Chaos created realms of new and different possibilities. The Domain of Sight was the first to specifically and intentionally create a new Domain. Chaos, appropriately enough, had no specific founder. Or he (she, it, they?) were lost in antiquity. Or confused, purposefully, by the House Chaotic itself. Or not. Or both.

Flux pulls power from the round.

With the addition of Chaos, Kendra saw ebbs and flows of power moving through the world. Tribes of Blood gained influence, Reckoners of Chaos tore them down or built them up on a whim. Children of Earth used the advice of Sight to better understand their own Ways, and then Chaos distracted them. Vast changes took place on scales much greater than ever before, and much more rapid. One group of Reckoners of Sight realized that change generates power in and of itself. It doesn't matter who wins and who loses, as long as there is a winner and a loser. Stability is less... energetic. To test their theories, they strayed from the Way of Sight -- which sought only to observe and record -- and introduced changes of their own. Small, at first, these "touches" began to affect greater and greater swaths of Reckoners...

And, for the first time, begin to draw Mundanes into the fray. Before this, there was no real contact between the two groups. Mundanes either perceived Reckoners as part of the world as they understood it -- a world devoid of Ways -- or they only saw enough to cause confusion and, sometimes, folklore. But Sight knew that even Mundane changes could hold power. That the fall of a great human city could provide energy Reckoners could use.

Ironically, war was something that the Domains learned from Mundanes. While there had been interaction between the Domains, real conflict between the Houses simply hadn't made sense. What use were the ties of Blood to Chaos? They'd split intentionally from that path. And while Blood relied on Earth for sustenance... well, so did Earth. And Sight, well... Sight just watched. There was murder, of course. Individual combat. Duels. Revenge. But for one Domain to fight another? Unimaginable.

Until Flux. The group of Reckoners who broke away from Sight and began to deliberately provoke hostility between Blood clans. To put Chaos in the path of Sight or to make their Ways break down. To draw Reckoners into

Mundane wars and make them choose sides. All in order to grow the power of their new Domain. Thus began the Reckoner Wars.

For more than two thousand years, the wars raged on. Every time there was a break in the fighting, Flux would intervene and tip the balance. Every chance for peace was ruined. The constant turmoil caused great suffering, but also great advances in understanding, power and lore. Mundane civilizations rose and fell as unknowing allies to the Houses. Entire city-states burned and were forgotten as Flux sought to maintain "the round" as they called the flow of fortune and loss, life and death.

Finally, the Domains had learned and gathered enough power to destroy the Earth herself. Ways of making that could call upon her core to create new creatures and structures. Ways of destruction that could wreak havoc on tides and seasons. Earth mourned, Blood raged, Chaos danced and only Sight understood how close to the edge of annihilation the Domains raced.

But Sight, by its nature, could not act. Not much. Maybe a little. Here and there. A touch.

And so, over hundreds of years, Sight hoarded lore in some times, and dribbled it out at others. Helped Blood in one battle and provided intelligence for Flux in others. Until they saw a moment. A moment where all the greatest warriors could be brought together in one valley, in one place. For a battle that would either end the world or end the war.

Kendra recognized that valley. And the army of creatures and Reckoners and their pet men. She saw Monday on his perch above the fray. And she saw his mentor, Aasher, start the slide of sand that released a sea's worth of water onto the battlefield, obliterating the greatest Reckoners from all the Domains. Ending the reign of Flux.

The Great Flood. The end of the Reckoners' War. More than 7,000 years ago.

Into that vacuum, the leaders of Sight provided gentle urging and hints of knowledge to certain groups of survivors. They intentionally split Flux into three Domains. There was no way to destroy a House, and so Flux survived, but its children would forever balance its power.

Increase seeks the gain of gain.

Unlike Flux, the Domain of Increase was not interested in change unless it was positive. What the elders of Increase learned from Sight is that, long term, gain is not aided by change for its own sake. That true growth may require alteration... but not loss or destruction. Ever since, Increase stood very much opposed to Flux in most situations.

Release opposes any bounds.

Essentially a check on all other Domains, the Masters of Sight provided the first generation of Release with lore that allowed them to create and develop Ways that only and ever worked in opposition to codes, laws and patterns. While other Houses often confuse the workings of Release with Chaos, nothing could be further from the truth. Chaos loved anarchy and disorder. Release just wants to be left alone. Any major effort on the part of another House to gain an upper hand was almost always met with a response from Release.

Ever balanced, poised Domains.
Each and every, all and one.

And the balance, the poise, each equal... that was the Law. Not so much codified after the great war as understood at a level below even instinct.

Seven equal, seven done.

Just as she had when Wallace had shown her the Way of seeing, Kendra heard/saw/felt/knew all this background history from Vannia's simple repetition of the Song of the Houses.

"Wow," she said. "That's a lot to take in."

Vannia smiled. "It is. But we grow up understanding our history in the same way you understand what 'mother' and 'father' mean. It's not learned, really. It's..."

"Bred," Kendra interrupted.

"Exactly. Part of being a Reckoner is, well... being aware of many of the paths and connections that created and shape the world."

"Walking the Ways," Kendra said, mostly to herself.

"Exactly."

The two girls sat there quietly for a little while, thinking and, in Kendra's case, enjoying the newfound clarity.

Finally, she asked, "So this 'Law' that Tess told me about, it's a codification of... what? By whom?"

"I don't know," Vannia replied. "I haven't studied that at all. I don't worry about it."

"Aren't you worried about, I don't know... breaking the Law by mistake?"

"I don't think it's laws like that," Vannia said. "It's not like shoplifting or speed limits or don't raise llamas in your backyard or all that Mundane junk. I think it's more about the Domains themselves, and I don't need to know about that. I just do what I want or what the Brothers tell me."

"The Brothers?" Kendra looked around, wondering if some new set of players was about to materialize on the scene.

"Yeah. The Red Brothers. The Hands of Chaos. First of my Domain, head of the House."

"And who are these Red Brothers?"

Vannia's wings became visible for a just a moment, twitching behind her and then settling back into invisibility. It seemed, to Kendra, that the question had made her nervous.

"I'm... normally I wouldn't be able to tell you."

"Why not?"

"We are Chaos. A known, acknowledged leader is much less..."

Kendra nodded. "Chaotic."

"Right. All the other Domains, they'll tell you right off." She ticked them off on her fingers. "Solomon Monday, Hahang Su, Gareth Ezer, Lady Percy and Sekhemib Senbi."

Kendra followed along, counting as she went.

"That's only five," she said.

"Oh, Earth doesn't have a leader. Earth is Earth."

OK... Well that explains... Nothing, thought Kendra.

"But your... Red Brothers..."

"That's what the first Hands of Chaos called themselves. Or himself. Or herself. Or itself. Nobody knows. Could have been one guy or ten ladies and a shehesagat. Knowing would be..."

"Less chaotic."

"You catch on fast. But," and here she raised a tiny finger, "We in the House know our own Hands. And, for some reason not explained to one as lowly as I... The Red Brothers have told me to name them to you."

Kendra frowned. "That sounds like a big deal. I'm not sure I want to know. I mean, why should I? Why would they..."

"Or he."

"Right, or he. Why would they or he..."

"Or she."

"Shut up. Why would 'your Hands' want me to know who they are?"

Parrot Girl just sat there grinning like an idiot, waiting for Kendra to figure it out.

Kendra almost got pissed enough to snap at Vannia. But instead, she just thought.

Finally, she smiled, too.

"More chaos," the two girls said at the same time.

"Good girl," Vannia said. "My Hands have told me to tell you that in this incarnation, the Red Brothers are the woman who is known to others as Shavain Orro."

Vannia reached into a pocket of her skirt and pulled out a plain, gold ring set with a small, round, red stone.

"Wear this," she said, handing it to Kendra. "If you need the help of Chaos, break the stone -- it's only glass -- and Shavain will come to your aid."

Kendra put the ring on and then looked back up at Vannia. "Or she won't."

"Ha!" laughed Vannia. "Well, I don't know. That's..." She stopped and looked puzzled. "Well, OK. I don't know for sure. But she told me that she had captured a Way of Chaos in the stone. If you break it, you will release the Way and, well..." She again fell silent.

"I like you," she finally said to Kendra, her child's face very serious.

Kendra chuckled. "I like you, too, Parrot Girl."

"So, I mean... Yes. I guess you're right. I have no idea what will happen if you break the ring. But it's from Shavain and I think... I think she means you well. I think she'd even like it if you chose Chaos as your House. That may be why she told me to tell you her name. Because if you join us, you'd have learned it anyways."

Kendra nodded. "OK. I'll take that at face value. But for now... I am hungry."

She stood up and dusted off the butt of her jeans. "Where can we get something to eat around here."

Vannia smiled. "You're with Chaos, honey. If we wander around these fields long enough, we'll trip on a picnic basket."

Kendra laughed. She knew a lot more than she had when she'd woken up that morning. And way, way lots more than when she'd fallen asleep in the topiary garden.

"How do you find a random, chaotic picnic basket?" she asked.

Vannia stood up and gestured for Kendra to take her hand. Together they went down the old, cold stone stairs and Parrot Girl explained several of the Ways in which Chaos called up its power.

"Rhyming," she said, "is an excellent start. Can you guess why?"

Kendra thought, hard, as they descended the stairs. "I'm sorry, but I can't."

"Why do words rhyme?" asked Vannia as they passed through what looked like a ruined guard chamber and out into the daylight.

"Because... some words sound the same?" she said. Lamely.

"That's the definition of rhyme, yes. Dummy." Vannia tweaked her ear as they wandered down the hill toward a nearby field. "But why do we care? Why do we even notice?"

"We like patterns," Kendra said without even thinking. That was just... true.

"Exactly! But what does the sound of a word have to do with its meaning?"

"Well... except for obvious onomatopoeia, like 'moo,' nothing. Really."

"Exactly!" Vannia said again, and skipped away into the tall grass.

And then it dawned on her.

Words rhyme, so we put them together in new ways to match them up. Ways that wouldn't be a pattern except for the rhyme. We purposefully confuse sound and meaning. It's a method of madness. And we like it.

"Chaos!" she shouted at her friend, who was now rolling in the grass, her wings extended beside her.

"Indeed!" hollered Vannia back at her.

Following Parrot Girl's lead, flopped down on her back in the field of long grass and rolled. She noticed the new, red ring on her finger and wondered if maybe it wasn't a powerful Chaotic Way. Maybe it was nothing but empty, ordinary glass. *Either way,* she thought, *it's pretty.*

* * * * *

When the Blood Thanes – a close-knit group of clan hunters—burst into the restaurant, Wallace of course knew them immediately for what they were. He could tell from their markings what clan they belonged to and that they had come to capture, not to kill. That fact was confirmed when one of them brandished a spirit glass at Kendra.

Interesting craftsmanship, Wallace had thought, looking at the object from less than a foot away. *One of ours, I think, though bound in Blood, of course.*

He wasn't afraid. There was no need to be. Reckoners might steal from each other or even cause each other some discomfort, but never real harm. There was drama, of course. Chagrin. Anger. Resentment. Loads of passive aggressive behavior -- he'd seen it all in his studies -- but very little direct violence. At least for the last seven thousand years or so.

Which was why he had been so surprised when the Blood Thane struck him across the face. Hard.

Kendra's disappearance was surprising, too... but everything about the girl had been... unique... thus far. Wallace didn't like unique. He didn't like extraordinary. His research was about finding patterns and seeing paths. Anomalies were to be understood only within the context of greater order. Either as examples of an as-of-yet unfound pattern, or as exceptions that required the discovery of other patterns.

Because, if you can see enough and know enough, everything makes sense.

Even a small girl with great huge parrot wings sliding down through the ceiling and flying off with your lunch companion.

A lunch companion who owes me information, Wallace thought as Kendra and "Parrot Girl" disappeared.

Some of the Mundane customers fled, seeing only gang-bangers with guns and knives and two girls running out of the restaurant. Their leader was scooping bills into a paper sack while the two by the door looked around, unsure of what to do now that their obvious quarry had vanished. Several other customers, both Mundane and Reckoner, held very still and shrank away from the robbers as much as they could.

"Excuse me," Wallace asked the confused Blood hunter standing by their table, spirit glass still brandished in his right hand. "Do you know if your glass was bound to Blood before or after the feedback line was set into the material?"

The Thane looked at Wallace as if he were an idiot, and speaking an entirely foreign language.

"The easiest way to tell would be if you knew whether there are other, similar tools in your..."

That was when the hunter hit him. A short, hard smack with the back of the hand that was holding the glass.

He'd never been hit hard before. Pushed, sure, a couple times by Mundanes or Reckoners who were trying to get by him. Those of Sight often stopped in odd places to observe... well... anything. He'd even tripped once and really banged his elbow pretty good.

But this was... really different. The surprise and shock adding to the pain in his cheek.

Before he could react, the leader of the gang hissed some kind of order and all four of them fled.

There was an odd moment of silence, and then the patrons all began talking at once, some of them now leaving quickly, too. The owner pulled out a cell phone, dialed and began talking to someone. The waitress sat down, hard, on the floor; not hurt, just shocked.

Tess now looked entirely like a young woman dressed in what Wallace would have qualified as "Goth-light." That is, all black and silver, but without enough "scary" make-up and piercings to make her seem anything but maybe... artistic or dramatic.

"We should leave," she said softly.

"Agreed," said Kaolyn. "Come on, boy."

The greenman helped Wallace to his feet and the three of them left just as a police car rounded the corner. Wallace could tell it was only Mundane cops, and so he had no worries about "trouble" (though what that meant was unclear in his mind at this point). But it might have taken time to deal with them.

"Leaving is smart," he mumbled softly. "Yes. I agree."

He was stumbling, and only Kaolyn's hand on his shoulder kept him from taking a fall.

"He's in a bit of shock," Tess said. "Let's get him back to the Library."

"No... no," Wallace insisted. "I... Just find me a cab. I'll go home. I work from home quite a bit. Nobody will miss me. And..." his hand went to his cheek, where he was sure a red welt was forming.

They stopped at the corner and Kaolyn flagged down a Mundane taxi while Tess took a look at Wallace's cheek.

"It's not that bad," she told him. "If it hurts, I can..."

"No. No, that's fine," he said. "I'll put some frozen peas on it when I get home."

Tess smiled softly. *You read that somewhere... I know you did. Maybe a month ago, maybe twenty years... Sometimes Sight can be so cute.*

Out loud she said, "That will take the swelling down, yes."

Wallace got into the cab and gave the driver his home address. As they pulled away from the curb, he turned and saw Tess become crow and fly away. Kaolyn stood and watched the cab until it turned a corner.

Home. Frozen peas. A text to his immediate superior to say he'd be working from home for a day or two. A shower. Some light reading and research for a Mundane client of the library.

Soon it was dark, and Wallace sat with a second bag of frozen vegetables (corn, this time) laying on his cheek as he watched *Casablanca* for the forty-ninth time. His face was numb and he suspected that he really hadn't been hit very hard, since there was barely any red left. But doing something... anything... felt good.

Just because you know it's the placebo effect, doesn't mean it isn't real, he thought.

At first, the decision to not tell his boss and Mr. Monday about the incident was simply a gut reaction. Part shame, part desire to avoid any kind of tension at work. Being "noticed" wasn't really a good thing in the Library, even for positive reasons. It was a distraction.

But then, while getting ready for bed, he realized that Kendra had intersected the Library and its workers several times already. As a professional and extraordinary "watcher of things," Wallace knew that coincidence was often a label applied to as-of-yet unrecognized patterns.

Maybe Kaolyn bringing Kendra to the Library when she'd been sprayed by skyblood had been an instinctive reaction.

Maybe Mr. Monday deciding to test her in his Way had been the simplest, most logical way to deal with that situation.

Maybe Kendra becoming a Reckoner in the Library was just a fluke. Highly unlikely, but essentially random.

Maybe Kendra bringing her uncle, a master of Release, into the library had been an unconscious decision on her part.

Maybe Kendra freeing Tess from Mr. Monday's study simply been part of the girl's own escape.

Maybe he, Wallace, had been with Tess during the attack at the restaurant because...

Too many maybes, Wallace thought. *I need to let Mr. Monday know what's happened. He'll decide if it's important or not.*

But then, just as he was drifting off to sleep, Wallace remembered how Kendra had felt in his arms as he'd brought her from the Library's outer area into Monday's office. She'd seemed so small, yet strangely solid. Her hair had smelled like green apples; shampoo, he'd assumed. And as he'd put her down, as gently as he could, she'd made a small noise; a kind of *mew* or a sigh.

When he'd heard, later, that she'd survived Monday's Way, he'd been strangely glad. He'd only known her for a minute or so -- and she unconscious for that. And she'd been, at the time, a Mundane. And they were, generally... well... less interesting.

But something about her stuck with him. The feel of her in his arms. The smell of green apples. The blue, iridescent mark on her collar bone. Something.

And as he drifted off to sleep, Wallace realized that he wasn't going to tell Mr. Monday about what had happened at the restaurant.

Not quite yet, was his last thought before slipping into a dream of crows and mirrors.

* * * * *

For the next two weeks, Kendra learned more and faster than she would previously have thought possible. Partly that was because she had, in Vannia, a constant and enthusiastic -- if sometimes mischievous -- teacher. Partly it was that she had access to new senses and resources that made it easier, with each lesson, to process the next.

But mostly, it was because she was having so much fun.

"The thing about Chaos," Vannia explained, "Is that things just happen. Sometimes. Other times, they don't. But you learn to ride the delta either way."

"The delta?"

"The difference between expectation and result. You order fries and they put onion rings in the bag. You can either be pissed and spend a bunch of energy and time taking them back, or..."

"Ride the delta," Kendra finished the sentence. "Enjoy the surprise. Live in the moment."

"Zackly."

Which discussion, of course, made them both hungry for onion rings.

According to Vannia, there were no good onion rings to be had in Europe or Asia. It was either off to Australia, or back to the Americas, and the latter wasn't an option with the search going on for Kendra. So they took the Ways to Australia.

Travel among Reckoners, Kendra learned, was less an issue of timing and expense, and more about preference.

"Let's start with the Narrow Roads," Vannia said. "They're fun and good for sightseeing, and we're not really in a hurry. Unless you need onion rings... you know... RIGHT NOW!"

That last was shouted, and as Kendra blinked her eyes, Vannia took two leaping steps and then landed on a strand of... something... that in her new vision seemed to Kendra to be a loop of viscous light.

It looked to Kendra's Mundane eyes as if Vannia was skating, on one foot, along a narrow, dirt path, at about fifty miles-per-hour. Shrugging, she took three steps and jumped on top of the weirdly pulsing strand of light.

Whatever it was, it caught her intention, and she sped off after Parrot Girl, grass and dust parting behind her in a gritty wake.

She focused a bit harder, went a bit faster, and caught up to her friend, skating behind and a little to one side of her. She felt that if she moved too far to one side, she'd lose the... grip.. of whatever it was she was riding, so she made sure not to do that. While she was pretty sure Vannia would take care of her, tumbling into a tree at highway speeds didn't seem to be a good idea, regardless.

She shouted out to Vannia, "How does this work?"

Vannia turned in place, still sliding along the ground at the same speed, and asked, quietly, "Why are you shouting?"

Kendra realized that, despite the speed, she wasn't being buffeted by her passage. In fact, there was no wind whatsoever. No whistling in her ears. No sting against her eyes. Vannia's hair was barely moving as they sped along, hanging almost straight down despite what would have been a pretty stiff blow had she been hanging out of a car window at this speed.

A stand of trees loomed up as they went over a rise, and Kendra started to shout a warning to Vannia, but the path swerved around it and they shot through a narrow gap in the woods.

Shaking her head a bit, Kendra repeated, "How does this work? These... Narrow Roads?"

Vannia gestured at the path. "This was created by Mundanes," she explained. "It's an ancient cow path or cart street or shuffle trail who knows or cares what they call it or whatever. Over time, as they used it more and more, their... intentions... soaked into it. We can ride those."

Kendra looked down. Other than the pulsing light that infused the path, it looked just like that... a dirt path through a meadow.

"I don't understand," she said.

Vannia scratched her head. "Almost any kind of energy can be harnessed as a Way," she explained. "The water in waves or rivers. Fire. Wind. There's the stuff that Mundanes can do with it, and there's the stuff we can do with it. A few thousand years ago, one of the Reckoners from Increase was able to figure out how to take the way that Mundanes thought about their roads and add a Way to it that we can use."

"Wait... I thought Mundanes couldn't use Ways?"

The little girl laughed. "Of course they can't. I mean, not without a Reckoner to guide them or provide passage. But this isn't 'using' a Way when they walk or ride or drive on a road. It's powering the Way. They only 'use' the Way the same way a horse uses a saddle or a river uses a water wheel."

The analogy made Kendra a bit uncomfortable. But she needed to understand.

"So... When Mundanes use the road, that provides some kind of... charge?"

Vannia made a rude, farting noise with her tongue. "Durned if I know, sister. It's an Increase thing. But as long as you can find one, any Reckoner can tap them. Not much good for long range travel, but often less exhausting and... more obvious... than some of the other options."

"So you can use a Way created by another House, but..."

"Sometimes," Vannia interrupted, sitting down on the ground which still flashed beneath her at, what Kendra thought, was increasing speed. "Depends on the Way. Some are locked to the Domain. You'd need to understand how it was created to even see or use it. Some can be shared, like with Mundanes, if you bring along the right friend. But some are just... for everybody.

"Like these," she finished, patting the ground.

Kendra realized that they were going faster, and that the path had become, while they spoke, more of a dirt road. Two streaks of packed soil about the width of a car shot under them now, and Kendra sat back and enjoyed the view speeding by. Soon, the road became smoother and wider and, here and there, crossroads began to run off from their path.

As signs of civilization -- post boxes, a parked truck, an old barn -- appeared, Vannia asked, grinning, "Ready for some real fun?"

Kendra nodded, grinned back, and at the next intersection, Vannia leaned to the left and they took a nearly ninety-degree turn onto a secondary, paved road... and nearly doubled their speed.

Houses whipped by. Other streets. Trees and fields and wells and more parked cars and trucks. Every time it seemed like they were going to slam into something, they simply swerved around without losing speed or any change of momentum. It was like the rest of the world was a set or a painting and they were simply changing their view on it.

The road wants us to go, realized Kendra. *I just need to accept its purpose.*

Parrot Girl leaned to the left again, and then to the right, and then another right... and they were on a minor highway. Paved, of course, with two lanes of traffic going in both direction. As they shot around cars and motorcycles that seemed to be standing still, Kendra estimated that they must be going well over a hundred miles an hour. Maybe more. She had lost her frame of reference.

At a traffic jam, they swerved up and over instead of around, lifting about ten feet off the ground to sail above hundreds of cars while still swerving around the trucks in the stream.

Right again, and they were on a major highway. Four lanes in each direction. And, at that point, they were moving so fast that Kendra stopped being able to see the cars or anything in nearby proximity. She tried, instead, to focus on the horizon or things at a distance. Tall buildings... maybe cities? A series of hills. More woods. Around her she'd occasionally glimpse or sense a color or a reflection. But it was like trying to read road signs directly out the window of a train. Not enough time to see the details.

Finally, with a number of leans and twitches, Vannia brought them to a stop just to the side of a road that paralleled a river. Standing, she dusted off the back of her dress, and gestured for Kendra to follow her down the bank to the water.

"Your turn," she said, pointing at the river. "Look. And tell me what you see."

Kendra concentrated... and saw... something. Different than what the Narrow Roads had been. But maybe of a similar flavor or tone. But where the Roads had been a long string of pulsing intention, here on the bank of the river, she sensed points. Spots of a Way that the river connected. Like knots on a rope, maybe. Or pearls on a string.

"I see..." she began.

"Here," said Parrot Girl, motioning with her hand. Suddenly, the points became clearer in Kendra's mind. She could tell that they were the places where the river had... decided?... to twist and turn. To go around a hard piece of land or burrow against soft clay.

"Whose...?" she asked.

"One of ours," Vannia said proudly, wiggling her fingers and making the knots of light and power glimmer even more brightly.

"Chaos," Kendra murmured. "Rivers don't know straight lines."

Parrot Girl leaned over and kissed her gently on the cheek. "You learn fast, sister," she said.

"Come on," Vannia said. "I'll show you..."

"Never mind," said Kendra. "I see it."

She stepped into the river and asked it to show her the story of its curves. The Way that made distinctive yet seemingly random loops and whorls in the landscape.

There was a shimmer, and Kendra disappeared. Smiling, Vannia splashed in the shallows for a moment before following her friend.

Chapter 7. Intersection

Wallace wasn't particularly surprised when Kaolyn sat down next to him on the park bench a few blocks from the library. He'd been expecting someone from their little lunch group to show up... either the greenman or the crow... and, at two weeks, it had actually taken a bit longer than he'd thought.

"I need to find the girl," the greenman said with no introduction.

"You mean Kendra," Wallace said unnecessarily. But while he wasn't surprised, he was still a bit uncomfortable. Naturals were some of the hardest creatures to truly see, since their Ways often disappeared into the fabric and flow of the world itself.

Kaolyn simply sat and stared at him. Waiting.

After a moment of nervous silence, Wallace replied, "I have no idea where she is."

The greenman nodded. "I didn't think you did. But I thought maybe we could work together to find her."

Wallace balled the crusts of his sandwich up inside his brown paper bag and plopped it in the trash bin beside the bench. He took the last few sips out of a juice box and then threw that out, too.

Standing up he said, "I don't think that's smart. Not for me. And why do you want to find her anyway?"

Kaolyn stood up, too. Easily a head taller than Wallace, he looked down at the man in a way that seemed to convey both concern and menace.

"My boss thinks she may be in danger. Serious danger."

"I think I'd agree with that," said Wallace, turning and walking back toward the library. "But it's still not a smart thing for me to..."

He stopped when he felt the greenman's hand on his shoulder. Always a slightly odd feeling, that. Like the difference between filtered, indoor air and a breeze from the outside, carrying a hint of dust or loam.

"Just tell me what you think you know," said Kaolyn. "I'm not asking you to go anywhere or do anything. I know that's... not your strength."

Wallace snorted, annoyed. Though... "True," he admitted, chuckling a bit.

Kaolyn gestured back to the bench. Wallace checked his watch, shrugged, and sat down again.

For the next fifteen minutes, Wallace and the greenman shared everything they knew about Kendra's situation. Kaolyn knew, of course, about how the girl had come to the library... he'd brought her there, after all. And he knew many more details about the fight with the aethereals. But Wallace knew more about the challenge Kendra had faced in the library, and about how she'd freed Tess.

"That was," he told Kaolyn, "the subject of much gossip among the staff for several days."

"I'd imagine," the greenman agreed. "For the Librarian to lose a tool like that. Very odd. And compounded with the other... oddness of the girl's awakening."

They sat quietly for a few moments, watching the Mundane traffic go by. Finally, Kaolyn asked. "How unusual is it? For a Reckoner to... sleep... like that? To not know the Ways or Domains?"

"It's very unusual," Wallace replied. "Not unheard of. I did some digging last week and found a couple dozen cases in the records. That's over the course of a thousand years or so. Most of the time it was a child who was lost among Mundanes for some reason. Abandoned or orphaned and then retrieved. Almost always within a short time, though. A baby lost very young and then recovered and returned to a House. But, again... still as a young child. Still at the age when we all initially learn to walk the Ways."

The greenman nodded. "You are all odd to us. My kind are born knowing."

"Of course," Wallace said. "You are more of a living Way yourself than a Reckoner."

Kaolyn chuckled. "A living Way. I like that. You may be a poet as well as a librarian, young one."

Odd to be called a young one, Wallace thought, *by a creature probably around four years old.*

"Poetry encodes more meaning than many other forms of..."

"Yes, yes..." Kaolyn interrupted him. "But back to the girl. It seemed, to me, from what she said in the garden, that she'd been on the kinds of drugs that Mundanes give each other to reduce their creativity and vision."

Wallace made a sour face. "That's a side effect. Not the reason. Many of them have a hard time with even the narrow slice of reality they experience. Theirs is not an easy life, I think."

"You sympathize with them?"

"Oh, of course," Wallace said. "How can you not? They are so much like us."

Kaolyn shook his head. "Mirkir is more like me than they are. But never mind that. If it is unusual for a girl to get to her age unawakened, my thought was that maybe those drugs hampered her the same as they do certain functions of the chronics."

Wallace nodded. "That's not a bad theory. Whether it was intentional or not? Who knows. A young Reckoner in the Mundane world might present as a schizophrenic or even a psychotic."

"I don't know those words."

"You wouldn't. But it's not uncommon among them. Their ability to perceive reality being so... narrow. It almost begs for misunderstanding and misdirection."

Kaolyn nodded. "Where would she get those drugs? From a parent?"

"A parent's permission would certainly be needed. Usually. But the drugs themselves? You generally need a doctor to prescribe them."

"I know of doctors. Can we discover which one gave her the drugs?"

Wallace nodded. "Trivial information to retrieve, especially since so much of that data is now online. Give me just a minute."

The young man removed a laptop from his backpack and fired it up. Kaolyn sat quietly and watched Wallace's manipulations of the device. He was doubly confused... both by the technology and the Ways of Sight that flowed through Wallace's fingers. But he was accustomed to waiting and watching and not really understanding the things held important by the "Young Domains" as Earth sometimes thought of the other Houses.

Finally, Wallace snapped the computer shut and returned it to his backpack.

"A psychiatrist named 'S. Lyonne.' Office isn't that far from here. We can walk."

Kaolyn nodded and held out his hand. Wallace took it and they slid onto a Narrow Road, speeding off in the direction of Dr. Lyonne's office faster than the nearby cars.

* * * * *

After her time of travel, tutoring and various juvenile (yet harmless) hijinks, Kendra felt pretty sure she wasn't going to join Chaos. If nothing else, it was simply too tiring. The adrenaline rush of not knowing exactly what was going to happen next was fun the first dozen times. After that?

"I need a break," she told Vannia. "I need to sleep in the same place -- preferably a bed -- at least two nights in a row. I probably should do that back at home so my mom doesn't worry or call to check up on me."

Parrot Girl paused from blowing notes on an empty Orange Crush bottle and nodded solemnly. "I think you're right. I've taught you as much as I can. I think one more stop, and you'll be ready to start figuring things out for yourself. Like which Domain you'll join. That's priority one after I drop you off."

It was Kendra's turn to nod. Vannia had explained to her that unaffiliated Reckoners were, while rare, not unheard of. And that they were often targets for either abuse, exploitation or outright murder. "The law adheres to the Way," she'd been reminded a number of times. And until you joined a House, you were unprotected.

"I'm still not sure why anyone would care," she said to Vannia. "I mean... how would my choice be of any concern to any Domain or person?"

Vannia rolled the bottle between her palms and asked, "Have you ever had an argument about something that doesn't matter? I mean, something that doesn't have any impact on you at all?"

"Uhm... Sure. I guess. I don't know. What do you mean?"

"Like about which band is better or whether a particular movie sucks or not."

Kendra nodded. "Of course."

"Why did you care what the other person thought? Or if you were right? Or if your opinion was better thought out or if you could state it more forcefully?"

That's a really good question, thought Kendra.

"I... I'm not sure."

"Ideas have power," Parrot Girl said seriously, putting the bottle down on the ground and spinning it. "I look at this bottle and see a decision making apparatus..."

The bottle continued to spin well after normal friction should have slowed it to a stop. Vannia gestured above the bottle and it danced a little, tilting up and down in a series of arcs and whorls.

"What do you see?" she asked Kendra, bottle still spinning, hands still waving slightly.

Kendra looked hard, the way Vannia had taught her. She saw the lines of probability and chance. She saw that, in this case, the bottle would make one of two choices; Parrot Girl or Kendra. It hadn't decided yet. Her friend was still suspending that choice. But soon... it would have to point mostly at one of the girls or the other.

Or the bottle could break, she thought. Kendra nudged it a bit herself with a tiny flex of her own volition and the bottle spun a bit closer to a little piece of stone jutting out of the pavement. Vannia didn't seem to notice, intent on making the bottle spin faster and rise higher on each pass.

Kendra nudged it a bit more. As the mouth of the bottle swung down, it hit the little thumb of rock and cracked. Vannia, surprised, released her control and the bottle skidded away, shattering against the brick wall Kendra was leaning up against.

Parrot Girl looked up at Kendra, smiled and said, "You win."

With that, she stood and held out her hand. "I'm going to take you to Bardonne's, now. And from there, you'll be on your own."

Kendra took her friend's hand and stood, asking, "What's Bardonne's?"

Vannia grinned and waggled her eyebrows. "A wretched hive of scum and villainy."

Kendra shook her head, amused. "Lead on, Obi Wan."

Parrot Girl's wings opened, obscuring the North African sun beneath a hazy shadow of soft green and they vanished.

* * * * *

The hardest part about breaking into Dr. Lyonne's office was waiting for her to leave the building. Since she lived in the apartment behind her office, Kaolyn and Wallace couldn't simply wait for her to "go home." Wallace planted a small observation Way across the street from her building and they went to a nearby Starbucks to wait.

And wait.

Nearly twelve hours later, Dr. Lyonne finally left the building and got a cab, leading the two to believe she'd be out for at least some time. Slipping unseen into a Mundane's building and office was no work whatsoever, but Wallace made sure they were careful to check for any hidden Ways that might betray their presence. The situation with Kendra was unusual enough that neither of them believed other Reckoners weren't involved.

Once inside, Kaolyn began carefully searching shelves, drawers and books while Wallace turned on the doctor's computer to see if he could discover anything there. Again, the kind of "security" that protected unwanted attention from other Mundanes had no real stopping power against even a junior clerk of Sight.

"According to her notes," Wallace said after a few minutes, "Kendra is suffering from some pretty severe issues, including paranoid schizophrenia and bipolar disorder. That's what they often say when one of them gets a glimpse of the world. Not surprising."

"Agreed," said Kaolyn.

"And," Wallace continued, "there's nothing else in her files that suggests Lyonne isn't simply treating Kendra as a Mundane with mental illnesses."

"So... No clues. Nothing to help find her."

Wallace shook his head, still clicking through pages of notes going backwards through the years of Kendra's treatment. "No. Adjustments to medications. New prescriptions when new drugs come on the market. Various comments about Kendra's personal life, but nothing you wouldn't expect from a girl with some troubling issues."

Kaolyn grunted in frustrated acknowledgement and continued to -- gently -- toss the office, looking under and behind anything that he could easily open, shift or lift.

"What is this?" he asked at one point, holding up a very nice set of shiny, metal balls on wires, all hung in a row from a metal frame.

"It's called a 'Newton's Cradle,'" Wallace explained. "It's just a desk toy. You swing the balls back and forth. Some Mundanes find it relaxing or entertaining."

The greenman put it down and set the balls swinging, all at the same time.

"Boring," he said.

Wallace smiled to himself but didn't explain the "proper" use of the toy.

"And these?" Kaolyn asked, holding up a handful of cards with seemingly random blotches on them.

"Those are ink blots," Wallace said, clicking back to the earliest record in Kendra's file, absently noting details that, later, he would be able to recall with perfect clarity if needed.

"Also a toy?" the greenman asked, flipping through them.

"No. They use it as a conversation starter, basically. You look at the patterns and tell what you see."

"I see messy spots," Kaolyn said, looking at another card. "They look like nothing."

"You have to be creative," Wallace explained. "You say what you imagine they look like."

"But they look like nothing."

"Bring them here," Wallace said. "I'll explain."

"No need, I assume it's useful for Mundanes, but..."

Kaolyn stopped at one card, looking carefully at it.

"But what?"

"This one isn't nothing," he said quietly.

"None of them are 'nothing,'" Wallace replied. "You have to..."

Kaolyn held up his hand and gestured for Wallace to come over. Shutting down Dr. Lyonne's computer first and returning the keyboard to its drawer, he did so.

"That's not nothing," the greenman said, turning one of the cards to face the clerk.

To Wallace, the image was as clear as a photograph would have been to a Mundane. It showed the Feast of Alleyanzee, a fable out of Reckoner mythology where the Chaos hero, Lying Tamrin, was tricked by Blood Priests into raising a family of snakes who eventually turned and ate him.

"Why would a Mundane doctor have such a thing?" Kaolyn asked.

"I don't know," Wallace muttered.

They looked through the other cards. Aside from the first dozen or so, which were standard ink blots as far as Wallace could tell, they were all scenes from Reckoner myths. All of them done in a style popular more than five hundred years before made famous by the Blood artist Mer'eket. To Mundane eyes, they would seem like a Jackson Pollock painting... just so many random spatters. Enough like Rorschach blots to not seem out of place in the same deck. But to any Reckoner... Not just obvious, but obvious and meaningful.

Turning one over in his hands, Wallace cast a minor Seeing and dropped the card as if it had burned him.

"What?" asked Kaolyn, bending to pick up the card.

"It's an original," Wallace said, holding out his hand for the rest of the deck. The greenman obliged, and Wallace passed his Seeing over each card in turn.

"These are all originals," the clerk whispered. "All eighteen of them. I knew the style was Mer'eket's, but I assumed they were copies or another artist's work."

"Why?"

"Because these are unknown. I mean, they are known. The pieces themselves. The pictures. We have a set in the Library vaults. But that's supposedly the only original copy done by Mer'eket himself."

Kaolyn looked at the images over Wallace's shoulder as he leafed through them again.

"Is that important?"

Wallace shook his head. "Yes. I mean, it must be. But I don't know why. The works of Mer'eket are all highly prized. Blood art is often... complex. Hard to understand. It works on levels that are closer to raw nature than anything outside of Earth."

"Earth doesn't create art," Kaolyn said. "Earth is art."

"I know," Wallace replied, putting the cards back down on the desk. "But the art of Blood can summon power that is, for other Reckoners, nearer to Earth than any other Way."

"Interesting."

They both stood in silence for a moment, contemplating the pictures.

Another coincidence, thought Wallace. *That makes... I don't know... five or six? That is... too many.*

He was familiar with the Mundane concept of "confirmation bias," though. Every string of perfect, unconnected accidents has an outcome. Seen from the beginning, you can track and trace those actions and know that, yes... they were all perfectly random. But if you only see the end point... then they seem inevitably connected. Because they are. But not by intention, simply by the final, combined effect.

"Coincidence," he muttered to himself. "Co-incidents."

The greenman hadn't heard him. "Where would a Mundane doctor get a set of priceless Blood-art originals?" Kaolyn asked.

"I have no idea."

"And once she had them, why would she show them to a damaged Reckoner girl?"

172

"I don't know."

"What would it to her, do you think? To see these?"

Wallace shrugged. "Again. No idea."

"But what..."

Wallace held up one hand. "Give me a moment, please."

The greenman nodded, and Wallace went into a kind of trance. He called up all the information he had about Kendra, about the doctor, about the events of the past weeks. He knew almost everything about Lane White, Kendra's mother, that a Mundane friend might know. And he suspected that there was more there. Small, strange inconsistencies in her history. Nothing that a Mundane would notice. And a Reckoner would never be interested enough in the life of an ordinary woman to scrutinize her through a Seeing.

Strings of dates, places and names wound through the clerk's mind. Comparing. Testing. Matching anything that might possibly be...

"Niles Fayton."

Kaolyn had sat down in the comfortable chair across from Dr. Lyonne's desk to wait. When Sight went into a thinking trance, it could be seconds or hours, after all.

"Who or what is Niles Fayton?"

"He's in the second circle of Release."

"So?"

"He's the only connection I can find between the Houses and Dr. Lyonne."

"And?" Kaolyn stood up and crossed to where Wallace was standing by the window, the afternoon light beginning to grow yellow and long.

"He's a collector of rare Blood art. We've done work for him on it at the Library."

"And?"

Wallace gestured back at the computer on Dr. Lyonne's desk. "Kendra's files. He's listed in the first entry as the referral source. He's the one who suggested that Lyonne treat Kendra."

The two stood quietly for moment before Kaolyn said, "That's a thin string, boy."

"I know. But it's the only one I can find."

The greenman put his hand on Wallace's shoulder. "OK, then," he said. "Let's tug on it a bit."

* * * * *

From the outside, Bardonne's looked like... well, like nothing. When Vannia pointed out the flat spots in the ground, she could see that some had stones in them. Like a paver that's been pushed down, flush, with the dirt and grass around it. Some of them were even buried.

"Look harder," Parrot Girl said. "Look deeper."

Kendra tried. It was getting easier to see the real world. Or more of it, anyway. So she stood back and took a deep breath and looked around her with the new senses she barely understood.

"They're connected," she finally said.

"Yes..." The tone clearly said, *Annndddd.....*

Looking harder, Kendra saw that they formed a double circle. Probably about fifty yards across, with about two yards between each ring. There was power there. Clearly a Way of some kind. But it seemed...

"It's blurry. On purpose."

Vannia clapped her hands. "Good girl. Come here!" She held out her hand and Kendra took it. Walking slowly, almost in a kind of marching step, Vannia led her between the lines and Kendra could now sense a kind of pattern within the pattern. Like striations on a rock or the rings on a tree. Seven of them, layering the rings as they pulsed beneath her and sent waves of power up into the air.

After walking around what felt like about a quarter of the circle, Kendra paused.

"There's a gap there," she said. Almost a question.

"Yup," agreed Vannia. "That's the front door. C'mon."

Still holding hands, they moved a bit faster and when they got to the spot in the Way that seemed less solid, they passed through it and into...

"Welcome to Bardonne's!" said Parrot Girl with a flourish.

The empty Scottish glade had been transformed into a noisy, bustling space that seemed half restaurant, half circus. There were tables and chairs and a high, domed ceiling made of, it seemed, slowly rotating black smoke. As it swirled, Kendra could occasionally see through it to the stars and moon they'd left behind. The walls were made of large bricks; *big, like the stones used to make pyramids*, she thought. They were all of a grayish material, but with hints of other colors.

Looking around, Kendra saw that the door they'd stepped through now appeared as a large archway in the wall, surmounted by an enormous capstone, on which was carved a huge, open eye. As she stared at the eye, it looked down at her and blinked.

Not the weirdest thing I've seen today, Kendra thought and followed Vannia into the hall.

A woman in jeans and a t-shirt with a nametag that said, *Hi, I'm Dotty,* approached them and asked, "Eat, watch or play?"

"Eat to start," Vannia replied. "Whatever the special is. And water to drink. Or iced tea if you got it."

"Sure thing, little sister," the woman replied. "Sweet?"

"Heck yeah."

"Kaykay," the woman said, making a note on a pad she took out of her back pocket. She seemed, to Kendra, to be entirely 'normal,' by Mundane standards. Athletic build. Not too tall. Dirty-blonde hair pulled back in a ponytail. Maybe twenty-five or thirty at most. But, as she wrote on the pad, Kendra saw that Dotty's skin was marked with loops and whorls of very fine, almost invisibly pale tattoos. That moved.

As Dotty turned to go, she said, "Good spots over by the fire, still, if you want to watch the next game. And if you want to play, remember that you gotta declare. No jacking, pinging or vendetta allowed."

"Yeah, yeah. I know. I've been here before. Door knows me."

"Just sayin'," Dotty just said and went off toward the far end of the space.

"So this is a... sanctuary?" Kendra asked. "But for who?"

Vannia grabbed Kendra's hand, leading her around the edge of the room to some open tables near a fireplace about the size of a minivan. She sat and motioned for Kendra to do the same, saying, "Sanctuary is a good word. It was called something else thousands of years ago, but now... The Mundanes come up with interesting vocab sometimes. For having a much less interesting worldview, they're remarkably poetic."

"So? You still haven't answered my question. Sanctuary for who?"

"For anyone, really," Vannia said, gesturing around. Raising an eyebrow, she asked, "Our server. What House?"

"Blood," Kendra answered without pause.

"Good girl. How'd you know?"

"How would I not?"

Vannia nodded. "You're getting more used to the signs. At first, like anything, you need to think about it. Eventually? A Reckoner or a Way will just... be obvious."

Kendra nodded. "It's like asking someone, 'How do you know something's cold?' The question doesn't even make sense once you know what the words mean."

"Right."

Parrot Girl paused to look around, and so did Kendra. It seemed, the more she looked, like a giant, stone tavern from a mix of ages. The huge fireplace had gothic carvings of faces across the mantel. Just to the left of it, though, was a neon Wurlitzer jukebox. And three Reckoners were shooting pool while another three or four looked on, under a hanging chandelier lit by hundreds of tiny, fey lights. The chain holding the chandelier disappeared up into the dark smoke of the ceiling, suspended by... nothing... as far as Kendra could tell.

It smelled good. It was amiably noisy. It wasn't too full, but it was comfortably... friendly. There was the kind of vibe you get at good concerts or minor league sporting events, where everyone was clearly there to share a common activity.

"It feels good here," she said simply.

Vannia nodded again. "Bardonne's is my favorite sanctuary. There are others. Dozens. Some smaller. Some much larger. This one has the best vibe, though."

Dotty arrived with a tray on her shoulder and put two plates and two glasses in front of the friends. The meal was a kind of shepherd's pie of some kind with a side of baked apples and some cubes of something Kendra didn't recognize.

"CB is still mixing up the iced-tea," Dotty said, handing them each a napkin bundled around utensils. "I'll be back in just a sec with a pitcher."

"Kaykay," Vannia said back to Dotty, which made the waitress smile.

"CB?" Kendra asked.

"Current Bardonne. The owner. Or manager. Depends on how you look at it. The guy in charge."

Kendra nodded and tucked into the meat pie. It had crust on the bottom and mashed potatoes on top and was a little too hot which meant it was the perfect temperature. By the time Dotty was back and pouring iced-tea, she was ready for a good, long drink to take some of the heat down a notch.

"Thab's is beally goom," she said around a mouthful of pie.

"I boe. Bight?" Vannia replied, equally eloquent around a too-large chunk of hot meat.

As they ate, Kendra studied the place more carefully. The walls themselves were fascinating. Again, she saw clearly that they had to be a Way of some kind. But it didn't jump out at her what it was for... other than the obvious; separate the space from the outside and keep the inside invisible to Mundanes.

"What did Dotty mean... 'No jacking, no pings or vendettas?'" she asked as she started in on the baked apples.

Vannia gestured at the open area directly in front of the fireplace. "Some sanctuaries are just for rest or conversation. Bardonne's also allows games. Fights, sometimes, too. Duels. A way for folks from different Domains to... get up into it."

"They can't do that outside wherever they want?"

"Depends. Remember, Houses aren't really allowed to fight each other. Individual Reckoners can. So if you have a deadly beef with someone, yeah. Declare vendetta and try to kill them in some dark alley and hope their clan or tribe or jangle or whatever doesn't find out and come after you."

"I still don't see how that's cool."

"Oh, it's not. We have lots of other rules and laws that govern all kinds of activities. Some of it would be the equivalent of what you'd call criminal law or civil law. Many of our contracts use Ways to bind them, and if you go off book..." she shrugged. "The Way can often enforce itself."

"I don't see how that's any different than what people... what Mundanes have."

Kendra picked up a fork and stabbed one of the little, soft cubes on Kendra's plate and popped it in her mouth.

"Good," she said. "Excellent gallaganash. You won't like it." She reached over and quickly scooped the remaining cubes onto her own plate.

Kendra frowned. "It's good. And I won't like it."

Vannia nodded around a mouthful. "Very much an acquired taste. And I'm doing this to make a point. Hang on." She took a gulp of tea to wash down the last bite of the stolen food and then gestured at Kendra's plate with her fork.

"I took your gallaganash. You don't have it. Suppose you had wanted it. Now you're pissed, right?"

Kendra nodded. "Sure. Let's assume I am."

"So you can ask me to pay you for it or make a stink to the establishment or steal my dessert when I'm in the loo or whatever. It's between me and you. You follow?"

Kendra nodded again. She was used, at this point, to Parrot Girl's roundabout way of teaching.

"Now... What if, instead, I go into the kitchen and, I don't know... tip over the whole vat of gallaganash. Or steal it all. Or poison it or whatever. And you come here and you want some and Dotty tells you, 'Sorry... some crazy fairy chuffed the whole load. No gallaganash tonight for you.'"

"Right. OK."

"So... Do you have a beef with me now? Or with Bardonne's?"

Kendra had to stop and think.

"I uh... Hmmm..."

"Think about it in terms of Mundane law. Do you, Kendra, have any legal recourse against me, Her Most High and Loveliest Princess Parrot Person? Or against the establishment?"

Kendra shook her head. "I don't think so. You didn't steal from me. And I might be disappointed with Bardonne's... but it's not their fault you pooped in the pot."

That made Vannia giggle. "Right. It ain't. But you still don't get your gallaganash."

That made Kendra nod and scowl. *The effect is the same, but the cause is very different,* she thought.

"Now," Vannia said, leaning way over the table and fixing Kendra with an overly dramatic stare, "Imagine that Bardonne's isn't mixing up gallaganash... but, instead, is the source of the highest power in the universe."

The light went on in Kendra's head. "The Law adheres to the Way."

Vannia leaned a little bit further forward and kissed Kendra on the forehead. "Good girl," she said, dropping back into her chair and slurping the last of her iced tea loudly through the straw.

"As long as you mess with an individual Reckoner," she said, "or even their family or clan or whatever. You pay whatever price makes sense. And if you're powerful enough, maybe no price at all."

"But if you mess with the Ways..." Kendra interjected.

"You bring the whole House down on your ass. And probably the other Domains, too."

Dotty appeared at that moment and asked, "You kids want any dessert?"

They both shook their heads. The meat pie had been very filling.

"I'll fill up your tea and you can hang as long as you like. Not too full tonight, so CB will go easy on the 'no drinky, no watchy' rule." Both girls nodded their thanks.

As Dotty turned to go, Vannia asked, "You want a roll?"

Dotty grinned. "Sure! Fun stuff. Haven't had a decent rando at table in a while. What you need?"

"What you like?"

The waitress tapped her pencil on her teeth, thinking. "Hair?"

"For hair I need some lemon and a mirror."

"Be right back," said Dotty, turning on her heel to go.

"What was..." Kendra started to ask.

"Just watch," Vannia said, digging a piece of string out of her pocket.

Dotty came back and pulled a chair over from the empty table next to them, sitting on it backwards, arms folded on the back. She handed Vannia a lemon and a small, cheap, round mirror that looked like it probably came free with a small, cheap purse.

"Here you go," she said.

"OK. Great."

Vannia took her table knife and cut the lemon in half. She squeezed some of the juice into one hand and motioned for Dotty to lower her head.

"And take the rubber band out," she said.

"Sure."

The waitress did so, and her fine, blonde hair fell down around her face as she leaned over the table.

Kendra watched as Parrot Girl flicked drops of lemon juice into the woman's hair and then kind of jiggled her hands around in it for a second, fluffing the hair up and around a bit. She then gathered it up into a new ponytail, and tied her piece of string around it. Then she squeezed a bit more lemon juice out onto the string and lifted Dotty's chin up with a gentle touch.

"That's it?" Dotty said.

"That's it," Vannia nodded.

"What did it..."

Vannia gestured at the mirror on the table. Kendra could see absolutely no difference in their waitress' hair.

But when Dotty picked up the small mirror and looked into it, she jumped up with a primal shriek of surprise and knocked her chair over backward. At that moment, there was a bright flash as the string around her ponytail snapped with the sound of a violin string being plucked.

When Kendra's eyesight recovered from the flash, she saw that Dotty's hair was now waist-length, thick, black and lustrous with a pattern of deep purple symbols shifting through it.

"You little..." Dotty had dropped the mirror and raised a hand as if to slap Vannia.

"Hang on, sister! Take another look!" Vannia was smiling like a fiend, scooting back in her chair to avoid a possible smack.

Dotty paused and recovered the mirror from the floor. With a nasty look at Vannia first, she glanced down at it, her anger slowly transforming to delight.

"Holy crap," she finally said. "That is... Wow. And it matches my carves. That's..."

Vannia leaned back, smug, crossing her arms and finished the sentence, "Totally awesome?"

The waitress nodded. "Yeah. I thought for a second..."

Vannia interrupted, "Yeah... sorry about that. It's the fear that triggers it. Whatever you think the absolute worst case scenario for your hair could be. That's what you'll see."

Dotty shook her head, both in wonder and to see how her hair fell, now. Clearly enjoying the cascade down her shoulders and all the way to her waist.

"It's gorgeous. Does it always work that well?"

Vannia snorted. "What do you think?"

The other woman shook her head again and laughed. "I guess you take what you can get when you roll with a roller."

"Especially if you ask for it," Vannia said, wiping the lemon juice off her hands onto her napkin.

"Truth," Dotty said. "Wow. Anyway. Nicely done, little sister. I'll bring you some more tea in a bit."

As she walked off, slowly tipping her head from side to side to test the weight and flow of her new hair, Parrot Girl said, "Tell me what you saw. Tell me what you learned."

I actually followed that all pretty well, Kendra thought. *Not exactly sure how... but it makes more sense all the time.*

"Roll. Roller. Rolling the dice," she said. "That's you. Chaos," gesturing at Vannia, who just nodded.

"The Way," Kendra continued, "was set up with the lemon and the string, but the trigger was whatever she saw in the mirror. Like you said. The worst haircut ever."

"Worse than that, even," Vannia interrupted. "But don't worry the details. Go on."

"So... you set up a Way for her. Rolled the dice. Changed her hair. She liked it."

"Right."

Clearly Vannia wanted to hear more. Something else.

Why?

"Why?" Kendra asked.

Without saying anything, Vannia made a, *look around and really see your world,* gesture.

Kendra looked. She saw people -- Reckoners -- eating and drinking. Shooting pool. Talking in small groups. Playing some cards in the corner. They looked the way she now saw all Reckoners; she could see their seeming and their true selves at the same time. The wings and horns and extra limbs no longer concerned her at all.

There was a doorway to the kitchen through which Dotty had just disappeared. Several other waiters and waitresses came and went. Somebody put a song on the jukebox; some Dylan tune that she didn't recognize.

People eating. People talking. Somebody on a cell phone.

Look... she told herself. *Really look. What am I missing? What do I expect that I shouldn't? Or what is different that I just don't...*

Suddenly it hit her.

"There's no money."

"Got it in one," Vannia said, leaning forward to give Kendra a little high-five.

Before Kendra could ask a clarifying question -- *so... you were giving Dotty a tip?* -- the room seemed to quiet down quite a bit all of a sudden.

"The night's first match will begin in five minutes," said a tall, bald man standing by the fireplace. "Get your drinks topped off, fetch a chair and place your bets. Ken Varr of Release challenges Dai Li 'Other Fingers' Sensu of Flux. This is a grudge spar to settle personal grievance. There can be no call of kanli. Fight is to submission, unconsciousness or death. No pinging or tagging during the match on penalty of lifeban."

He glanced around the room, seeming to make eye contact with a few folks. He was, Kendra now saw, a very tall man with a fantastic, muscular build. *Like a caber-tosser,* she thought. *Or a blacksmith.* His arms nearly split the seams of his clean, gray t-shirt and she could see his abs through it as well.

"CB. Good looking dude," whispered Vannia.

"Uh... Yeah," agreed Kendra.

People pulled up chairs around the fireplace, two other patrons asking if they could sit with Kendra and Vannia. They nodded, and the two newcomers -- an older man with a rainbow ring of light around his head and a thin woman with purple-black skin -- sat down and turned the chairs toward the fire. Parrot Girl just reversed herself in her own chair, and Kendra looked around the room, waiting for the match to begin.

* * * * *

Half a world away, Wallace and Kaolyn waited somewhat less than patiently outside the office of Niles Fayton. They'd called first, and his secretary had said that, yes, Mr. Fayton could spare a few minutes for them today. At the end of the day. Come around five. Thank you.

It was about half-past five, and they weren't even sure if Niles was in his office. If so, he'd been in there for more than an hour without making any noise or showing any signs. Kaolyn was about to get up and ask the secretary, again, for an update, when the door to the office opened.

The man who came through was, Wallace thought, the most indescribably bland person he'd ever seen.

His hair could have been described as light brown or dark blonde. Or maybe a kind of gray with a touch of color in a short, standard "businessman's cut." His skin wasn't pale enough to be called pale, but he also didn't have any real tan or coloring. His eyes might have been green or hazel or brown. Just... eyes. Not interesting or penetrating or unusual. He wasn't particularly tall or short. Probably a bit under six feet, Wallace estimated, rising alongside Kaolyn to greet the man. Fayton was dressed in a dark gray sports coat and white Oxford shirt, no tie, and light brown chinos.

He looks like a mid-level marketing guy, Wallace thought. *Or a lawyer who's working on the weekend.*

Wallace, trained to look for and recognize details, realized that he'd have a hard time describing or remembering this person. He looked entirely like a Mundane... no obvious Reckoner-specific traits. Though, to be fair, Release didn't often encumber themselves with a lot of jewelry, costumes or flair.

Neither handsome nor ugly, fat or thin. *Supremely average,* Wallace thought as the man held out his hand for a thoroughly average shake. *Unusually average,* he continued to himself, smiling on the inside.

"You must be Wallace Bradstreet," Fayton said. "From Sight. And Mr. Kaolyn. Of Earth, of course. My secretary said you were looking for information about some works of Mer'eket. I'm sorry I couldn't see you earlier. I was on an international call that went long. Please come in."

He gestured for the other two to enter his office and closed the door behind them.

The office was as bland as the man. A desk, a desk chair. A small conference table with four side chairs. A bookcase with books and a few corporate knickknacks. A painting of a ship. Gray drapes on either side of a modest office window with a view of the building next door.

"Please, have a seat," Fayton said, gesturing at the table. He sat in one of the side chairs and waited for his guests to join him.

"Now," he said, resting his elbows on the table and leaning forward in a friendly way, "How can I help you?"

Wallace looked at Kaolyn, who looked back at Wallace and shrugged. Wallace looked at Fayton, then back at Kaolyn, that back at Fayton, who was waiting, patient and friendly. He seemed uncommonly good at sitting still and waiting.

Wallace decided to go into "reference interview mode." It was one he was more comfortable with in front of strangers.

"We're wondering if you can provide us with any information about a young woman named Kendra White," Wallace explained, trying to sound both authoritative and firm. "She has been missing for some time, and her Mundane doctor's records indicate that she was referred by you. As we've run out of other leads, we thought you might know something useful."

Fayton nodded as Wallace spoke, appropriately serious but, still friendly.

"Yes," he said after Wallace finished. "I know Ms. White. And I knew her father. And I know her mother. A very sad story, of course."

Wallace and Kaolyn exchanged another confused look.

"Sad story?" Wallace asked.

Fayton leaned back in the chair a bit, frowning slightly. "I assumed that Dr. Lyonne would have told you. Since you got my name from Dr. Lyonne's records, as you said."

Well... that was pretty lame of us, thought Wallace.

"Wallace is from Sight," Kaolyn interjected. "He's good. Didn't need to know the doctor to know the know."

Fayton scowled a bit more. Now looking concerned as well as interested. *But still,* thought Wallace, *remarkably unremarkable.*

"I see," Fayton finally said. "I do not know where Kendra currently is. I'll confess, I'm not sure I'm comfortable telling you much more than that. If you don't personally know Dr. Lyonne or Kendra, then..."

"Oh, we know Kendra," Wallace interrupted. "We're... friends of hers."

"Who don't know where she is?" asked Fayton, eyebrows up.

"Nobody knows where she is," said Kaolyn, leaning forward toward the other man. "That's the thing. And some folks think she may be hurt or in danger, and we'd like to help is all."

Fayton nodded again, still serious and seemingly unconvinced.

"I don't know where she is," he repeated plainly. "I haven't actually ever met her, to be honest."

"You said you knew her," said Wallace.

"Ah, yes. Well, I know who she is. And I did know her father. And I still know her mother. Quite well, actually. She worked for me at one point."

"She's from Release?" asked Kaolyn.

"Yes." Fayton frowned again. "Well, she was. As I said... a very sad story."

His two guests sat looking ignorant and uncomfortable. Sighing, Fayton finally said, "I will tell you some of what I know. What I'm comfortable you could find out yourself, young librarian, had you probed the right records or made the right inquiries."

"Thank you, Mr. Fayton," Wallace said, triggering a minor Way that would, essentially, record the entire rest of the interview across all senses, catching details for others to review that he, in the moment, might miss.

Fayton stood. "Can I get either of you a drink? Bottled water? Coffee?"

They both shook their heads, and waited a moment while Fayton ducked behind his desk to open a small fridge and extract a bottle of chilled mineral water. He returned to the table, took a swig, and replaced the cap.

" Elaynia, Lane that is, Geary was a very lively, very attractive, very creative young woman. She worked for me, as I said, as a security consultant and assistant from time-to-time. She was good at crafting subtle locking Ways. Layers of locks that would let some people in, keep some out. She was so good that we eventually got many requests for her work. Especially from Increase."

Wallace nodded. "I would imagine that they require plenty of locks."

Fayton made a weighing gesture with his hands. "More than some, fewer than others. Your master, Mr. Monday, has also been a customer of ours quite often."

I did not know that, thought Wallace. *I don't know that I've ever sensed a Way of Release in the Library. That's something to check out later, maybe...*

Playing with the water bottle, Fayton continued.

"Most of our Domain is more interested in the escaping of locks and bonds, of course. But it renders some of us uniquely qualified to create them. And those that do, such as Lane, often become popular... both for their Houses, and for... personal reasons."

Wallace looked confused.

"People want to take somebody out without a killing, locks is a good thing to have," Kaolyn explained.

"Ah. Sorry. I'm less familiar with your House than others," Wallace apologized.

Fayton waved the apology away. "No worries. Anyway. At one point, Lane was doing a job for Increase and happened to work with a Reckoner named Morgan White. An attraction formed, and the two of them were seen together quite frequently."

"That's unusual," muttered Wallace.

"Indeed," agreed Fayton. "As was commented on at the time. After years of friendship, Morgan convinced Lane to first marry him, which she did, and then convert to Increase."

Kaolyn chuckled and Wallace looked horrified. "That's... almost unheard of," the librarian said.

"More... 'heard of' than you might think," said Kaolyn. "Except for naturals and constructs of Earth, of course. Like me. Young Domains... fickle." He shook his head, dreadlocks swinging back and forth.

"Your greenman friend is correct, Mr. Bradstreet," Fayton said. "It happens often enough that there are even practitioners among Release who can assist in the transition. And it happens between Flux, Increase and Release more than the other Houses."

"That makes sense," said Wallace. "Flux birthed those Houses. And Release would be... handy... in a situation like that.."

"It is successful... about half the time," Fayton continued, tilting his hand back-and-forth. "It requires commitment. It often takes considerable time. The Reckoner almost always has less power in his or her new Domain. Sometimes there are other side effects. And in Lane's case..."

"She lost her reckoning," filled in Kaolyn.

"You knew that?" asked Fayton. "But you didn't know the rest of the story?"

"I guessed," said Kaolyn. "I've met Lane. She is... different."

"That she is," agreed Fayton. "There are very few cases of Walkers so thoroughly separated from the Ways."

"That is... just... awful," muttered Wallace.

"Indeed. The... transition... was so deeply traumatic for Lane that she, essentially, developed a kind of permanent amnesia about her former life. At the time, she was also carrying Kendra, which neither she nor Morgan were aware of during her... injury. When he found out, he demanded of Release that the child be taken from Lane and raised by Increase."

"Demanded?" asked Kaolyn. "Of Release? I assume that didn't go over well."

Fayton shook his head. "No, it did not. Lady Percy does not take kindly to demands of any kind. And she was already quite angry at Morgan over the attempt to convert Lane. We were all deeply troubled and confused by her decision. While we in Release were not happy to lose a promising young Reckoner, she had made her choice and we honored it. But after she became, essentially, a Mundane and we knew she was with child..."

"Right," said Kaolyn softly. "That's another story."

"Yes," agreed Fayton. "A potential new member of our House. But Morgan didn't see it that way. When he found out about the baby, he became... highly agitated. Wouldn't take 'no' for an answer. Lady Percy finally went to Ezer and had him... discourage further attention in the girl."

"Discourage?" asked Wallace quietly.

"I didn't inquire too closely," Fayton answered. "But, as far as I know, Morgan White has not been seen since that time."

Wallace swallowed hard, but Kaolyn nodded, understanding. "The Ways must be preserved."

"That is correct, my good greenman," replied Fayton.

The three sat in silence for a moment. Then Fayton continued. "The rest of the story is, if you'll pardon the pun, somewhat Mundane. Lane raised Kendra as her own, Mundane child. At a young age, it became clear that the affliction of her mother had caused the girl some severe psychological trauma. We in Release kept an eye on her, and when Lane expressed to her pediatrician the need for Kendra to see a counselor of some kind, I provided the recommendation of Dr. Lyonne. While Mundane herself, she is an associate of Earth and highly regarded in matters that... crossover... jurisdictions."

Kaolyn nodded. "A tag."

Fayton made a sour face. "An associate. Please. I run several international non-profit companies and a dozen art galleries. I'm not a gangster, Mr. Kaolyn."

Trying to get back on track, Wallace asked, "So... Kendra started seeing Dr. Lyonne, and you continued to keep tabs on her?"

"Oh, no," Fayton replied, taking another sip of his water. "Between Release and Increase, the decision had been made that she should be, essentially, 'hands off' as far as the Houses are concerned. The conclusion of our combined leaders was that the child would probably go mad before adulthood. Her interaction with Dr. Lyonne would, we hoped, simply make her more comfortable in the interim. As I said, I never met the girl and haven't seen Lane since before she gave birth."

Answers only father more questions. Wallace quoted the Sight parable to himself silently.

They were quiet for a moment, then Fayton leaned further forward. "Perhaps if you were to tell me what the circumstances of her disappearance were, I might have some perspective."

Wallace looked at Kaolyn, who shrugged. Wallace gestured for Kaolyn to begin, and the greenman tipped his chair back and said, "I found her in one of Rain Vernon's gardens. The topiary that houses a number of bound aethereals... "

* * * * *

Kendra missed the first few seconds of the fight because, when CB clapped his hands to begin the match, there was a blinding flash of light that everyone else knew about and turned away from. By the time her vision had cleared, she saw that the two Reckoners -- Varr and Sensu -- had already begun to grapple like wrestlers.

Ken Varr was a big, hulking dude wearing only a black t-shirt and jeans. Shaved head, no moustache or beard, arms like legs, legs like trees. He looked, to Kendra, like a biker or a bouncer. His opponent, Dai Li Sensu, was almost comically unlike him; lithe, dark-skinned, with long hair tied back in a queue. He wore a robe that seemed to change color, size, pattern and style as he moved.

Which, at the moment, wasn't much, as Varr had him in some kind of complex arm/wrist/finger lock that kept Sensu pinned to the floor.

The big, bald man applied more pressure and Sensu grunted, the first noise either of them had made. The crowd seemed to grunt or growl in appreciation, and Kendra turned up her new, Reckoner senses, now that the spots swimming in her eyes had calmed down.

She saw streams of power from Varr which seemed to wrap his opponent in straight lines, right-angles and regular patterns. This was one strength of Release, she knew. The ability to create locks, to fence things in. Because to get out of traps, you had to be able to build them. Vannia had explained it to her, though it still seemed contradictory to Kendra.

The lines and boxes looked like those patterns at the top of walls on some old Greek buildings, she thought. Right angle loops and swirls. They started out thick near Varr's hands, but seemed to get thinner and finer as they snaked across Sensu's back.

But what is Sensu doing? What is his Way? I can't...

Then she saw it. Into the complex yet rigid tangle of energy, Sensu was applying small, almost imperceptible taps of some other kind of influence. She couldn't quite fathom it...

Varr's Way makes total sense, she thought. *I can see him trying to box Sensu in. Forms and rigid requirements that, like the arm lock, keep him from doing what he wants.*

Then, it became obvious to her. Rather than fight the entire Way, Sensu was attempting to alter key junctures in the pattern. Like weakening individual stones in a wall. And she saw the pattern to his changes, too. Saw what was going to happen when enough energy got stored up in Varr's Way.

Yeah, she thought. *Like a wall. Weaken the stones at the bottom, and then when someone builds the wall up too high... Crash, crumble, fall.*

Sensu was Flux. The Domain of change. *House of the Pendulum, Vannia called it,* Kendra remembered. *For every action, an equal and opposite reaction.*

Around her, she heard people betting. She couldn't make hide nor hair out of the things being wagered, but that they were gambling was entirely clear.

"Four trundles on Varr!" shouted a man from behind her.

"I'll take that," said the purple-black woman next to them. "And two more at mark."

"Done!" shouted the man behind her.

191

Varr bore down harder and Kendra couldn't believe that everyone couldn't see through Sensu's subtle ruse. He knew that the big man was going to add power. And he wasn't even really weakening anything...

Brilliant! He's just keeping the intersections at their original strength. That's amazing. So subtle. If anything, it looks like Varr's lines get stronger faster because the Way is flowing around those connecting spots. To Varr it must feel like he's winning even more. But the strength is flowing around the most important points...

Turning to Vannia she whispered, "Do you ever gamble?"

Parrot Girl looked deeply offended. "When do I not?"

"Right," Kendra acknowledged. "Whatever. Anyway. Bet on Sensu if you want to make some... whatever. Bet big."

Vannia looked at her, scowling, for two heartbeats and then said, in a voice much stronger than made sense coming from such a little girl, "Five rolls on Other Fingers."

Two people jumped and signaled or shouted to take advantage of that. Vannia gestured at one of them and turned to look at Kendra.

Are you sure? her raised eyebrow seemed to say.

Kendra simply nodded once.

"One roll on Other Fingers, all takers," Vannia called out.

Bedlam. Probably twenty, maybe thirty people all called out at once, offering competing wagers. Vannia just kept nodding and Kendra saw that CB was hard pressed to notice them all while still keeping an eye on the fight.

As the betting noise waned slightly, Sensu grunted again as Varr poured more energy into his Way, tightening the structures around the thinner man.

Sensu fell to one knee and cried out. Varr fell with him, still holding tightly to his hand and arm, now wrapping his other elbow around Sensu's neck. The symbols and lines twined around the other's dark hair, flowing toward the ground.

"Will you yield?" grunted Varr.

Barely able to move, Sensu shook his head a tiny bit and Varr pressed down harder, tightening both his physical grip and the lines of force now covering them both.

Parrot Girl cut Kendra a glance. Kendra just smiled.

Taking a deep breath, Varr leaned forward and Kendra could almost feel the power flowing off his Way. In fact, she could feel it... the runes made her sit up straighter. She could feel her legs uncrossing of their own will, and she saw that others were doing the same in the rows nearest the fight.

And then Sensu closed his eyes and whispered the word, "Drowning."

Varr shook as if he'd been hit by a taser. His head snapped back and the arm around Sensu's neck went slack, dropping to his side. He retained his hold on the other's wrist, but fell back a step, the runes of his Way shrinking and fading in intensity.

With a single, loud, "Kiai!" Sensu rolled forward taking Varr's wrist in both his hands. The larger man was pulled forward and his Way completely broke, scattering shards of light and symbols into the air as it disappeared.

Rolling Varr onto his back, Sensu landed astride the big man's chest and removed his wrist from the other's grip. Then he placed both hands on Varr's chest and asked, "Will you yield, old friend?"

The fight went out of Varr and all the tension left his frame.

"I yield," he whispered. For a pause of several heartbeats the club was silent as the two competitors maintained a quiet, immobile tableau. Then those who had bet on Sensu -- not as many, Kendra suspected as had bet on Varr -- began to cheer.

The slim, dark-skinned man stood and offered the big brawler his hand. Varr took it and stood, head down, seemingly ashamed of something. Sensu gripped him in a short hug, and then walked away toward the kitchen.

"The match is to Other Fingers," shouted CB. "Payment due on demand. All is recorded. All is balanced. All will be made whole or answer to me."

Varr collapsed on the floor in a heap and a few others, friends Kendra supposed, picked him up and carried him to a far table.

"I don't understand," she said to Vannia.

Parrot Girl was looking at Kendra like she'd grown a third eye. "You don't understand. And yet you called the match at the point when Varr looked like the sure winner."

"I understand what was going on with the Ways," Kendra said. "But not the bit about 'old friend' and the hug and all that."

Vannia looked at her sideways, frowning a bit. "It was a grudge match. There was something personal between them. Now it's settled. The details aren't important. I mean, you could ask either of them if you wanted... but that would be seen as a bit rude."

Kendra nodded. "OK."

A nice looking young man in a white jump suit with eyes made, seemingly, of liquid metal approached the table. "I've come to settle," he said to Vannia.

"Pay the Brothers when they call," Vannia said. This made the nice young man swallow nervously.

"I'd rather settle with you. Now," he said.

"I'm sure you would," Vannia said, turning her head and grinning at Kendra. "But the terms don't work like that, do they?"

He thought for a moment, then said. "Double now."

Vannia shook her head.

"Triple?"

Vannia seemed to think about it, clearly enjoying making the man uncomfortable.

"OK," she finally said. "Triple. Now. In waymarks."

He nodded. "Of course," seemingly both relieved and a bit chuffed. He took a small pad of paper out of his jumpsuit pocket and wrote a series of numbers on it, finally tearing the sheet off and handing it to Vannia. She glanced at it, nodded, and put it in her pocket.

"Nice doing business with you," she called after the man as he went away.

Kendra scowled. "What was that all about?"

"I'll tell you later. But now... you tell me how you knew Sensu was going to win."

Putting her thoughts in order, Kendra explained, "I think Sensu set a trap from the beginning. Something that... channeled.. Varr's final push of energy into changing the Way he'd set up."

Vannia nodded. "Makes sense. But how did you see it?"

Kendra thought for a moment. Then another moment. Vannia waited patiently, sipping her iced tea.

Finally, Kendra said, "I'm not sure."

Slapping the table, Vannia gestured at another one of the patrons who'd betted against her. "Fair enough, friend. We in Chaos don't need to understand everything. What would be the fun in that? Now... let's get paid!"

* * * * *

"... And she disappeared up through the ceiling of the restaurant with a little girl who looked like Alice."

"Alice?"

Wallace remembered that not all Reckoners were as familiar with Mundane literature as he himself. "A character from... never mind. A small, blonde girl."

"With wings," Kaolyn added, Wallace nodding in agreement.

Niles Fayton, seeming a little distracted, leaned forward on the table. "This happened -- she was taken away -- right after the Blood warriors were about to... do something or other to or with her."

"Right," Wallace agreed.

Fayton shook his head. "It makes no sense to me," he said. "She was... wakened or affected, somehow, greenman, by the garden of your master... this Rain Vernon."

Kaolyn nodded. "Whatever happened to wake her to the Ways, it was in the garden, yes."

"And then she was further... altered... by her experience in the Library."

Wallace nodded. "Yes. Mr. Monday's Way had two outcomes. Either her mind would break and she'd die, or she'd enter fully into the Ways as an unaffiliated Reckoner."

Fayton took a sip of his water and scowled. "I'm surprised he has that... authority."

Making a *don't-misunderstand-me-please* gesture, waving his hands around a bit, Wallace said, "Oh, no. It's nothing to do with authority. It's simply a Way that leads to one of two conclusions, determined entirely by the perception of the walker. He didn't make her into a Reckoner. He just presented her with, essentially, two paths. She had to fight and find the one, or slide down the other."

"Poetic," Fayton muttered.

Wallace blushed a little and Kaolyn snorted a laugh.

"Something is funny?" Fayton asked.

"You other Domains," the greenman said. "Wanting the 'how' and 'why.'"

Both Fayton and Wallace looked at Kaolyn for more of an explanation, but that was apparently all the greenman was prepared to say on the subject.

"Anyway," Fayton said, coming to some kind of conclusion and standing up. "I still fail to see any reasonable connection between all these... odd events. The girl awoke to the Ways. Somehow she offended Blood, or they wanted her for their House. Either as a member or for one of their... rituals. Someone else sent another girl to rescue her."

"A girl with green wings," Kaolyn reminded them again, not too subtly chuffed at being ignored.

"What. Green wings? Yes, yes..." That made Fayton stop and think. "Wings. I missed that from earlier. Do you have an image of her handy?" he asked.

Wallace made a small pass with his hand, calling up a minor Way of Sight, and a full-color, three dimensional image of the winged blonde girl appeared on Fayton's table.

Niles shook his head and pointed at the figure. "Yet another House involved. I recognize her. She belongs to the Brothers. Name is Vannia Tacitus. First circle, if I remember correctly, within Chaos."

Wallace perked right up. "I looked through the archives," he said, "but I couldn't find anyone who matched her looks."

"Not unusual with Chaos, is that?" Fayton asked.

Wallace shook his head, agreeing. *They don't like to have their pictures taken. And they change appearance so often, too...*

"Could that help? Knowing her House?" Fayton asked.

Wallace nodded. It just might. Even Chaos has habits. Favorite places. Hidey holes. I can ask some questions. Consult some sources." After a pause, he asked, "How did you recognize her?"

"I saw her once at a meeting with the Red Brothers."

Wallace and Kaolyn both leaned forward, eyes wide. The greenman spoke about a second before Wallace, "You've met the Brothers?"

Fayton chuckled, moving toward the door in a not-too-subtle cue that the meeting was over. "I've met with Reckoners of Chaos who spoke as them. More than that... I shouldn't say."

Wallace and Kaolyn rose, understanding that their time was up. At the door, the greenman turned and said, "Thank you for the help. And your time."

At which Wallace seemed to remember his manners, mumbling, "Uh... Yes. Thank you."

Fayton waved their thanks away. "I'm sorry I couldn't be of more help. Lane was a dear colleague and her troubles are still of interest to Release. If something has happened to her daughter, that would be more sadness in her life. If I think of anything else, I'll contact you through the Library."

At that, Wallace turned, a little too startled and scared looking. *Damn it,* he thought. *Did it again.*

Fayton grinned and said, "Or you could leave your direct number with my secretary."

"I'll do that. Thanks," said Wallace to Fayton. But the other man had already turned and closed his office door, silently, behind him.

As Wallace wrote his number on a Post-It note, Kaolyn muttered, "Idiot."

It wasn't until much, much later that Wallace realized he'd never brought up the subject of the strange, Blood-art cards.

Chapter 8. Alignment

After the warmth of the club, the cool night was both refreshing and a bit of a shock.

"All this globetrotting," she said to Vannia, "makes it hard to know what to wear."

"Peh," said Parrot Girl, looking down at the piece of note paper and mumbling to herself.

"That's a 'waymark?'" Kendra asked.

They were standing outside the club. Vannia had spent the better part of an hour collecting on the various bets that had been made with her. For some reason she didn't want to do it inside the place, but kept ducking back in to pull out other customers to settle their accounts. Kendra had sat on a nearby stump for awhile, just looking at the stars with her newfound senses -- *they seem to be talking to each other...* -- and absentmindedly keeping an eye on her friend. There were laughs from time to time. And some harsh words. And, once, something that sounded like begging in an Asian language she didn't recognize. But, in the end, Vannia collected everything she was owed and then signaled for Kendra to join her.

"Yup," the little blonde girl answered.

"You want to tell me what that is?"

"What what is? Oh. Wait. Hang on. Yeah." Vannia folded the note up and put it back in her pocket.

"It's a map, kind of."

"To what?"

"Ways that aren't usually visible to those outside their created House."

"And that guy has a list of them because..."

"Because he's from Sight. And they trade -- or in this case, gamble and lose -- information."

Kendra nodded. "Makes sense."

"Couple good ones on here," Vannia said, patting her pocket. "Two that I didn't know about. And at least one that I think is a lie. But it's hard to tell if that kid was trying to short me, or if he's just honestly wrong."

"And if he's shorting you?"

Vannia grinned a not-at-all-nice grin and said, "You don't stiff the Brothers."

Kendra nodded again and looked up at the night sky again. "It's late," she said. "Where are we going to sleep?"

"We can stay here. They have some rooms that they rent. Simple. Clean. Safer than almost anywhere else on the planet, really. The Ways that wrap the sanctuaries are crafted by all the Houses. You can get killed in a legit fight, of course, but unless you declare... the walls themselves would pretty much stop anything other than an army from doing you dirty. Well, the walls and CB."

Remembering the tall, well-built man, Kendra said, "I imagine he's... impressive in a fight."

"You have no idea. Anyway. Let's get a room."

* * * * *

Knowing that the little blonde girl who flew away with Kendra was from House Chaos was a start. Knowing her name? Wallace was just about guaranteed to find her within...

"Got her!" he said, less than an hour after they'd returned to his apartment. Kaolyn had taken the opportunity to sleep, curled up on the rug in Wallace's small living room.

"Where?" said Kaolyn.

Wallace jumped a little. The greenman had moved across the apartment almost instantly and in complete silence. *That's a bit unnerving.*

"Uh... Hi. Where? Uh, at a sanctuary. Bardonne's. She was gambling and there's chatter about..."

"Is Kendra with her?"

"Unknown. Nothing specifically indicates her, but that's not..."

He got no further, as the greenman was already headed to the door.

"Kaolyn? Wait for me. I just have to lock up this..."

But the greenman was gone, door left open behind him, and Wallace was left to wonder, *Should I follow him? He came to me for information and I got it for him...*

He glanced at the clock on the wall. It was still too early to go to the Library for an official day's work. He could still take "personal research time" and not get in trouble.

But do I want to? Why should I care?

Caring about the subject of research was... unusual... in the Library. Knowledge for its own sake was the rule. His patrons? Of course they cared. And he cared that they received good service from him. But one person might want to know how to care for a sick tree and nurse it back to health, while another might be looking for information on how to deforest an entire county's worth of woodlands.

Not my business.

And yet he remembered how determined Kendra looked while confronting Mr. Monday. How delighted she seemed at the discovery of her new Reckoning. How quickly she'd managed to acclimate herself to the Way he'd used to show her the events of the Reckoners' War.

She learns very fast, he thought. *That's something I can respect.*

And then, at exactly the same time, two very different thoughts occurred to him.

She would make an excellent addition to Sight.

and

She felt so small in my arms.

Hurrying to secure and pack up his laptop, Wallace considered eight or nine different Ways he could probably get to Bardonne's before Kaolyn. He'd never used any of them before, but knew about them because, well...

librarians know things. The quickest one would definitely be the most uncomfortable and, possibly, even a little dangerous. But he believed it would certainly be faster than any of the Ways of Earth.

Sometimes information is less important than experience, he thought. *Or maybe experience is a kind of information? That's an interesting line of thought... I'll need to come back and refer to that.*

He slammed the door shut on his way out but left it unlocked. Power still on to various screens and appliances. Windows wide open. He didn't notice and he didn't care. His apartment knew what to do when he left, shoring up various wards to keep the place under complete surveillance and reporting. The door locked itself, the devices went into sleep mode and the window slid shut and latched itself quietly.

* * * * *

Kendra woke up to a gentle pressure on her shoulder. When she opened her eyes, a very handsome, very bald man was smiling down at her.

"There are two men downstairs fighting over you," he said quietly, more than a hint of amusement in his voice. "I told them that our policy is not to disturb guests who are sleeping, but they seem to be close to the point of... doing something stupid. I said I would at least check and see if you could come down and arbitrate whatever their issue is."

None of that makes any sense at all, Kendra thought, rubbing at her eyes and sitting up. She'd slept very well and very deeply and seemed to remember dreaming about a lamp post.

"What?" was all she managed to get out.

The man stood up, still smiling, still gentle in demeanor, and held out his hand for her. She took it, unthinking, and he helped her to her feet.

"You're CB," she said, waking up just a little bit more.

"That's right."

She looked around. Vannia was still asleep, nestled between her wings, the knuckles of one hand resting on the floor beside the bed.

"She looks so cute asleep," Kendra said, not really aware she'd spoken aloud.

CB chuckled. "Unless you know her well, yes. Very cute."

Kendra looked a question at him, frowning.

"I take it you don't know her very well?" CB asked.

"I thought I did. I mean... We've been together non-stop for the last couple weeks. And... I knew her as a child."

CB nodded, smiling more broadly. "You're a friend of hers, then. That's good. For you, anyways. I don't worry about her breaking sanctuary while she's here, of course. But you seem like a nice kid, and I wasn't sure if this was the... first act... of one of Vannia's special assignments."

"Special assignments..." Kendra wasn't sure she wanted to know what that meant.

"I'll let her tell you," CB said, turning toward the door. "Her business. Or yours. Not mine. What is my business is the two idiots downstairs who look like they'd risk kanli to be the one who talks to you first."

Kendra turned her head in a circle, cracking her neck vertebrae and opening and closing her jaw to relieve some of the stress of her nightly teeth clenching.

"What if I ask nicely?" she said, bending over to get her backpack from the floor.

"Ask what?"

"About Vannia's special assignments?"

CB looked down at her from a height difference of well more than a foot and folded his arms across his chest. She was, all of a sudden, acutely aware again of what great shape he was in. Not just fit or athletic. But really, really intentionally strong. *He looks like he could break me in half with one hand,* she thought.

He scowled a moment longer, then finally shrugged. "If it was another House, I don't think I would tell you. But with Chaos? They don't mind a little mixy. I'm not breaking canon or rule or oath, so what the hell.

"Your cute, winged friend is sicaria to the Red Brothers. Chief assassin. Has been for about three hundred years. Her current form, and her current name, is relatively new. Very few people would recognize her for what and who she is. But the Bardonne's... we have long memories. And our walls have eyes."

With that, he waved her toward the door. "Enough of Vannia's colored past. It's time to deal with your own messy present."

Kendra nodded. Surprised but, strangely... not really shocked. She looked back over her shoulder and saw that Vannia was drooling a little onto her other hand, the one nestled between her chin and the pillow.

As they descended the long, curved staircase from the rooms above to the bar area below, CB said, "Oh, one other thing. She loves movie quotes. You probably know that. If you hear her say, 'Red Leader, standing by'... I'd get the hell out of Dodge."

* * * * *

As she entered the almost empty bar area, Kendra saw Kaolyn and Wallace stand up from where they'd been sitting at two different tables. The only other person in the large room was one of the wait staff from last night that she hadn't really met. A man with curly red hair and a long, lumberjack-style beard to match who was doing some general neatening and straightening.

I get the feeling he's also subtle back-up, she thought. *Nothing obvious. Just an additional pair of hands for CB if things got weird.*

Wallace and Kaolyn spoke at the same time.

"You need to come with me."

"Hi, Kendra. It's... I mean... I think we should talk."

CB stopped and sat on the bottom step with a good view of the whole room, leaning back against the banister. Kendra moved forward to stand in front of and pretty much equidistant from her two visitors.

"What the hell are you doing here?" she asked. Again, they both answered simultaneously.

"You need to come with me. To see Rain. It's important."

204

"I wanted to talk to you about the Library."

She shook her head. "One at a time, geez. Can we all sit down, please? I just woke up. I could use some water and some coffee and something to eat and I'm not going anywhere without Parrot Girl."

"You mean Vannia?" Wallace asked.

"Yes. Vannia. My friend. The one who rescued me from those Blood dudes."

She's much more confident than before, Wallace thought. *She's learned a lot. I can tell.*

They all turned as Dotty came out of the kitchen, a tray in her hands. She put coffee, water, OJ and a plate of various breakfast pastries on the table nearest Kendra.

Kendra didn't even think to be surprised that Bardonne's knew what she wanted. She just said, "Thanks," and took a seat, pouring coffee into a mug and grabbing a cruller.

"C'mon," she said, talking through a full mouth. "Sit. Eat. Drink. Or not. Whatever."

Wallace and Kaolyn spared each other a quick, suspicious glance and sat down on either side of Kendra. Wallace helped himself to a cheese Danish but Kaolyn just sat, leaning back in his chair and waiting.

After she'd had a few sips of the insanely good coffee and a few bites of the average cruller, Kendra finally asked, "Now... What's up. You go first," gesturing to Kaolyn.

Leaning forward, the greenman seemed very earnest and concerned. "Mr. Vernon has been trying to find you since you were taken," he said. "He's worried about you. Not just because you disappeared. But because of what you are, now."

She nodded. "I get that, and I appreciate it. I assume he wants me to pick a Domain."

"I don't know what he wants," Kaolyn said. "He just asked me to find you and bring you to him."

Kendra nodded. "And you, Wallace? You're a long way from the Library. What's up?"

Wallace brushed a few invisible crumbs off his chin and looked... awkward. He tried to say something. Stopped. Tried again. Shook his head. Looked off into the space above and to the right of Kendra and was clearly working out exactly what he wanted to say.

Wow, Kendra thought. *I guess even Reckoners can be socially retarded.*

She had plenty of friends like that. Super smart, nice people who had trouble communicating, especially with other super smart, nice people. Rather than interrupt or suggest what she thought he wanted to say, she just waited.

Finally, he came to some kind of conclusion and said simply, "I think you should apply to the Library. For a job. You'd be good at it. Eventually. After a lot of training, I mean. I think."

He looked worried. So she smiled at him and he seemed visibly relieved.

"I don't think so, Wallace."

His eyebrows went up and he looked like he was starting to work on another long, well-thought-out, pre-saying-something pause, and this time she did interrupt him.

"I know he thought he was doing the right thing. But your boss basically tried to kill me. And then he was a complete dick about it. The first thing? I guess I understand it, now. Not sure I agree with the methodology, but it was well within his rights. But to put somebody through that and then... well... to basically wave me off with almost no explanation or help. That was pretty douchey."

Wallace nodded. He pretty much agreed with her, so it was hard to argue. Nevertheless, he thought he should at least try.

"He's... not an easy man. And... doing stuff... isn't his forte. Watching is Learning. But he's consistent. And he's a good man. Just... not easy. Or really friendly. Or approachable. Yeah. Kind of a dick."

CB laughed from his perch on the stairs. They all turned and he held up his hands saying, "I'm just glad, for your sake, that you said that in here. You call Monday a dick beyond these walls..." He laughed again.

"That's a good point," agreed Wallace, turning a little pale.

"Don't worry," said Kendra, smiling. "I won't tell."

Turning to Kaolyn she said, "Now you. You want me to come with you to see Mr. Vernon?"

The greenman nodded silently.

She thought about it silently.

The only sounds were Dotty humming in the kitchen and the clack of clean silverware being laid out on the tables.

"I think that makes sense," she finally said, rising.

Wallace, Kaolyn and CB all stood up after her, and she turned toward the owner (*or whatever*) of Bardonne's and said, "Thank you for your hospitality. For the food, the drink and the entertainment. And the courtesy."

He smiled (*God he's handsome*) and bowed a little. "Ever at your service. You know how to find us now."

Kendra nodded and said, "When Vannia wakes up, tell her I've gone to see Rain Vernon. We'll meet..." she turned and looked at Kaolyn... "in the topiary garden?"

It was a question and the greenman nodded.

"After that, if she wants to find me, I think I'll be back home for at least a few days."

She hefted her backpack onto her shoulder, turned and gulped down the last of her coffee, and said to the greenman, "Let's see a man about a garden."

They walked side-by-side toward the big stone door beneath the staring eye. When she'd first come in, it had seemed threatening and ominous to her. Now?

It feels like I'm leaving a place where I was watched over. A safe place.

One hand on the stone arch, she turned back and said to CB, "When Vannia gets up, will you give her a message for me?"

The tall, muscular, handsome man smiled handsomely and nodded.

"Ask her, 'If you wake up at a different time in a different place, could you wake up as a different person?'"

CB frowned. "I don't know that one."

Kendra chuckled and waved, "I think she will."

* * * * *

Rain Vernon sat in his car outside the topiary garden and fondled the envelope Gareth Ezer had given him. He'd heard from Kaolyn that they'd located the girl and that she was on her way to meet him here, within the hour.

The envelope was sealed, of course. And not just with glue and wax, of course. Rain suspected that if he opened it -- and very bad things didn't happen immediately-- it would seem to contain a blank sheet of paper. Probably nice, thick, soft stationary that felt like it was the child of heavy cream and Egyptian cotton sheets.

Protecting a message from eyes other than those intended was trivial.

For many, unprotecting the message would be, while not trivial, certainly achievable.

In personal battles that often lasted centuries, communication and information were both powerful and complex weapons. In this regard, Rain envied Sight just a bit. The ability to both see and "see through" would be extremely handy sometimes.

Even if he thought he had a good chance of opening the envelope safely and reading the actual message he would not have done so.

It is not wrong to fear a power greater than yourself, he thought. *It is wisdom. The sea will drown the strongest.*

Nevertheless, he resented it. Within his own House, there were few Reckoners as powerful as Rain. None had as many followers. None had so much wealth accrued in real estate, minerals, artifacts and favors. He had many friends. Actual friends. People who liked him regardless of his own power and wealth. Friends from long ago. Even some prominent Mundanes who were, he had to admit, occasionally more interesting than Reckoners, simply because they were so different, so headstrong and foolish in their lust for life.

They eat every meal as if it might be their last, because it truly might, he thought. Unlike the Naturals, such as Kaolyn, who understood that death and life were so intertwined as to be sides of the same coin. And unlike Reckoners, who could live in ways that a Mundane would never understand.

Maybe they are so beautiful because they live between those worlds and reflect them both, he thought. *That deserves some thought. Maybe a poem...*

His reverie was disturbed by a sharp clicking on his passenger side window.

He turned and saw a large, black crow sitting on his rearview mirror, pecking at the glass. He made a shooing gesture, but the bird just kept pecking. Some kind of repeated pattern, he realized.

Tap-tap-a-dap-dap... Tap-tap. Tap-tap-a-dap-dap... Tap-tap."

Finally, it came to him. *Shave and a haircut... two bits.*

Ah. Not just a bird, then.

Not particularly surprised, as messengers can take many forms in Earth, he rolled down the passenger side window and the bird hopped onto the frame, head inside the car, tail still sticking out.

The bird then spoke in a language that Rain hadn't heard in more than three thousand years, saying, essentially, "I know you, and I see you and you will listen carefully."

Struggling to retain a modicum of calm, Rain replied in the same language, "I hear and will hear."

"Good," the bird said in English, cocking its head, shiny black eyes fixed steadily on Rain's.

"You are planning to offer the girl a place in your House, I believe?" asked the crow, continuing in an American-accented English. *A slight Boston accent, maybe?* Rain thought. *But Brahmin. Back Bay. Not Southie, certainly.*

In response to the bird's question, Vernon simply nodded.

"And if she says 'no,' you will give her that message," the bird dipped its head in the general direction of the envelope resting on Rain's thigh.

Rain nodded again.

"One of two things will happen when the girl reads what's in that envelope," the crow said. "Either she will change her mind and agree to join your House, or she will not."

Niles frowned. The statement was, at its face, obvious.

The crow continued, "If she accepts and becomes a Reckoner of Earth, then all is well. You will train her and she will make an excellent addition to your Domain, I believe."

Niles nodded, still frowning. "That is what I'm assuming will happen."

"And if she does not?"

Now Rain looked a bit confused. "I believe she will."

The bird simply repeated, head cocked to one side, "And if she does not?"

"I'm..." he stopped, because Gareth hadn't told him, really, what to do after that. Just that he should give Kendra the envelope if she wouldn't join the Domain of Earth.

Again, a third time, the bird asked, "And if she does not?"

Did a parrot ever sound that grim? Rain wondered, surprised at his own inner levity.

"If she does not... I will... let her go. I will have fulfilled my duty."

The crow hopped onto the dashboard, sitting just a foot or so away from his face. She -- somehow he knew the crow was female -- had to duck down a little to avoid brushing her head on the windshield and it made her look even more menacing. Like she was crouching before a pounce.

Or examining a crushed raccoon in the road to make sure it's truly dead, he thought.

"If she will not join you, then you will kill her," the bird said simply.

"That's not..."

In that other language, the one that sounded like wind across a desert and stones tumbling into a dry well, the crow said, "I tell you: this is Law."

Without even thinking, Rain replied, "I hear the Law."

I have to find a way to contact Gareth before they get here, he thought. *He didn't tell me what to do if she wouldn't join Earth. I just assumed...*

But the crow cut short his frightened planning. Returning to English, she said, "Good. I trust that a Reckoner of your abilities will have no trouble destroying an untrained, unaffiliated youngster within a Way of your own making. Since she will have no House, you have no need of an excuse. It is not even vendetta. But if asked, and you feel you have to answer, blame her for the undeclared murder of your greenman."

"The killing of..."

But before he could finish his question, the bird croaked once, turned and flew out the open window. He heard her caw again, from a spot that sounded like it was atop the roof of the building that fronted the garden.

She's watching, he thought, and looked up just in time to see Kaolyn and the girl come around the corner toward the black, iron gate of the topiary.

* * * * *

As they approached the gate of the topiary garden, Mirkir, the stone gargoyle, appeared from around the corner of the entrance tunnel. He sat calmly on the other side of the iron bars, looking to Kendra like a big, goofy dog just waiting for his master to finally come home.

She reached into her backpack for the iron key, but then heard a voice behind her:

"Kendra. So nice to finally meet you in person."

The man stepping out from behind a nice town car was, Kendra thought, the Platonic Ideal of the suave, elegant, slightly up-tight European business patriarch. His hair, while a bit thin on top, was neatly coiffed and was at that stage of salt-and-pepper where "experienced" turns into "distinguished." His skin was the deep olive of a Mediterranean native, either Greek or Italian Kendra guessed, and was only lined at the corners of his mouth and eyes. More smile lines than wrinkles, really. He was wearing a neat, tan suit with an open-collared, cream-colored shirt.

As he stepped forward and extended a hand to her, Kendra noticed that his cufflinks were made of dark green gems of some kind, backed by gold.

She shook his hand and it was the nicest, firmest, most friendly handshake she'd ever experienced. Not too strong, like he had something to prove. Not weak and timid. Not too warm or too cold. Just...

Alive... he feels alive. And he feels like he knows he's alive and likes it.

This was a man to be trusted. A man to be liked or even loved. His eyes, Kendra now saw, were light gray, like sea foam, and had a little merry twinkle to them as he smiled.

What a great smile, she thought. *Such a nice man. He seems so friendly.*

She realized that he was what she'd hoped he'd be. His correspondence about the job had always been friendly in a business-like manner. But she'd imagined that a man that owned and cared for such beautiful gardens would have to, himself, be wise and beautiful.

And it seems like he is...

"Mr. Vernon..." she said, a little nervously. "I'm glad to meet you, too. I've always wanted to thank you in person for the job. It's been great."

He waved away her thanks, gesturing toward the gate. "It's nothing. Why don't you come in and we'll talk about your recent adventures. I'd love to hear all about your travels."

He held out his hand and Kendra gave him the key. After he unlocked the gate and was swinging it inward, Mirkir scooted outside and jogged around Kaolyn, sniffing at the greenman's legs and backside.

"Bardonne's," the stone creature said simply.

"Yes, yes," Kaolyn reached down and thumped Mirkir a few times on his stony head. "But I didn't bring you any crusts. Sorry. No time."

If a stone, winged fu-dog can look crestfallen, Mirkir did. Kendra almost laughed at how comically similar he seemed to a fat bulldog who'd been denied a treat.

As Rain swung the gate fully open, another voice called from behind them, "I'm not sure you should go in there, Kendra."

They all turned, and there was Wallace. He looked... disheveled... to say the least. There was dirt on both his knees, his hair was in a wild state of messiness, he had a little blood caked on one nostril and...

"You're missing a shoe," Kendra said to him.

Wallace looked down, looked back up, and looked down again.

"Yes. Ah. Well. It's back in..." he gestured behind him. Thought better of explaining and simply shrugged. "I wanted to get here as quickly as possible."

With a gracious and sincere smile, Vernon said, "You're welcome to join us, son. We can get you cleaned up. Maybe a spare pair of shoes. There's nothing we'll talk about that needs to be a secret from..."

"I don't need to clean up," Wallace interrupted. "But I would like to... listen... to hear what you have to say. Kendra may have some questions. Some questions that I can help with."

Rain nodded, still smiling. "That's fine. Come inside. As I said, you're welcome to..."

"I don't think she should go in there."

Kendra looked at Mr. Vernon. Very patient, very wise, very friendly. And then at Wallace. Very dirty, very agitated, very nervous.

I trust agitated and nervous more than patient and friendly, she realized.

"There's a juice bar just around the corner with some tables and chairs outside. It's a nice enough day. Let's get something to drink and we can all hang out and have a chat."

Vernon looked like he wanted to argue the point, but decided it wasn't that big a deal. Nodding and smiling, he handed the key to Kaolyn who locked the gate and waved for Mirkir to follow him.

"Whatever's best for you, dear," he said and gestured for Kendra to lead the way.

As they walked, Kendra realized she could hear Mirkir's stone feet tapping on the sidewalk and the shuffle-slap of Wallace's one-shoe-off gait. She could hear the birds chirping and the traffic and the breeze. The faint sound of people talking in the distance or in apartments with the windows open. It seemed as if the world became more alive to her every day since her... awakening.

Leading the small group around the corner, she asked, "Does anybody else want something? I'm really thirsty."

Rain and Kaolyn shook their heads, but Wallace said, "Just some water, please," and Mirkir growled, "Something crunchees."

"Sure thing."

Inside the juice bar, she experienced the same awareness of her senses, but this time for smell. There was the clean scent of a shop well-scrubbed. The aroma of coffee drinks and cream and sugar. A mix of fruits that, when she tried, she could separate out into orange, strawberry and banana. And something fake. Some kind of sugary, syrupy taste/smell that wasn't anything ever grown on a vine, tree or bush.

"Can I help you?" the young guy behind the counter asked.

A Mundane, she thought, without even realizing it.

"Yeah... A bottled water... An OJ Fizzy... and..." she looked through the glass at the snacks, "... A couple of those biscotti."

"Sure thing," the guy said. She could tell without trying that he was twenty years old. That he had just gotten over a cold a few days ago and was still feeling a bit logy. She knew, without knowing how, that he was left-handed, had an iPhone in his back pocket and was going to have to have his wisdom teeth out within the next year or so.

"What kind of biscotti," he asked, opening the case.

"I don't know," she said. "One of each."

He nodded and put three differently marbled pieces into a paper bag.

As she handed him a five, he looked down at her hand and said, "Nice ring. Looks vintage."

She nodded, having forgot about the red, glass ring that Vannia had given her.

Just two weeks... but it seems so much longer, she thought.

"Keep the change," she said, tucking the bag beneath her arm and taking the drinks in her hands.

"Thanks," he said behind her as she pushed the door open with her hip.

Outside again, Wallace took the drinks from her, put them down on a cheap wrought iron table, and pulled out a cheap wrought iron chair for her. Mr. Vernon and Kaolyn were already sitting.

Good thing we didn't all want food, she thought, sitting down, *these tables are barely big enough for a couple drinks.*

Remembering the biscotti, she opened the bag and let them fall out onto the ground next to Mirkir. He wagged his little stumpy stone tail twice in thanks, and began to crunch one of them with such gleeful violence that the sound drowned out any chance of conversation.

"Mirkir..." Kaolyn chided. The gargoyle looked up, the stump of a biscotti sticking out of his mouth like a little cigar, and Kendra laughed out loud. Which made Mirkir smile. Which made him drop the biscotti. Which made everyone smile.

"Take those off a bit, will you," the greenman chided gently. "And don't choke on them."

Mirkir scooped all of them up in his mouth sideways and carried them off a ways, chuffing happily. While they could still hear the crunching, it wasn't close enough to be distracting. Just funny.

"On behalf of my friend, thank you, Kendra."

"No biggie," she said. "He seems like a fun little guy."

Vernon and Kaolyn shared a bit of a meaningful look at each other, but said nothing.

Kendra shook her head. "I know, I know. I assume he's also a terrifically dangerous and powerful mini-god or something. But he also seems like a fun little guy."

Kaolyn chuckled and Vernon smiled a bit wider, saying, "I imagine you've seen a lot of things like that over the past weeks. Both interesting, fun and, maybe, a little dangerous."

Kendra nodded, sipping at her drink through a large, purple straw. *I have to remember to drink this slowly,* she thought. *They always give me brain freeze.*

"It's been a weird time, for sure."

"And I assume you have some questions."

She nodded again. "Lots. But one in particular."

Rain Vernon smiled and spread his palms in a gesture that said, *Ask whatever you like.*

"Did you know I was a... potential... Reckoner when you hired me?"

Rain remembered what Gareth Ezer had said about truth: *a rather blunt instrument.*

But it's all I have, the moment, he thought.

"I did know."

Kendra nodded. "I figured out as much. Too much..."

"Synchronicity?" Wallace ventured.

Slurping slowly, she nodded. "That. Yes."

They were quiet for a moment, Kendra sipping and thinking. In the distance, she could hear Mirkir licking the sidewalk with his stone tongue, which sounded like a cross between sandpaper on cement and crushing ice in a blender.

"Is that it?" asked Vernon. "No other questions?"

Kendra put down the drink so that the icy junk could melt into juicy sludge. "Oh, no. Plenty more questions. But that was the most important, I think."

"What's the next most important?"

"What's wrong with my mother?"

That's not what I was expecting.

"What do you mean?" Rain asked aloud.

"She has a half-brother who's a Reckoner. A guy from Release. Name is... Bran. Bran Alix. He's the one who helped me get out of Monday's puzzle."

"I see," Rain said. "But not about something being wrong with your mother..."

"I'm a Reckoner that somehow got... I don't know what to call it. Stunted. Turned off. Abandoned. Whatever. Cut off from the Ways."

"Yes."

"And my mother seems very... I don't know. 'Cut off' seems like as good a term as any. Absent, in some sense. Like she's..."

"Missing something," Wallace interrupted.

"Shut up, Wallace," Kaolyn said, a hint of anger in his voice. "Let her ask questions."

"It's not going to work like that," Wallace said. "I'm here to help Kendra make a good decision. An important one. And that means giving her all the information we have."

"What information?" Kendra asked, leaning in toward Wallace and taking one of his hands in hers.

He drew back, pulling his hand away, looking a bit shocked at the contact.

"Your mother was a Reckoner of Release, too," Wallace said. "She lost the Ways when she tried to switch over to Increase to be with your father."

"My father... I never heard anything about..."

"That's the truth," Vernon said. "And, Kaolyn, there's no need to keep anything from her."

The crow's prediction -- *the undeclared murder of your greenman* -- stuck in his mind and Rain felt the need to keep the greenman calm. Not that he wasn't. Just... Better to be friends.

Kaolyn nodded, his face serious.

"My understanding," Vernon went on, "is that, yes, your mother lost the Ways during an attempt to switch to Increase at your father's request. While she was pregnant with you. She was badly... changed... during the attempt and there was a fear that your life might be at risk if you were raised as Reckoner. Thus, the drugs and therapy with Dr. Lyonne."

Kendra nodded. "And you took me on as a gardener to keep an additional eye on me?"

Rain nodded. "If you could have made it through to full adulthood as, essentially, a Mundane, we believed you would, then, be safe to lead a normal life."

"As a chronic," Kaolyn put in.

Vernon held up a hand to silence the greenman. "Yes. As a Mundane. But, somehow, something in you triggered the Ways in my topiary. Then, not knowing about your history, Kaolyn brought you to the Library where..." he spread his hands in a *we all know the rest* gesture.

Kendra frowned. "That reminds me of another question I wanted to ask. Why did you take me to the Library, Kaolyn?"

The greenman looked at Vernon quizzically. The gardener nodded. "Just the truth, my friend."

Kaolyn shrugged and said, "I had disappointed Rain recently. If I'd done so again, it might have had... implications... for my future."

"You were scared of getting in trouble?"

The greenman sighed. "Yes, pretty much. I knew I could get the topiary cleaned up before that night's... before Rain would notice anything had gone wrong. I assumed the Librarian would, I don't know... find you to be an interesting problem. They like puzzles, Sight. And that would get me out of it."

Kendra nodded, and sat thoughtfully toying with the straw in her drink.

Finally, she asked simply, "And my father?"

"His name was Morgan White," said Wallace. "I looked him up while some of my Ways were out searching for Vannia and you. He was fairly high up in Increase. There is a record of an internal judgment against him that was made public so that the other Houses would know that he didn't represent Increase anymore. Beyond that, there are no details that I could easily find."

"According to my sources," Vernon added, "he was banished from Increase and was killed in a duel less than a year after your birth."

"That can't be true," Kendra said.

"Why not?" Kaolyn asked.

"Hang on," answered Kendra, and she fumbled through her pack for a bit, finally finding the copy of *The Magician's Nephew* that she had, somehow, brought with her out of the first part of Monday's Way.

Opening it to the title page of the book, she saw...

It's gone. The inscription is gone.

"It's gone."

"What's gone, my dear?" Vernon asked.

The world seemed suddenly very quiet and still, and, for a moment, Kendra wondered if everything that had happened to her since she stopped taking her meds was, in fact, a hallucination.

That would be comforting in a way, wouldn't it? she thought.

I could go back on the meds. Maybe even more of them. Maybe spend some time in a program or a hospital or whatever they call the loony bin these days. Somewhere where girls don't have wings and roads don't move under your feet and the stars don't talk to each other.

"Kendra?" Wallace asked. "Are you all right?"

I am not all right. Something is not right, she thought. *I'm missing a piece. Of myself. A piece of me is missing.*

Rain reached out and touched her shoulder. Kindly. Warmly. She looked up at him and he was smiling slightly in sympathy. "Come with us, dear. You love working in the gardens. You have a knack. Mirkir clearly likes you," he nodded down at the stone creature who was looking up at her saying, *More, please?* in the universal language of dogs and, apparently, gargoyles.

She looked up at Wallace.

She's confused and scared, he thought. *I understand that.*

"You don't have to join Sight," he said. "But you can come to the Library until you figure things out. You're a Reckoner now. We can help you find out whatever you need to know to choose a House."

"I don't know," she said softly. She had the book. The book was real. It had come out of the Library, that was for sure. *Maybe I pulled it off a shelf in there?* she thought. *And the rest was a dream?*

Vernon waved his hand, indicating the day around them. Beautiful blue sky. Little puffy clouds. The smells of summer in the air and the sounds of birds and children. His gesture seemed to say, *All this can be yours.*

"You are not a watcher, Kendra. You are a creator. A doer. A gardener, in whatever soil you finally choose. I don't think the Library would make you happy. And you don't have to choose today. But I tell you, truly, that I think Earth is the right Domain for you."

Shaking off her confusion, Kendra closed the book and looked at Rain Vernon, making a decision.

"No. Not Earth. Not today. Not ever. You knew about my past. About my parents. And you didn't tell me anything. I think you're a nice man and were trying to do the right thing, but I couldn't ever forget that."

Rain frowned, looking disappointed. "I'm sorry you feel that way. Are you absolutely sure?"

She thought about it one last time. Though he seemed very nice, in the back of her mind was a whisper that reminded her, *He created the sky woman and the sky cat. His pleasant, mild, European professor bit isn't all there is to him.*

"No. Not Earth. And not Sight. I'm not sure about the others, I'll have to..."

Rain reached into his jacket pocket and took out a white envelope about the size of a Hallmark card. Maybe a bit bigger. Placing it on the table between them, he gestured for Kendra to open it.

"Uh... What is that?" she asked.

"It's for you," he said simply.

"So I figured. But what is it?"

"Open it and find out," Vernon said. Wallace was scowling, looking suspicious and Kaolyn seemed impatient for the entire situation to resolve itself one way or the other.

Whatever it is, it doesn't matter, she thought. *I'm going to find Vannia and maybe join Chaos and maybe get a job at Bardonne's or maybe another sanctuary where it's safe.*

Hesitantly, she slipped a finger under the flap of the envelope. It had clearly been closed by a Way, and she felt it melt under her touch. A seal that anyone but her wouldn't have been able to easily break.

She opened the envelope and pulled out a single, folded piece of heavy paper. On it was written, in the same handwriting she remembered from the inscription in *The Magician's Nephew,* the following:

My Dearest Elaynia,

I know you are afraid, but you must quit your House and join me in mine. The danger you've been warned of is not real. It is a tale told to frighten children and to keep the Houses in line. No Reckoner has ever lost the Ways by changing Domain.

If you wait much longer, if your pregnancy begins to show, Lady Percy will absolutely forbid you to join me. And if Gareth knew what we are planning, he too would forbid our union.

Meet me under the willow by the boat house. Once we are together, truly together, we will find peace.

Yours,

Morgan.

It makes sense, thought Kendra. *People in love do stupid things. Morgan... my father... must not have known that it really was possible to lose the Ways like that. Like what happened to her.*

She read it three times, then looked up at Rain. "Mr. Vernon? Is this real? Is it true?"

With profound sympathy, he nodded. "It was given to me by someone whom I trust. And who told me, explicitly, that it was the truth."

Earth, Sight, Release and Increase... all with some kind of hold on my past or something that makes me distrust them, she thought. *That leaves Blood, Chaos and Flux. My mom's father was from Flux? Right? And I like Vannia... but she's apparently an assassin. And Blood tried to kidnap me. I think. In the restaurant. That leaves Flux, which I know nothing about...*

"What are you thinking, my dear?" Vernon asked kindly.

"That I need more time to think," she said softly, standing up. "I'm going back to Bardonne's."

Wallace nodded in agreement.

Vernon heard a whisper on the wind: *If she will not join you, then you must kill her.*

"No. You're coming back to the topiary with us," Vernon said firmly. "You can think there. And I honestly believe that you're better off in the Domain of Earth than anywhere else."

Kendra looked at him blankly. "No," she said simply. "I'm going to Bardonne's."

"Bring her to the garden," Vernon said to Kaolyn. "I have a call to make. And then I'll be back. Very soon. And lock the gates once you're in. All of them this time."

The greenman looked back and forth between Vernon and Kendra, clearly a bit perturbed.

"Must I repeat myself?" Vernon asked, and Kendra heard steel in his voice for the first time. The flip side of the kindly European professor.

The general who will not be disobeyed.

Kaolyn shook his head. "I understand," was all he said. He motioned for Mirkir, who looked more confused than usual. "If she runs," he said to the gargoyle, "bring her back."

Mirkir nodded seriously. But then he looked up at Kendra, broke into a wide smile and said, "It's OK. I found a Frisbee yesterday."

She laughed and almost went along with the greenman and the stone creature. But then she remembered the writing in her book and the sky woman and that Mr. Vernon had, apparently, known about her for many years. He'd done nothing to help with her condition. Maybe even...

Pulling away from the table slightly, she asked, "Mr. Vernon... Did Dr. Lyonne know about my parents?"

Mirkir scooted a bit closer to her under the table.

Vernon thought for a moment, then said, "Your therapist? I don't think so. She's a Mundane, after all."

That's a mistake, Kendra thought. *Dr. Lyonne said she had never heard of you. So why do you know her?*

She decided to push that wedge a little harder.

"That's weird," Kendra said. "Because, looking back, she had a set of therapy cards that I could swear were laced with some kind of Way. I didn't know that at the time, of course, but if I think about it... Yeah. I'd bet they were made by a Reckoner."

Vernon looked confused and, now, a little impatient. "They might have been a gift. We don't keep completely apart, you know. And it might have been a gift... or a curse... who knows... from a Reckoner. Why do you ask?"

Somewhere above them, a crow cried out.

In his mind, Vernon heard, again: *If she will not join you, then you must kill her.*

"Kendra... Let's go into the garden. I will make some calls to some friends and we'll get you more information. You don't have to make a decision now, but you should stay where we can keep you safe."

"So you don't know anything about the cards?" Kendra asked.

"No. I don't know anything about any cards," Vernon said.

"Dr. Lyonne never mentioned them to you?"

"No, she never did. She wouldn't talk about a patient, I don't think. Confidentiality and all."

There it is. A blatant lie, either from her about him or vice versa.

She took another step back. Mirkir moved closer to her again, and Kaolyn stood up. As did Wallace.

I missed something, Vernon thought. *Something changed. What? All I said was that I hadn't ever heard anything about any cards. Which is true. Why should that matter to her?*

Then it clicked. *As far as Kendra is concerned, I don't know Lyonne.*

Kendra could see that Vernon now realized his mistake. "Dr. Lyonne said she'd like to meet you. She was impressed by the idea of using computers to track plants."

Vernon thought for one moment about trying to cover his tracks, trying some other little lie or covering tactic to smooth over what he'd said. But, frankly, he'd had enough.

Two weeks of Ezer breathing down my neck wanting this girl. Years of keeping tabs. Years of pretending to befriend that sycophantic Lyonne... chronic... All for what? To make sure that this girl didn't become a Reckoner. And then it happens anyways. By mistake. In my garden. Which Ezer told me to let her into in the first place. For the love of the Mother...

Though Earth has no single Warden or Ruler, she has just a few masters. And Rain Vernon was one. And he was tired of acting the flunky, the messenger and the babysitter.

The change that came over him made Kendra physically flinch, and Wallace actually backed up a few feet, stumbling off the curb. It was like watching a blue sky turn gray very quickly as a summer storm raced in. A storm with clouds that held the promise of lightning.

"Take her to the garden and keep her there," Vernon said quietly to Kaolyn. "I'll be back in an hour or so."

The greenman reached out and held Kendra's arm in a strong, slightly painful grip. She noticed, again, that he had an extra knuckle on each finger. Though that no longer seemed strange to her. Just part of the new world she'd discovered. A world that was now dragging her down a path that made her afraid.

"No," she whispered, but he either didn't hear or didn't care.

As she looked at his hand, she realized that the greenman was casting a Way on her as well. Something like vines were seeping out from under his palm and beginning to creep up her arm.

She didn't know what to do.

I'm frightened, Parrot Girl, she thought. *You helped me last time. When the Blood soldiers came for me. Will you help me again?*

But there was no winged Alice, no girl flying down on great, green wings.

I guess I'm on my own, then.

She looked more carefully at the Way as the vines spread further up and down her arm. She could feel them holding her, stopping her muscles from doing what she wanted. Cold, like clear water in a stream. Like rock in winter. In a moment they'd be up around her neck and then she'd have to go where the greenman led.

Time seemed to slow. She saw Vernon looking at her, waiting for her to follow Kaolyn back around the corner to the topiary. Mirkir was still grinning, still looking forward to having a new playmate in his yard, she supposed. The vines were at her shoulder. Her arm was numb. And she was beginning to feel sleepy. Disconnected. As if the vines weren't just holding her, but sapping her energy.

She could feel Kaolyn's Way the same as she'd seen Varr's back at Bardonne's. Saw that he was applying his knowledge of the world, his understanding and his power and his will. Earth was powerful and still. Earth grew vines that choked trees and crushed rock over time. Earth could wait and turn and wait again and, eventually, she would turn and follow and...

Just as the vines were about to creep around her throat, her head lolled forward and she caught a glimpse of shiny red... a ring. *Was I wearing a ring? I should do something with the ring...*

Hardly thinking now, she leaned over and brought her fist down, hard, on the metal table top, shattering the red glass bauble in the ring Vannia had given her. A pulse of power ran up her arm and mixed with the vines, merging into them, turning them a sick, blackish red.

Kaolyn, surprised and angry now, tried to release her but couldn't let go of the Way. He brought his other hand around to pull at her shoulder, trying to pry his hand off her arm, but it got caught, too.

The black, bloody color moved up the vines and into his fingers, over his skin. First his hands then his arms then his chest and neck turned the color of dried, corrupted clay. Kendra could see it happen as if the instructions for the Way were written in clear, precise words.

It's not Chaos, she realized. *It's Flux.* And Flux was change, turning power back on itself.

Growth becomes cancer, she thought. *Growth becomes blight. A swarm of locusts, a cholera epidemic, poison too... they are all of Earth. They all grow.*

Kaolyn made a sound in his throat like a tree collapsing in a forest, a far larger noise than should have been possible. His entire body had gone tense, and he looked as if he was going to shake apart. Kendra looked around, but it seemed that none of the Mundanes had heard. And if any Reckoners were nearby, they were keeping a distance from the spectacle.

The unhealthy, black-red color crept up into the greenman's face, surrounding his eyes. Looking down, Kendra could see that the vines of his Way were turning gray and starting to flake off. She pulled hard and they ripped away, taking three long fingers of his hand with them, still clinging to her arm. She brushed at them with her other hand and they crumbled into moist chunks of dust.

The greenman turned his head down to look at Mirkir, who seemed confused. Then he looked up at Vernon and seemed to find some kind of peace, the muscles of his face and neck relaxing. Without a word, he turned his face to the sky and exhaled one last time, the whites of his eyes finally filling with the red sickness.

When he fell, his body burst into hundreds of dried, rotten fragments that the wind began to pick up, breaking them into flakes that looked like ash.

Chapter 9. Conclusion

"I... I... I didn't mean for that to happen," Kendra stuttered, backing away from the pile of dissipating rot that had been the greenman.

Rain Vernon stared as if seeing her for the first time.

"That should not have been possible," he said simply.

"It's not... I didn't..." she was still unable to fathom what had happened. The ring had released the Way. Not her. She hadn't had anything to do with it.

"You are not of Flux. The Way should have spilled. Or even turned back on you. What did you do?"

"I have no idea..."

Wallace was standing in the street looking shocked. Mirkir was nosing in the remains of what had been his master and friend, trying to understand, by smell, what none of them could understand by sight.

The gargoyle turned on her and growled. "Not good," it said in its low gravelly voice. Then, louder. "Not good! NOT GOOD!"

As the gargoyle lunged at Kendra, Vernon heard the crow's voice again: *Blame her for the undeclared killing of your greenman...*

How did it know?

But just as Mirkir's sharp, stone teeth were about to clamp down on Kendra's leg, a brown flash shot between them and brought the creature up short.

It was a squirrel. Racing in to pick up a random chunk of the biscotti that Mirkir had somehow missed.

But Kendra knew better. She could see clearly now. Wallace had tossed the piece of pastry on the ground. Then he'd cast a Way of Sight to enhance a nearby squirrel's perception, drawing it to the food. And another, an UnSeeing, to keep it from noticing Mirkir until it was too late. Until...

"MINE!" shouted the stone dog, leaping after the now surprised and terrified rodent. The squirrel took off at top speed. Barking and wheezing, Mirkir shot down the block, across the street and was gone from sight.

Kendra almost laughed, and looked at Wallace who, too, seemed on the verge of laughter. Or at least hysteria.

Then she looked back at Vernon. And everything like laughter died inside her.

He looked like an earthquake. Like a tornado. Like a tidal wave. She could see the power in him. Hundreds, maybe thousands of years of studying the Ways of Earth. Of coming to know the wind and rain on the surface, the rock beneath, and the fire below.

"I am sorry," he said softly. "You would have made a fine gardener."

He didn't even gesture theatrically. No raised hands, no cry of power, no mystical rune. He just looked into her and she felt...

Time.

That most basic of nature's powers. The turn of the world, the circle of life and death. The seasons. Water in the clouds falls to rivers flows to the sea and rises back to the clouds. Trees to ash and loam and back into the dirt where new trees grow.

She could feel herself aging. Which, she supposed, had always been the case.

But now... It was obvious. And terrifying.

Every moment, every cell in her body ticked off a little mark on a ledger and she was a tick closer to her final breath. Her blood ran just that much thinner. Her bones just that much more brittle. Her muscles growing a little less flexible.

And it was speeding up. Or, rather, everything around her was going much, much more slowly.

Wallace was caught mid-step, one foot raised above the other as he climbed the curb. A scrap of waste paper was caught in a tiny whirlwind and she barely saw it move. Even the light, she realized, was slower. *And that's not possible, I don't think.*

Her thoughts weren't slower. She saw all these things around her and could have reached out and plucked the paper from the air. She could have slipped it under Wallace's foot before it came down. She was breathing and blinking and thinking so much faster than they were. Like they were sloths and she was...

A gnat, she realized. *Or a hummingbird. Or a bee.* She remembered reading that the lifespan of some bugs was measured in weeks. And she'd wondered, at the time, if that felt like a long, full life to them.

I wonder how long Kaolyn would have lived, she thought. *And Mirkir... maybe he'll be around for hundreds of years.*

She realized she was daydreaming. Distracted. She should move. Go somewhere. Do something. But while her mind was able to maintain its internal speed, her body was still stuck in "normal" time and she couldn't move it at all.

She tried everything. Her feet were stuck to the ground. Her hands, still soiled with the gunk of the greenman's death, were frozen mid-air. The only thing that seemed unstuck was...

My eyes. I can still move them.

She looked up and saw Vernon staring at her. Sad and powerful. His Way wrapping her in loops of time that did these things to different parts of her. Speeding up her perception of time, keeping her will and ability to move at bay.

She managed to look a question at him: *how long?*

He seemed to understand and said, amidst the silence of the world, "Does it matter?"

Which made her frightened. *I could be stuck like this, aging and frozen, for... sixty years!*

She could feel herself feeling it. The terror of living with the body of a tree and the mind of a girl. A sharp mind. An active mind. But all the while... decaying. Unmoving. Doing nothing. Nothing. Just...

Dying.

And that, all of a sudden, made her not just scared... but angry.

None of this was her fault. But, like Monday, Rain was being an ass about it. Sure, people died all the time. Innocent people. They get caught in the crossfire or have an accident or are in the wrong place at the wrong time. But she didn't know anything and now, here he was, about to age her to death because she wouldn't join his Domain.

That's just... mean.

He seemed ready to wait for a long, long time. And Kendra knew that it didn't matter. Whether it seemed like a thousand years to her... She was going to age and wither and die before Wallace's foot came down on the curb.

She could feel Vernon's Way in detail. All the subtle patterns and shifts. The blending of several flavors of time. The life of rocks that didn't move on their own but were cracked by water and ice. The roots of trees that moved down so slowly, ever so slowly, to eat and drink. The leaves that came and went much more quickly. At least compared to roots and rocks. And waves that came and went with a fast, short rhythm against the shore. All natural. All these patterns of time. All of them at war in her body, now, tearing her mind from her body and her life from her will.

But whatever time I have, I might as well spend seeing the world with my new eyes.

She turned, then, as much as she could, from looking at Vernon and looked at the Ways around her. The many little scraps of power that Reckoners had left behind. Tiny trails of Seeing. Little loops of Chaos. And the larger, yet more subtle flows of power, like the Narrow Road that ran down the middle of this street in her home town.

I have often walked down this street before, she sang in her head. *But the pavement always stayed beneath my feet before...*

She was losing it. Something about the time flows was making it hard to think. Was blurring the lines between her conscious thoughts and her memories.

The Narrow Road, she thought. *Right there all along, and I never saw it.*

Powered by Mundane travel. Directed by Increase. Used by any Reckoner.

Any Reckoner.

And she saw them. Like the negative space on the ink blot cards that made the frightening pictures. Like the spaces that Dai Li "Other Fingers" Sensu of Flux manipulated in his opponent's Way of Binding. Like the blue hole out of which had stepped the sky woman at the beginning of this whole mess.

She saw the places between the Ways. She saw where they almost touched. Which, because they were created by Reckoners from different houses, they never really did. Except when they were in conflict, like the grudge match at Bardonne's. And, even then, it wasn't really about the space between the Ways. Nor the overlap.

What she saw was... different. She didn't have a Way of her own to cast. Even the red ring was gone.

But she had her eyes and she had her mind.

And for a long, long, seemingly long time she thought and thought and knew that, yes, soon it would be over because the loops and whirls of time would tear her apart but there was still time left for...

One question... please?

She looked straight into Rain Vernon's eyes and willed him to understand what she was saying to him. What she was thinking. What she wanted to ask.

He was mountains and their valleys. He was the river and the delta. He was Earth and Earth was forever. Changing but eternal. *And you have no fear of one tiny, young, homeless girl,* she thought with all her might.

"One question," he allowed, and freed her lips. Knowing that as soon as she spoke, time would catch her up again in its relentless grip and age her flesh instantly to bones and bones to dry dust in the moment before the scrap of paper landed and Wallace's foot came down.

Into the throbbing of the surf and the turning of the world, holding back the last tick of her soul's clock, Kendra whispered:

"When is seven less than none?
What road is only ever one?"

Nonsense, Vernon thought. *Doggerel.* But it recalled the Song of the Houses, which every Reckoner knew. *But the rhyme is wrong. It shouldn't be "none and one," it should be "one and done."*

A silly riddle. About a road? But why should that be her very last question? Why not, "Why?" Or... something about her fate. Or a request to, yes, please, let me join Earth and not die today.

He looked at her and she was smiling. Perhaps a bit mad. *But that's to be expected as conflicting Ways of time pull your mind from your body and soul.*

Even frozen in his own pattern, Wallace saw it before Vernon did. Seeing things was his specialty, of course.

The riddle, the rhyme was a distraction. A tiny drop of Chaos on her tongue. A way to make someone search for a pattern where there was none. To make a connection between...

Something moved, Rain thought. No. Wait. *I moved.* But he hadn't intended to.

What's happening? he thought.

And then, in a flash of insight, he, too saw what Wallace had perceived. To him, so familiar with the shapes in the topiary, it was like a transition mold; a negative Way triggered by the space around it. But he was only familiar with molds crafted of sky and branch and water. Not...

The Ways themselves.

This cannot be, Vernon thought, as his ancient, powerful mind began to fall apart.

In that last second of his life, he saw what she had done and was terrified. Of the simplicity of the idea. Of the complete confusion it would create in the Houses. Across all the Domains. Of this new power he had, somehow, helped bring forth, even accidentally.

The channeled might of the Narrow Road churned along despite Vernon's murderous Way of time. Of course it did, because it was crafted by another Domain. And now, because of the distracting rhyme, because of the drop of Chaos she had thrown into his mind, the speed and power of the road twisted in and around and through his own Way.

The Narrow Road took him by the mind, where the silly rhyme still rung in his ears. He felt it grip his skull the way he'd felt it pull at his feet a thousand times. At a speed magnified by the intentional speeding up caused by his own Way. With a thought, Kendra allowed the Narrow Road to sling a thousand miles of travel at him and through him all at once.

Rain's last thought was a question of his own: *Raven... Did you know?*

And time returned to normal. And the scrap of paper fell on the little metal table. And Wallace's foot came down on the curb. And Kendra sat down, hard, on the sidewalk.

And Rain Vernon's headless corpse flopped down on the street, emptying its blood into the gutter.

And the police would never find his head, because it was, simply... gone... smeared across a thousand miles of tarmac.

Chapter X: Conclusions

Mr. Monday sat back in his office chair and stared at Wallace Bradstreet. Stared at him hard. But Wallace didn't flinch or shrink in on himself.

The boy found some spine out there, Monday thought. *That's something anyways.*

"So you let her go?"

Wallace actually smiled a little. And then clamped it down. "Sir. She had just done something I'd never even imagined much less heard of or seen. She created what, to me, seemed like a Way built from three Ways, all of different Domains. It was as if the... difference... between them was what created the force. It was... somewhat distracting."

"You're a librarian," Monday reminded him. "You should be able to observe, record, catalog and preserve almost any information without emotion."

"She exploded his head into a cloud of red vapor and blew it instantly over the length of a Narrow Road. Sir."

"Yes. Well. I did say 'almost,' didn't I."

Wallace stood quietly, waiting for... well... whatever came next. Finally, Monday motioned him to take a seat on the couch. He'd never been asked to sit in the Librarian's office before. He stood stock still for one second more, until Monday, with an exasperated sigh, motioned again.

"Thank you, sir."

The older man pressed a button on his desk and asked into the intercom, "Mrs. McKey. Could you please bring us both some coffee?"

"Of course."

Monday sat back, waiting, until his chief assistant returned with a tray, a carafe and two cups. Black, the way he liked it. He didn't inquire if Wallace wanted milk or sugar. *One step of familiarity at a time,* he thought.

As Wallace took a sip, wincing a bit at the bitterness (he did, in fact, prefer it with sugar and cream), Monday asked him, "Where do you think she went?"

Wallace shrugged, looking at the iron hook where the crow had once perched. *Why would he keep that,* the young Reckoner wondered.

"Make a guess," Monday said.

"If I had to guess, I'd say she probably went to find her friend from Chaos. I mean, other than us, Vannia is the only Reckoner Kendra really knows."

"Possibly to Bardonne's, then, where they were last together."

"At least long enough to make contact, yes."

Monday nodded. "And the book she gave you? What was her request again?"

Wallace knew that Monday had clearly heard his initial report and could, certainly, repeat it back to him word-for-word. He also knew that the Librarian often liked to ask the same question more than once to see if new or differently worded answers would provide more context.

"She said, 'I'd consider it a favor if you'd find the message that used to be written on the title page.'"

"And that was all."

"Yes."

"Nothing else?"

She kissed me on the cheek, Wallace thought. *That's not really important. So I don't need to tell him about that. I don't think.*

"No, sir. Nothing else. Just that she was going 'walkabout' she called it, and would I find the message."

Monday looked up at the ceiling. "A message that 'used to be' written on the title page."

"Yes."

"I think that's an excellent project for you. Or one part of a larger project, actually."

Monday stood up and held out his hand. Confused, Wallace stood up and shook it.

"Congratulations, boy. I'm promoting you to Section Head. And you'll be in charge of the 'Kendra Project.' You'll have a coven of seven and a budget. Talk to McKey about the administrative details. She knows those things. I don't care. I expect a weekly update on progress, and immediate notification if anything... interesting... happens. Understood?"

"Uh... Yes. Understood. Thank you. Thank you, sir. I'll... I won't let you down."

"I know you won't."

Monday patted the boy on the shoulder -- *they seem to appreciate a patting at times like these,* he thought -- and ushered the boy out.

"No calls, please, Mrs. McKey," he said. "I'll be studying. I'll see you tomorrow."

"Of course, sir. Have a lovely evening."

"You, too, Mrs. McKey."

He closed the door to his study and felt his own Ways radiating out around him. All the stored power and closely held secrets. The subtle, spider-web strings that led to all kinds of watch stations. The more obvious lenses that focused attention on major players and events.

All of them now...

"Vulnerable," he said aloud.

He sat down again and ripped off a few pages of his Dilbert calendar, bringing it up to date. Then he poured another cup of coffee, leaned back in his chair and removed the small notebook from his coat pocket.

Much less editing to do on this story than I had originally thought. No cutting at all, actually. Not for me. Not for now. Maybe not ever.

Solomon Monday, Librarian, Master of Sight, looked at the iron perch where once his crow had sat. *I wonder where she's gone to, as well,* he thought. *Too many questions. Not enough information.*

But, secretly, he was a little pleased to have a mystery or two to unravel. It had been a long time since anything really... interesting... had happened around the Library.

He closed his eyes. And as he sipped his coffee, the sight and aroma of apple blossoms and the sound of an alarm clock made their way out of his notebook and down a Way to the archives where Wallace and his staff would pore over them in shocking detail.

ABOUT THE AUTHOR

Andy Havens is a writer, poet and gamer. He sings while doing the dishes.
He plays the ukulele and the mountain dulcimer (not while doing dishes).
He lives in Columbus, Ohio, USA. He prefers basset hounds as pets.

He is one-third of the "Chris and Andy Show,
Now With 100% More Dan."

He has perfect hair.

54634608R00143